Chapter One

"**Y**ou and Taylor are standing under the mistletoe, so you have to kiss," Matty Brennan Currick proclaimed to Cal Ruskoff over the background noise of a party in full swing. Then she embellished. "Otherwise it's bad luck for the whole new year."

Ambushed.

Cal looked from Taylor Anne Larsen, standing beside him with a flush rising up her neck like a long, slender glass being filled with rosy champagne, to the dancing eyes of Matty and knew he'd let himself be ambushed but good.

As the owner of the neighboring Flying W Ranch, Matty was Cal's employer. Which was one reason he was here at the Slash-C at her New Year's Eve party. She was also nearly the only friend he could claim, which was the other reason he was here.

"Never heard that," Cal grumbled.

"Me neither," Taylor declared staunchly. She stood beside him, as if they presented a united front, at the same time angling her face away from him. He saw only her light red hair and the turn of her jaw heading toward a pointy chin.

Maybe she'd been ambushed by Matty, too.

"You haven't heard of it because neither of you grew up around here. Dave!" Matty snagged her husband's arm as he headed toward the noisy hub of the party in the family room.

"Dave, isn't it true that if you stand under the mistletoe with someone and don't kiss them, it's bad luck—*terrible* bad luck for both people, all year long?"

Cal could see clear as day that Matty was focusing a compelling look on her husband. Dave Currick's lips quirked, but he nodded solemnly.

"Terrible bad luck," he concurred.

Matty beamed at Dave, then turned triumphantly to Cal and Taylor. "You see! And with Taylor as my partner for the Dog Rescue League, I don't want to take any chances of having to share terrible bad luck. *Awful,* terrible bad luck."

"In fact, it's such strong awful, terrible, bad luck," said Dave with a remarkably straight face, "that even if you're three feet away from the mistletoe and don't kiss, you can get hit with it, so…"

He swept Matty to him with one hand at the small of her back, and Matty cooperated fully. There was no time to look away before their lips met in a brief but sound kiss. But it wasn't the kiss that had Cal feeling as if prickles had gotten under his skin—it was what followed. Still molded against each other, the husband and wife exchanged a look that spoke of remembering past moments and of promising there'd be more—and soon—that would be well worth re-membering.

Cal didn't envy Matty and Dave having this. He just hated feeling like a starving kid with his nose pressed against the damned pastry shop window, watching what he wouldn't ever have.

But maybe on New Year's Eve, a night somehow separate from both the past and the future...for just a moment...

"Oh, hell," he growled, then pulled Taylor to him in much the same embrace Dave held Matty.

Only Taylor didn't lean into him, pliant and willing. She remained straight, even arched slightly back against his arm, as if to avoid contact with the front of his body. She didn't entirely succeed, and they shifted to keep balanced.

Her head jerked back.

Shock.

That was what he saw in Taylor's wide green eyes. Shock.

He couldn't blame her. Taylor Anne Larsen was a nice woman. Even if she was a lawyer. The kind of woman who wouldn't care for lies of either omission or commission. Polite, a little shy. He hadn't meant to shock her. It wasn't her fault he hadn't had a woman in too long to think about. It wasn't her fault that when he had thought about it lately her red-haired image had come to mind too often for comfort.

Well, there was no hiding his response from her now, so what the hell.

He pressed his mouth to hers.

Shock.

That was what he felt popping and sizzling and crackling through his bloodstream and nerve endings. Had to be.

Soft lips. Soft warmth. Soft skin when his mouth trailed off to one side. Soft hair that brushed against his cheek when he shifted the angle. And all around, a soft scent like...like something he couldn't quite name.

He sought deeper for it, finding an opening between her lips and sliding his tongue inside.

She gasped and pulled her mouth free.

He didn't even realize he was reaching to kiss her again until she stepped back, abruptly leaving his arms empty.

"So now we're safe against bad luck for the coming year." Taylor smiled, but her voice wasn't steady. She stood barely beyond arm's reach. "Excuse me, I see Lisa, and I want to talk to her about, uh, the dog rescue project."

She took one step, then she looked over her shoulder, her gaze going from one face to another, and said, "I'm sure I'll see you again before midnight, Matty. And Dave. But I'll say Happy New Year now, Cal."

She walked away.

Something in Cal's chest felt tight and heavy. It took an extra couple of beats for him to realize she'd just declared that she didn't expect to see him again for the duration of this party. Didn't expect to, or didn't want to?

"Cal." Matty laid a contrite hand on his arm, then murmured, "I'll go talk to her."

"Not on my account."

But Matty was already gone.

"I'm not sure if that's mud in your eye, but I'm positive that's lipstick on your mouth." Along with the comment, Dave offered a small paper napkin.

Cal shook his head and dragged the pad of his thumb hard across his lips. A smear of red showed on his thumb. Not bright red like the candles Matty and Dave had all around. More like the bow on that Christmas wreath Matty had insisted on putting on the grill of his truck after a month of sun and wind and snow. Soft.

He rubbed the smear against the side of his index finger until it disappeared from both spots.

"Gone," Dave confirmed.

Cal cursed. "Don't know why grown people would go hanging mistletoe around their house in the first place."

"I would think that would be obvious. Sometimes the pagans had the right idea."

"If you say so. But why put mistletoe here?" Cal said, pointing above him.

It had seemed a safe place to mind his own business. He'd been leaning against the doorjamb, not quite in the room, finding it the most isolated position to park until he could make a quiet exit, when Taylor had appeared from the hallway behind him. That's when Matty had pounced.

"I'd think that would be obvious, too, Cal." Dave nodded his head to the hallway at Cal's back. "That leads to the bedrooms."

Cal stayed only because it was easier.

By staying till midnight, he wouldn't have to listen to Matty yapping at him about being a recluse and a hermit and living like a monk. At least not as much.

Yet, as much as she got after him, she'd never pried into how he'd come to be here in Wyoming, not when she'd visited the Flying W before her great-uncle's death and not since she'd taken over. Maybe because at first they'd both been too busy working as hard and fast and cheap as they could to try to set the Flying W back on its feet. More likely because she hadn't wanted him probing into her secrets in return. Like the one that she'd still loved Dave Currick a half-dozen years after he'd broken off their youthful romance.

But since she and Dave had gotten back together, all that had changed.

Matty was happy, truly happy.

That would be good news if it ended there. But she was bound and determined that everyone else around her was going to be happy, too. He grimaced. She didn't even care if her efforts to make someone else happy made them miserable.

"Thirty seconds till midnight!"

The announcement acted like a switch on a slow-motion mixer. People started moving, shifting across the room, seeking out the person they meant to be beside at midnight. Matty and Dave and several of the other married couples came together in quick order.

"Fifteen seconds!"

Dates shifted near each other in varying degrees of self-consciousness. A group of unattached men started to coalesce near the kitchen door. A knot of women formed in the center of the room.

"Ten!"

"Nine!"

"Eight!"

"Seven!"

Someone said something he didn't hear. There was laughter, and the knot of women shifted toward the fireplace, apparently craning to see something.

"Six!"

"Five!"

"Four!"

All except Taylor Anne Larsen, who remained in the very center of the room, momentarily isolated.

"Three!"

"Two!"

And then Brent Somebody-or-Other visiting from Salt Lake City separated from the other single men, heading straight toward Taylor.

Cal pushed off from the doorjamb.

"One!"

He reached Taylor's side as the final shout went up.

"*Happy* New Year!"

He took her shoulders between his hands and turned her to present Brent Whatever with her back. He had one second's impression of her surprise, mixed with a glimmer of something else, then he muttered, "Happy New Year, Taylor." The last word muffled as their lips came together.

Hers were parted. He stroked his tongue into her mouth, once, then again.

He slid one hand down her back, closing the space between their bodies. The other formed to the curve of her skull, supporting there even as the press of his mouth arched her neck.

He felt her hands clutch—one at his shoulder, the other above his elbow.

The scent was there again, all around him, a freshening breeze blending the lemon tang of freedom and the jasmine richness of gracious comfort.

And then it deepened and heated as her tongue slid against his, first touching, then seeking.

Her fingers skimmed the back of his neck, slipping under the ends of his hair, where the skin was tender and never exposed.

Someone jostled against his right side so hard that both he and Taylor had to take a step to keep from losing their balance, ending the kiss.

Their arms still around each other, their bodies together from chest to thigh, his wanting her was no secret to either one of them.

"Cal."

That's all she said. Almost a question.

A question he couldn't answer. Not ever.

He'd never felt further from getting what he wanted in his life.

He turned around and got the hell out of there.

From the passenger seat of Matty's four-wheel-drive vehicle, Taylor looked across the snow-dusted, windswept landscape passing beyond the windshield, and felt deep gratitude for efficient heaters.

"I don't understand how anyone could leave a puppy at a rest stop," Matty said. "It's February in Wyoming, for Pete's sake."

When word came in of an abandoned dog during their stint on duty for the Rescue League, Taylor had packed the gear they'd prepared, and Matty had picked her up twenty minutes ago.

"But at least the truck driver who spotted him called in the report," she said. "Those long-distance guys are on such a strict schedule it's probably unreasonable to wish he'd brought it in."

"Yeah," Matty responded with an absentness that indicated her thoughts had shifted. "Time probably really flies by for them."

These first six weeks of the year had taught Taylor caution in responding to Matty's comments. Although she couldn't see danger in this one, she kept her answer neutral. "I suppose."

"I read somewhere that a sense of time condensing happens a lot. I mean, can you believe it's been more than a month since New Year's Eve?"

Uh-oh. Now Taylor saw the danger.

"It was a great party, wasn't it?" Matty was saying. "I can't remember giving a party I enjoyed more. As long as we're on the subject, I was wondering—"

"Don't wonder, *please*."

"I was just going to—"

"Ask me again if Cal Ruskoff has called me. He hasn't. He isn't going to. I never thought he would. I told you that."

"But he—"

"But he kissed me on New Year's Eve. Yes, I know that. You know that. I wouldn't be surprised if all of the Rocky Mountain region knows that."

"He didn't just kiss you. He *kissed* you."

Taylor really wished Matty hadn't said that. Not that way. Not the way that reminded her all too clearly of how thoroughly kissed she'd felt New Year's Eve. The external sensations of Cal's arms encircling her, his hard body pressed against hers, and his lips firm and sure on hers. The internal sensations of coiling heat and rushing blood. And the desire to let go, to let his hold be all that supported her, to rely on what his kiss told her and made her feel.

All those sensations just made it more difficult to remember that behind the heat in those compelling blue eyes she'd seen such incredible bleakness. And despite all that heat surrounding her and inside her, she'd wanted to shiver.

"Believe me, he's experienced complete, utter and absolute New Year's Eve kisser's remorse."

"You're making jokes, but I'm serious. Cal needs somebody like you. Other than Dave, there's not a man I—"

"I'm serious, too," Taylor interrupted, not wanting to hear Cal Ruskoff's virtues extolled. It was bad enough having to contend with the unshakable vision of his square face under ash-brown hair nearing hers in those split seconds before he'd kissed her. "The guy exhibits all the symptoms. Crossing the street and sudden U-turns out of the café when he sees yours truly seated inside."

She didn't tell Matty that each of his evasive moves had left her simultaneously relieved and disappointed.

"Maybe I should—"

"No, Matty. Don't do anything. Don't say anything. Just let the whole matter drop."

"But—"

"There's the exit, Matty. C'mon, let's go rescue a puppy." *And forget Cal Ruskoff.*

The first impression of the puppy tied to a fence post near the men's bathroom was of a fuzzy toy with woefully inadequate stuffing. A piece of cardboard with "Free" traced several times in blue ink was tacked to the post. He was lying on a faded blue towel, worrying a corner of it.

As soon as he saw them, he stood, with the fabric still in his mouth, making him look slightly roguish. His long, fuzzy tail wagged slowly as he watched them with intense interest and a hint of wariness.

"Hi, baby dog," crooned Matty, drawing off a glove.

"Matty, you should leave your gloves on."

"He won't be able to get my scent if I do."

"He won't be able to bite your hand, either," Taylor noted dryly. "Remember what the manual said—most dogs react to fear of being hurt by running, but some attack."

Just like men.

"I grew up with enough strays coming by the ranch to know when one's mean. This one isn't. Are you, sweet boy?" The animal stretched his neck to sniff.

"Boy?"

Matty looked over her shoulder. "You *are* from the city, aren't you?"

"Suburbs. Where dogs wear identification and are nearly always connected to a human, who will tell you nicely if it's a he or a she. And whether or not it's friendly."

"Oh, Baby Dog's friendly, aren't you? Taylor, untie the rope from the post."

Matty kept talking in a crooning tone while Taylor started on the knot. "Let's see, light caramel brown with white markings, pointed nose, ears that tip—well, one tips. I think you're a collie, aren't you, Baby Dog?"

"A collie, really?" As Taylor tugged the knot loose, the puppy took a step and promptly sat down. "Oh, Matty, he's weak. He can barely stand."

Matty lifted the puppy. He made one feeble effort to get loose, then subsided. "Get the towel and let's go. I want to get him to Dr. Markus."

"This towel is filthy." But she was already following the order. An envelope fluttered from it, and she automatically snatched that up, too.

"We can wash it, but it's the one thing that's familiar to him."

Cal saw Taylor heading his direction from down the street.

He'd avoided her up to now, but surely enough time had passed to temper temptation. Surely he wouldn't respond as strongly as he had New Year's Eve. That had been an aberration. A combination of too long without a woman, an unsuspected streak of sentimentality over the holiday and—okay, yes, no sense denying it—the woman.

But now...

With his head down as if examining the menu propped in the café window, even though the offerings hadn't changed in the nearly three years he'd lived here, he fingered the scrap of newspaper in his jacket pocket, the one he'd clipped from this morning's *Jefferson Standard*.

Under the brim of his hat, he watched her walk toward him, her movements easy and smooth.

He had good cause to talk to her now. As a lawyer she'd know the ins and outs of wills, might be able to tell him what some of his options were.

Her gaze seemed to focus on him, and she stopped dead. With his head dipped, he still caught the motion of her looking around, as if seeking an escape.

Pivoting away from her, he started across the street.

It had been a bad idea anyhow. She couldn't have given him any useful advice without his telling her some of the story, and he'd be a fool to do that.

No, he'd stick to his first decision, to ignore the whole thing and go on as he had been. Although he would confirm the information first, get a few more details.

Without looking in her direction, he went into the Knighton library.

Taylor had washed the towel twice, using bleach. It would never be a thing of beauty, but it looked considerably more reputable than the puppy did the next afternoon, dripping flea-bath soapsuds into her bathtub in a second go-around of bathing. Once just hadn't been enough.

And there was a dauntingly good chance that he looked considerably better than either she or Matty did as they leaned over the bathtub, hair damp and mussed, clothes spattered and faces flushed. The scent of flea shampoo tickled Taylor's nose and she sneezed.

"Tell me again, Matty, why we couldn't have let the groomer wash him?" She rubbed suds behind his ears. The puppy half closed his eyes in apparent bliss. She smiled and kept rubbing.

"I see no reason to spend Rescue League funds on dog-washing when we can do it ourselves." Matty reached for the animal's far hip.

"That's because it's not your bathroom," Taylor said morosely, though she knew she had the better end of the deal—literally—at this moment.

"Would you have wanted Baby Dog to stay here without a bath?"

"*No!*"

"Then start rinsing."

Finally Matty sat back and announced grandly, "I believe we are ready for the first towel."

"It's right here." Taylor reached behind her. "Just don't let him—oh, no!"

Taylor turned back in time to get a dog-shaken spray full in the face. If any surface had previously avoided being spattered, it wasn't missed this time.

"Don't you laugh, Matty Brennan Currick. Don't you dare laugh."

"I can't help it. Sorry. It's just... I was thinking of what Grams used to call it—the most efficient water dispersal system known to man."

Taylor stifled a chuckle, handed her friend a towel, and said sternly, "Dry."

It took two more towels each.

"He cleans up pretty good," said Matty. "He's past the ball of fluff, adorable stage, but he'll grab somebody's heart."

The puppy trotted to a pile of old towels, curled up and promptly went to sleep.

Taylor had an odd lump in her throat. "He's still adorable."

Matty gave her a look, but Taylor shook her head. "Don't even think about it. Even if my landlord would let me, it wouldn't be fair to an animal in this tiny apartment." She looked around. "All we have to do now is clean up, then find a home for Baby Dog—and fast, before my landlord, Hugh Moski, finds out I'm keeping a pet."

"You promised you'd deliver Baby Dog to the new owner, right?"

"That was our deal. Why?"

"You know who needs a dog? And doesn't have to worry about the landlord objecting?"

"Who?"

"Cal Ruskoff."

Chapter Two

"Matty—"

"Collies are herding dogs, so that's perfect."

"*Sheep!* They herd sheep, not cattle," Taylor said. Arguing about the animal kingdom seemed much safer than her real objection. She was not ready to face Cal again, especially on his turf.

"He'll adapt," Matty said blithely. "Besides, Cal needs the company. With me living at the Slash-C, he lives all alone on the Flying W, and getting him out of there takes a crowbar, dynamite and a list of needed supplies a yard long. And don't get that look on your face. It's not because of you, so get that out of your head. New Year's might have made it worse—"

Taylor gave an involuntary groan.

"—but it wasn't the cause. Cal's been like this since he hired on. After Dave and I got together, I realized how solitary Cal keeps himself." Matty gave her a serious look. "It's not right. He's a good man, but he keeps such a high wall between himself and the world, it's like he lives in a...uh..."

"A shell?"

"I was going to say 'cave,' but 'shell' works. And I think you're the one who could bring him out. You two have a...a *connection*."

"You just said he's been worse since we, uh, since New Year's Eve. You can't have it both ways."

"Sure I can." Matty pulled the plug in the bathtub. "That made it worse because he's hot for you."

"Matty—"

"The fact that he wants you is the reason he's pulled back so far. If you didn't threaten his wall—his shell—he wouldn't fight so hard to keep you away. All you have to do is spend as much time as possible around Cal, and pretty soon those walls will come tumbling down, like Jericho."

And what about her? All that time spent around Cal, waiting for walls to crack. What if Matty was right, and they did tumble? Even if they didn't fall *on* her, squishing her flat as a bug, there were other dangers.

Cal was a powerful presence as it was, with his will and his personality and his...desires clearly held under a tight curb. What would it be like if he let go?

She used to think she was strong, that she held to certain unbreakable, even unbendable, principles. But her life before she'd come to Wyoming had proved her wrong. Could she risk getting involved with a Cal Ruskoff who was no longer curbed by his own walls?

And, of course, this was all presuming Matty was anywhere close to being right in the first place. Two kisses— even those two kisses—did not a powerful connection make. Necessarily.

"Uh-oh."

Taylor was so dizzy from her own circular thoughts that she even welcomed that "bad news" interruption by Matty.

"What?"

"The water isn't going down the drain."

"Hugh is going to shoot me. How am I going to explain this?"

"Tell him you were shedding?"

Taylor glared at her. "Oh, God, I can't keep Baby Dog here after I tell Hugh about the drain."

"I gave you a quick solution. Otherwise you'll have to wait until I work the phones, looking for the right home for Baby Dog. And we'd have to check those people out. But we know Cal, so we wouldn't have to check him out. It's the quickest solution."

As solutions went, it might be quick, but it certainly was dirty—or at least nerve-racking.

"What a sweet Baby Dog," Taylor crooned, as she ran her hand over the downy fuzz atop the puppy's head. As long as she concentrated on the animal, she wouldn't have to think about the fact that she was going to face Cal.

If he ever came back.

The puppy, momentarily tired of exploring, sat beside Taylor's feet and leaned against her calf, a nice added warmth as the air chilled rapidly with the waning daylight. She wasn't sure how much longer she could—or should— sit on the steps to Cal Ruskoff's small home, waiting for him to return.

The first fifteen minutes had been fine, with the structure behind her serving as a wind block and the sun exerting some winter strength. She'd had plenty of entertainment from the puppy. Keeping him from an apparently fascinating mud puddle beside the steps had been nearly a full-time job.

But for the past ten minutes, doubts had crept in along with a chill.

"Not even Cal Ruskoff could say no to such a sweet Baby Dog." Was she reassuring the puppy or herself? "Look at that face. So sincere."

The puppy obligingly tipped his head back until his face was nearly upside down.

She was chuckling when she became aware of a shadow looming against the brilliance of the setting sky. Cal walked slowly toward her, pulling off first one glove, then the other.

His squared-off jaw was firm beneath a sensuous mouth drawn neutrally straight. A groove curved from the outside corner of his nose to beside his mouth, echoed by a longer groove from just under his high cheekbone to his jaw. She had seen those grooves deepen with both anger and amusement. But they, too, were neutral at the moment.

She scrambled up, automatically brushing at the seat of her long jacket.

"Hi, Cal. I hope you don't mind us waiting on your steps." She became aware his eyes were following her brushing motion and stopped it immediately.

He was slow answering, as if hoping she might disappear or run off before he needed to make the effort.

"Taylor. What brings you here?"

It didn't qualify as the most unfriendly greeting she'd ever received, but it didn't rank far down the list.

The puppy wagged his tail. Maybe he liked Cal's unhurried tenor voice. There was no doubt it had an effect on her.

"He does," she blurted out.

Cal's brows met at a deep groove over his nose. "Who does?"

"The puppy."

His gaze followed the direction of her gesture, to where the puppy was settling down in the center of the mud puddle. If she hadn't known better, she'd have thought Cal looked relieved.

"Oh, no! We just gave him a bath." She grabbed the old blue towel from the supplies she'd hauled to the steps, and wrapped the puppy in it. It engulfed him, so only his nose stuck out, looking like a fuzzy fox in an oversize babushka.

"The dog's the reason you came out here?"

If his question held a hint of suggestion that she'd come here as a personal overture of some kind, she'd have been embarrassed. Instead, he sounded as if he was trying to eliminate some other cause. She didn't have a clue what that might be, but as long as he didn't think she was chasing him, that was fine with her.

"Of course. He's really a sweet puppy. About four months old, the vet thinks. Remarkably healthy, considering. All collie, Dr. Markus said. They're known for being intelligent, loving and loyal." She set Baby Dog on the ground. Wherever his fur had contacted the mud, it stood straight out in pointed tufts. "This little guy's coat isn't the best yet, but it will get better as he gets regular meals and—"

"Why the sales job?"

Taylor drew a deep breath. She was doing this all wrong. Now she had his suspicions up.

"He's a Rescue League dog. Matty and I took the call on him." She told him the story. She left too many details in but couldn't seem to edit herself. It could have been that she was a little nervous. "When we found him, he was dirty and hungry and skinny—"

"He's *still* skinny."

Taylor had no clue whether Cal's murmur was meant to be humorous or critical, so she ignored it. "We're trying to find a home for him. Matty thought you—"

"If he's so lovable, why don't you keep him?"

"My landlord says absolutely no pets." Especially not after he'd fixed the bathtub drain, complaining all the while about the smell of flea shampoo.

"Then let Matty take him."

"Dave's allergic."

He frowned as he looked to the animal now sniffing his

boots with audible interest. "He doesn't look much like a collie."

Taylor bridled. "Were you expecting Lassie, with all her Hollywood groomers? He's a puppy. And he's been neglected. Maybe abused. You wouldn't look so good if you'd lived such a hard life."

You wouldn't look so good... Oh, Lord, how had that come out of her mouth? Nothing like telling the man she thought he was appealing. *Appealing, Taylor? Try a hunk.*

His ash-brown hair was lighter around his face from the sun. Brows a shade darker than his hair dropped at the corners, just as his eyelids drooped lower at the corners over brilliant blue eyes.

His shoulders were as square and straight as his jaw, his jeans showed taut muscles, and his chest had been wide and firm enough to have left an apparently indelible impression on her nerve endings from their New Year's Eve embrace.

"That doesn't change that his legs are too long for his body and he's knock-kneed."

Her lips parted to vehemently deny that charge. Then she realized he was talking about the puppy, not continuing her mental catalogue of his attributes.

"You want an aristocratic dog? Are you planning on hitting a show ring?"

"I'm not planning on anything, because I don't want a dog."

Had he overheard her comment about not even Cal Ruskoff being able to resist this puppy? He certainly seemed determined to put the lie to it.

"Matty said you could use a dog around here. He can alert you if strangers are coming. And with the main house empty, he can help keep guard."

"Strangers don't usually come, because they're not invited," he said pointedly. "And I've had no trouble keep-

ing the main house safe from marauders. If Matty thinks
otherwise, she can fire me. She's the boss.''

Taylor wasn't a lawyer for nothing; she jumped on the
opening.

"Yes, Matty *is* the boss. And she said you should take
him. She said he could become a working dog. Would you
refuse to care for a colt she bought, even though it wouldn't
be ridden for another year?''

She had him there, and they both knew it.

"He's not a cattle dog."

"Collies have strong herding instincts," she shot back,
echoing Matty's argument.

"For sheep—that's where the instincts are. And it's not
wise to mess around with instincts."

A glint flared in his eyes, and the word *instincts* no
longer applied to the gangly bundle of fur at their feet, but
to something else entirely. The sensations of their kisses
New Year's Eve swept in like a chinook, warming her so
suddenly and unexpectedly that she shivered with it.

Taylor tried her best to ignore that shift. "Are you going
to argue with Matty?''

He tucked his fingers in his front jeans pockets beneath
his winter jacket, and rocked slightly from heel to toe and
back.

"I've been known to."

Did he mean he'd argued with Matty about her, Taylor?
Had Matty been urging him as she'd been urging Taylor?
And there it was again, the conversation sliding from the
dog that stood between them to this other thing between
them.

"Are you going to make me go back and tell Matty you
turned down her request to take this puppy?''

"I've never cared for a dog."

In another man it might have been an admission. Cal
made it a flat fact. But Taylor wondered what was behind
that fact.

"The basics are pretty obvious, Cal—food, water, shelter, attention. It's actually a lot less complicated than caring for a horse, which you do all the time. So, what's your answer? Should I tell Matty you refused to take him?"

His posture remained inflexible, but he said, "No."

"Good. I'm glad." Their eyes met, and the intensity of his blue stare was overlaid by the memory of another look...after he'd kissed her at midnight.

She shifted her shoulders, dislodging the memory, then turned toward the supplies she'd brought.

"There's enough puppy food here to get you started. The proper amounts are listed on the back. Try to make meals the same time every day. That should help with house-training. He's been really good so far.

"He has a new collar and leash. There's a brush, toys and puppy treats. He likes this towel. He had it when we found him. You'll need a couple bowls for him—one for food, one for water. He's really very good."

"Good grief." Cal looked around at the puppy as if trying to match all he'd heard to that one small creature. "What's that?"

"His crate. He sleeps in it. Travels in it in the car. It helps with house-training. There's a booklet on using the crate in the bag, too. But as I said—"

"He's really very good," he filled in, using her earlier words.

Cal obviously didn't believe it, but she answered, "Yes, he is. Any other questions?"

"What's his name?"

She almost smiled. A man as entirely indifferent to an animal as he posed at being wouldn't care about a name. He was softening.

As soft as Cal Ruskoff probably ever got. Soft was not what she associated with him. Those kisses on New Year's Eve had told another story, a story of heat and hardness.

The drift of her thoughts sent her eyes from his wide shoulders to his narrow hips...and below.

She jerked her gaze to one side and took two slow, deep breaths.

"He had no tags, no collar. Matty and I call him Baby Dog."

"I'm not calling—"

"He's your dog now," she interrupted. "You name him."

"He's the Flying W's dog. I'm taking him as one of my duties as foreman."

"Make it another of your duties to name him." She started off, then turned back. "One more thing."

"Now what?"

"You have to have him neutered."

"Neutered? You want me to *castrate* this dog?"

"No, I don't want you to personally castrate him. I want you to take him to the clinic in a couple months, and Dr. Markus will do it for free if you remind them he's a rescue dog. I don't know what the big deal is—you do it to cattle all the time without batting an eye."

With that, she turned on her heel and got in her car, backing out with more speed than finesse.

For fear she'd laugh in the man's shocked face.

She knew exactly what the big deal was. Despite his best efforts, despite his tough words, despite his harsh attitudes, Cal Ruskoff had begun to feel a kinship with the stray puppy.

Maybe that shell could be dented after all.

"She doesn't know what the big deal is, huh," Cal muttered as he put away the last of his supper dishes.

"You do it to cattle all the time," he mimicked in a voice entirely unlike Taylor's memorable contralto.

"Yeah, but when we do it to cattle, it's a prelude to fattening 'em up so we can eat 'em. I don't suppose she'd be too happy if I decided to eat her precious puppy. Do you?''

He turned around to leer at the animal who'd been dog-ging—literally—his footsteps all evening. But he'd disap-peared.

Cal gave the main room a quick look, checking in the corner behind the wing chair by the window before passing on to the single bedroom. The floor was bare except for one throw rug beside his bed.

He was on his way to the bathroom—the only other open door—when something out of place caught his eye.

The dog. On his bed.

The blue-and-white quilt had been tugged off one pillow and crumpled into the semblance of a nest. The dog was curled up inside it, his head resting comfortably on the pillow, as if to demonstrate what palomino hair might look like against the white pillowcase. Not that palomino had been Cal's fantasy. Taylor's hair was redder and—

"Get down."

It was one thing to know he couldn't risk bringing Taylor Larsen to his bed, but he'd be damned if he'd share it with a *dog*. Two long strides took Cal to the side of the bed. He took a firm hold on the collar and repeated, ''Get down,'' while he tugged enough to ensure the animal did.

''That's where you sleep,'' Cal added, pointing through the open double doorway to the crate in the kitchen.

The animal heaved a sigh, then circled around and before Cal could back away, sat on his feet, covered only in heavy socks.

Pain shot from Cal's feet and up his legs, bringing water to his eyes and a muffled curse to his lips. He jerked his feet free of the torture and the animal stood up.

''You have got the boniest butt in creation, dog!'' Cal shook one foot then the other. No wonder the animal had sought out something with some padding—he had none of his own.

He's been neglected. Maybe abused. Taylor's words echoed in his head with a good deal more meaning than they'd originally had. This puppy had missed more than a couple of meals.

"All right, you made your point," Cal muttered as he headed for the cupboard.

Damned if he wasn't starting to sound like Taylor, thinking about dogs making points.

Which made no sense, because all Cal Ruskoff and Taylor Anne Larsen had in common was living in Knighton, Wyoming. She'd arrived shortly after he'd been hired on by Matty's great-uncle. Her degrees and connections and history were common knowledge, and she'd settled into the life of the town and made friends. For almost two years he'd seldom left the ranch, and he'd shared none of his past with the people of Knighton.

Then Matty, an entirely different kind of boss, inherited the Flying W. She'd needed a good lawyer. But she hadn't wanted to go to Dave last spring when they had not yet untangled the emotions that led to their now being happily married. So, she'd signed on with Taylor, the town's other lawyer.

And in between Matty inheriting and when she and Dave worked things out, Cal and Taylor had stood up as witnesses at their wedding and even engaged in a bit of subterfuge to help the couple along. Their cooperation hadn't altered the fact that there was a gulf the size of the continent between their lives.

When he'd first seen her sitting with the dog on the steps of the foreman's house, two possibilities had hit him almost simultaneously.

New Year's Eve was the first possibility.

She's working for them was the second.

They were equally unlikely.

If she'd had any thought of following up on what happened on New Year's Eve, she hadn't acted on it in these past weeks. Which just saved him the effort of withstanding further temptation.

As for the other, his trip to the library had not only confirmed what he'd read in the newspaper, but added a nasty surprise to it. But it was a big leap from that to anyone knowing where he was or who he'd become. That was the reason he'd dismissed that second possibility. Not from any starry-eyed notion that Taylor Anne Larsen wouldn't sign up for the job. Dangle enough money in front of them, and most people would take on any kind of work.

So, having her sitting on his front steps in order to foist off a homeless dog on him was actually good news.

None of that meant he would start thinking like her, especially about the scrawny animal watching his every move. Next thing he knew he'd be calling the creature something like Muffin.

He's your dog now. You name him.

He wasn't his dog. A man in his position couldn't afford to own anything he wasn't prepared to leave behind any minute.

Still, after Cal selected a blanket and two towels, he grabbed an old pillow for good measure and added it to the crate.

Three hours later, he moved the crate to a corner of his bedroom.

Self-defense.

A man couldn't sleep wondering what the critter was doing in the other room. But at least he'd come up with a name for him—and one Taylor would have to approve.

"Are you going to tell me, or are you going to make me ask you?" Matty propped her hands on her hips.

Cal knew what she wanted. They'd covered a fair amount of information about the Flying W's operations in the past hour, but only in between her questions about the puppy and his brief answers. If she expected him to wax poetic, she'd have a long time to wait.

"Ask me what? You already asked me every question under the sun about this animal. From his eating habits to his burps to his emotional state."

"You still haven't said if you like him."

"He's all right."

"What a ringing endorsement. Looks as if he thinks more highly of you."

"I feed him."

"Just goes to show those old wives' tales aren't always right—like the one about dogs being able to tell good character."

He grimaced. But she was looking beyond him with a faraway look.

"Maybe I should tell Taylor she was right, that you're not the right one to have this puppy, and she needs to come and take him back."

Did Matty really think he was that easy to lead? That he'd declare himself devoted to this canine and beg her to let him keep it or that he'd protest Taylor's low opinion of him? "Maybe you should."

"It *would* be nice for you to get to see Taylor again so soon, wouldn't it?"

He should have known Matty wouldn't be that obvious. It was Taylor she wanted him to declare his devotion to, not the dog. Or maybe both. He used his most reliable defense: silence.

"Dave's got some legal dinner tonight," Matty went on. "Taylor will be there. Probably going to wear that green dress she wore when the two of you stood up for Dave and me at our wedding. I'm sure they wouldn't mind one more."

He said nothing.

"Would you like to come?"

"No."

"Would you come as a favor to a friend?"

"No."

She gave a sigh. He'd like to think that meant she'd given up on this for good.

"Come by the Slash-C so we can go over the spring planting plan—day after tomorrow, okay? I've got all that stuff in the computer there and it's easier."

"Sure. 'Bout ten."

"Good. Plan to stay to lunch."

"Okay."

She swung up onto Juno's saddled back with accustomed ease. "Hey, Cal."

"Yeah?" Squinting up at her, he thought she was fighting a grin.

"You know it's safe for you to fall in love with Baby Dog. He won't bite. For that matter, neither will Taylor…unless you want her to."

With a wicked chuckle, she rode away. Leaving him trying to gain control of a certain part of his anatomy that was dealing with the image of Taylor—

"Damn!"

The first time he'd seen Taylor there'd been that stir of interest. He'd kept a lid on it, though. But since last spring, with their coming across each other more because of their associations with Matty and Dave, so much steam had built under that lid that it had become practically a full-time job holding it down.

If Taylor were the type to just take to bed, maybe he'd have accepted the risk and gone for the steamy, sheet-twisting interlude his mind kept conjuring and his body craved…but she wasn't. He had no doubt that she'd tell him she believed every bit in the fairy tale of love.

So, he couldn't let anything happen between him and Taylor.

His life depended on it—at least this life did.

Chapter Three

"You want all this filed?"

Taylor looked up at the question from Lisa Currick in surprise. Dave's younger sister ran Taylor's law office with a firm, organized and self-sufficient hand. Rarely did she consult Taylor on such matters as office equipment or expenses, much less filing.

"What is it?"

"Papers on that rescue puppy you took out to Cal Ruskoff. I filed one copy of your receipt from the vet, and other papers. But I thought you might want to take copies to Cal. Medical information on the dog and such."

Taylor shot her a look that should have made most employees scurry to check their severance package. Lisa looked back at her, knowing her job was in no danger.

Lisa was a gem as an office manager—organized and utterly dependable. Most times, Taylor knew she'd be crazy to ever let her go. Sometimes, however, Taylor thought that if she were really Lisa Currick's friend, she would fire her, so the younger woman would go find what she was really meant to do. What might make her happy.

She suspected the answer to the mystery of Lisa Currick rested in the gap between Lisa's happy years growing up on the Slash-C with Dave and their parents and her apparently content life now, dividing her time between more than full-time work and more than part-time school. But Lisa never talked about that gap, and Taylor respected her privacy.

Perhaps, Taylor also didn't want to risk Lisa asking about certain segments of *her* past.

"Mail them."

If she'd known about this a few days earlier, when she'd spotted Cal heading into the Knighton Library for the second time in a week, it would have been entirely reasonable to call out to him and tell him to come by and get the information. Reasonable, but not comfortable. Would he have ignored her? Made an excuse not to come? Or would he have complied, treating it as absolutely no big deal while her stomach acted as if she'd been on a solid diet of Mexican jumping beans?

"I can do that," Lisa acknowledged.

"Good."

"'Course, there's a weekend coming up. Probably wouldn't get there for oh, three, maybe even four days. If something should happen in the meantime, it could make the difference between that poor little puppy living and dying."

Taylor glared at her. "It's not like he has a rare medical condition, Lisa. Dr. Markus said he was basically healthy."

"You might never know," the other woman said, "not until it's too late. I'd hate to have it on my conscience that I didn't do something that could have made the difference."

Taylor was not a fan of conspiracy theories—to her way of thinking, people could do enough craziness on their own—but she was beginning to get suspicious. Was Matty behind Lisa's sudden push to have Taylor hand-deliver these not-urgent papers to Cal?

"Fine, then you take the papers out to the Flying W."

"Can't. Got a class tonight. Midterm exam." She dropped the folder onto the desk, an inch from the contract Taylor was reviewing.

Taylor pointedly ignored the folder. Continued ignoring it even after the door had closed behind Lisa. Ignored it until she had to acknowledge that she was spending a lot more time wondering how Baby Dog was getting along with Cal—and vice versa—than she was reviewing the Gibson contract.

With an exasperated sound, she grabbed the folder.

She'd assure herself that there was nothing in the papers that couldn't stay a few days in the U.S. postal system, shove them into an envelope and send them on their way.

She skimmed the receipts she'd already seen, looked more closely at the detailed medical information from Dr. Markus and checked the list of vaccinations given and future ones needed. She indulged in a humph of vindication. All routine.

In the back of the folder she found the battered cardboard sign with the ballpoint ink-printed "Free" on it.

Taylor was flipping the front cover of the folder closed when she noticed the corner of an envelope protruding from behind the cardboard. She pulled it out and recognized it as the one she'd absently picked up at the rest stop.

It bore the imprint of a cut-rate motel chain. Taylor couldn't think of any around Knighton. It was smudged and wrinkled, with no name or address on the front, but a few canine teeth marks on one corner. The flap was loose.

Taylor opened it and took out a single sheet, raggedly torn along the bottom and folded unevenly.

When she finished reading the brief message, her eyes were wet.

There *was* information in this folder Cal Ruskoff should see.

But she wasn't going to be the one to show it to him. The last thing she needed when she was facing the enigmatic man who made her hormones do the samba was having her emotions close to the surface.

She folded the note along its original crease and put it back in the envelope.

How would Cal respond to the sentiments in this note? Would it touch him as it had her? Would it open a crack in that shell of his? She shook her head. *Pollyanna Larsen* strikes again. That's what her study group at law school had called her for her hopeful views. That had been leached out of her in the years with the firm in Dallas, until she'd felt like a skeleton left in the desert, devoid of flesh and blood and heart.

But during these past two years in Knighton, she'd felt a return of her hopefulness.

Maybe too much hopefulness, in the case of one Cal Ruskoff.

Even if something opened a crack in his shell, who was to say what she might see through the crack? Another shell? Or would she find something darker.

Just because her intuition said he was a good man didn't mean she was right. What proof did she have that there even *was* anything beyond his cold exterior? Although she did have proof that there was some hot blood behind that exterior.

Still, what he showed to the world might be what he was, through and through. Thinking she'd seen glimpses of more really wasn't any better than a hunch. And a hunch was no basis for building a case.

Or for running a life.

She plastered a sticky-backed note to the folder, wrote ''Send copy of entire contents to CR'' on it, and forced her mind to get back to work.

* * *

"Uh-huh. I understand. Okay, Lisa. I'll see what I can do."

Matty finished her conversation with her sister-in-law and hung up the kitchen phone in the Slash-C main house in time to hear her husband emit a humph.

"Humph, what?"

She asked the question from reflexive curiosity. She already had enough on her mind without adding mysterious humphs. Dave might maintain that, when she got her mind set on other things, she was blind to her fellow human beings' emotions, and even sometimes her own, but she'd have to be on another planet to have missed the separate but equally lousy moods Cal and Taylor were inflicting on the rest of humanity since New Year's.

So she was doing something about it.

Unfortunately, Lisa had just reported that Plan A hadn't sent Taylor out to the Flying W, the way Matty had hoped.

Time to think of a Plan B.

Cal and Taylor needed to spend time together. That had worked for her and Dave when they'd both been too stubborn to see that they loved each other and belonged together. Of course, she and Dave had been married by a temporary deal at first, which made spending time together hard to avoid. Getting Cal and Taylor to marry each other at this point might be a task even beyond her determination. So far, even her efforts to get them face-to-face weren't working. She had to think of something else.

Dave's voice brought her back to the present.

"I was listening to the weather forecast. That snow they've been predicting? They've moved it up to arriving late this afternoon. Storm's developing fast. And they're saying it's going to be a big one."

"Yeah?"

"Could get nasty." Dave looked out the window toward a line of gray along the northern horizon of the otherwise blue sky. "I'm going to stop by and have a word with Jack before I head into Knighton. I've got to be in the office for an appointment about ten, but then I'll head back. You don't have to go anywhere, do you? You're squared away over at the Flying W?"

"Hmm?"

Dave touched her arm, drawing her attention away from the fast-clicking thoughts in her head. "Are you okay?"

"Yes. Of course. Sorry. What were you saying?"

He looked at her quizzically, and she returned her most limpidly innocent smile. He looked more worried. "I said are you squared away at the Flying W? You and Cal, have you got things set for a storm like this?"

"Sure."

"Then why do you have that look?"

"What look?"

"The look that says somebody better look out."

"Don't be silly. Except..."

"What?"

"You better come back here before the storm hits. All the years we've known each other, we've never been snow-bound together."

Worry was wiped from his expression, replaced by some-thing she enjoyed much more. And something that prom-ised even greater enjoyment later on. "We'll see what we can do to remedy that."

"Good."

"You aren't thinking about going over to the Flying W, are you? Storm could hit early. I don't like the idea of you getting caught out in it."

"No, I thought I'd stay here. I have a phone call to make."

Taylor opened the car door and took a blast of cold, wet, stinging snow in the face.

What was she doing out here at the Flying W instead of in her snug office getting more work done?

Taylor interrupted her own thoughts with a hard shudder and amended her question to what was she doing here besides freezing? And watching the snow come down harder and faster with every passing minute.

She was here for a puppy, that's why.

"Oh, Taylor, I've never heard Cal sound like that," Matty had said on the phone less than an hour ago. "Said he's at the end of his rope."

Fear had clutched Taylor's throat so tightly she'd hardly recognized her own voice. "Is he all right? Is Cal hurt?"

"Cal? No, he's not hurt." Had Matty sounded gleeful? Taylor had thought so, but with her friend's next words, that impression disappeared. "No, it's the puppy. Cal said he's totally fed up. Wants him out of there. Today. Or he won't be held accountable."

"Oh, no. I can't believe it. They seemed so..."

She'd started to say *attached*. But that word didn't fit Cal Ruskoff.

"I know, I thought so, too. But if you could have heard him. He was totally fed up...."

Matty's voice trailed off into ominous silence. Taylor had a bad feeling she knew what was coming, but she made a stab at preventing it.

"So what are you going to do?"

"Oh, Taylor." Matty was not a wailer, but she came close. "I don't know what I *can* do. Dave's not here and my truck won't start and on top of that Juno's thrown a shoe, so I can't even ride her. But somebody's got to get there."

"Okay, Matty. Don't worry. I'll go."

"You will? Oh, Taylor, that's such a relief. You'll have to go right away."

"Of course I will," she said staunchly. It wasn't as if she were braving great danger. Just six feet of irritated male. "I'll pick up the puppy and bring him home. But you have to start making calls to find this puppy a new home—before Hugh sees him. Right this minute, you understand?"

"You know I'm not sure that'll be necessary. Cal might relent, you know. You have to try talking to him first, okay?"

"If he's so fed up—"

"Oh, I know, but promise me you'll talk to him first."

"Fine. I'll talk first, but that puppy deserves a home where he'll be loved, and if your foreman isn't—" She clamped her mouth shut before she could add *capable of love*. She was getting too worked up about this. A dog surely wouldn't feel a sense of rejection because a certain man looked at it with cool disinterest. "Promise me you'll make those calls to find a new home, Matty."

"I tell you what, if you really think the puppy can't stay with Cal, Baby Dog can stay here with us until I can talk sense into Cal."

"What about Dave's allergy?"

"Aller—? Oh! Of course! What was I thinking? That just shows how upset this has me. I better go, Taylor. You do what you think best, but give Cal the benefit of the doubt, okay?"

Halfway from town to the turnoff to the Flying W, snow had started. By the time Taylor had followed the ranch road around the front pasture and past the main house to the cluster of barns, sheds and utility buildings on one side and the foreman's house on the other, it was coming down thick enough to keep the windshield wipers fully occupied.

She could almost imagine that their rhythm sounded out the word "doubt," over and over.

Give Cal the benefit of the doubt.

Well, she sure had plenty of doubt. She wasn't so sure about the benefit.

She climbed out of the car, slung her large bag over her shoulder and pushed the car door to close it. The wind caught it and made it slam. Over the sound, she heard a high-pitched bark from the old, often-patched barn.

If Cal Ruskoff had left that poor puppy alone in the drafty, cold barn during this weather…

Potential outrage drove her across the open ground to the single human-sized door set in the barn's wall to the left of the main double doors that could let in wagons and tractors. Inside, the gloom stopped her progress completely and abruptly.

The strong scent of hay hit her. Another scent reached her, of animals' bodies enclosed in the building.

Sounds separated into identifiable shiftings of animals, a hoof thudded against wood, a creaking of leather, a rustling among hay, a jangle of harness. And then a short, high yip of greeting.

She turned toward the yip. Her eyes had adjusted enough that the puppy's white markings were like a beacon from an open stall across the aisle. It took another heartbeat to realize the puppy stood beside Cal Ruskoff, who was adjusting a strap around a horse's head, while he stared right at her.

He'd obviously seen her the moment she stepped into the barn, but hadn't bothered to acknowledge or greet her.

"Sin. Sit."

And the dog did, though only after first yawning hugely and then heaving a theatrical sigh. Sort of obedience on a time delay.

"Good dog."

Taylor would have thought she'd heard a thin undercurrent of pride in Cal's voice if she hadn't known better. And then something else he'd said snagged her attention.

"What did you call him?"

"Sin." He laid a pad over the horse's back, smoothing it carefully with his palms. He glanced up from his chore and for an instant she thought humor glittered in his eyes.

"Sin? You named a puppy *Sin?*"

She had the niggling feeling she should be defending the animal's innate innocence, but at that moment, the puppy shifted to sitting on one hip, with his tongue lolling out the side of his mouth, his eyes nearly shut and one ear standing straight up. He looked like the canine version of a loafer lounging outside a pool hall with a cigarette dangling from his lips and squinting against the smoke.

She choked on a laugh that turned into a cough, and Cal reached out to thump her on the back, while he answered in an aggrieved tone, "Actually, you named him. You're the one who said it fit him."

"*I* did?" Her voice reached an octave closer to the rafters as she twisted around to look at him, or maybe to avoid the contact of his broad palm against her back, even through her jacket, sweater, blouse and bra.

That was a mistake, because it brought their faces close. Too close. His blue eyes were alight with a glint that it took her a moment to recognize as mischief. His mouth—his wonderful mouth with that shadowed spot under his lower lip—quirked up at the corners. He hadn't lowered his back-patting hand, so her pivot had brought it to rest high on her arm. He stroked slowly up over the point of her shoulder and back.

"Yeah, you said he looked sincere."

His gaze dropped to her mouth. She sucked in air that suddenly felt as heated as the summer sun. In fact, all around her and even inside her the winter freeze had given way to a sultry warmth.

She stepped back, two hurried, awkward steps. Reaction flashed across his face, too fast to categorize, then his expression shut down. For another heartbeat and a half he stood still, with his hand suspended in air where her shoulder had been, then he deliberately turned away, reaching for a saddle resting atop the open stall door.

"Sincere," she repeated, trying to recapture the thread of conversation. "Sin is short for Sincere?"

"Yup. And now that we've settled the name issue—" he swung the large saddle up and settled its weight with surprising gentleness onto the horse's back "—tell me why you're here."

"When I heard the puppy bark, I, uh…" It was hard to finish that sentence by saying she'd been worried about the animal's welfare, since he was wagging his tail and practically grinning at her. "Wouldn't he be better off in the house where it's warm. You know he still doesn't have much coat to protect him from the weather."

"Tell Sin that. Okay," he added to the dog, and the puppy jumped up and made a beeline for her. "He wouldn't stay in the house. Insisted on tagging along."

The notion that the gangly pup could *insist* to Cal almost surprised another laugh out of her. She stifled it as she bent down to pet Sincere. Considering what the last laugh had triggered, a second would definitely be ill-advised.

"But I didn't mean why you're here in the barn," Cal said. "I meant on the Flying W."

Too late to do much good, she saw with absolute clarity that she was here on a fool's errand. He wasn't fed up with this dog. He wasn't demanding they take the puppy away.

How on earth has she fallen for Matty's rigmarole? Because she'd been concerned about the puppy, of course. Because part of her wanted to see the man, too? She just hoped that part of her was taking notes on this humiliating lesson so it would mind its own darn business next time.

"I came to, uh, talk to you."

He stopped adjusting the saddle and swung his head around to face her. "You chose today to come out here for a chat? Did you happen to notice the weather? I already sent the other hands home."

"I'm from Ohio. I know how to drive in snow."

He snorted and resumed his task.

She clenched her mouth closed to keep from arguing with that snort. The more she tried to defend herself the worse she'd sound. She'd used that tactic in deposing witnesses for the opposition—she wasn't going to be caught in it now.

She was rewarded when he finally broke the silence. "What's so important that you had to come out here in a snowstorm to talk about?"

That was the flaw in her case. She wasn't going to tell him Matty's fib—not so much because she didn't want to expose Matty as she feared what believing it might expose about herself.

And then she remembered the last thing she'd snatched up from her desk and put in her bag as she'd headed out the office door.

"Snow's not a big deal to me. I thought you should have this information."

She drew out the folder Lisa had given her and extended it toward him without closing the gap between them. He seemed to consider whether it was worth stopping his tightening of straps to take it, but at last he did.

He skimmed the papers. "Sin's medical records. Okay. You've officially handed them over."

"No, wait. There's one more thing—in the envelope. Read it."

He gave her a look that said he'd do this one more thing, but no more, then he tucked his right hand between his body and his left arm to pull off his work glove so he could draw out the single sheet.

From where she stood she couldn't make out the specific words in the childish scrawl. She didn't need to. She had it memorized.

Please take care of Buster. Dad says we can't be feeding him anymore, even though he doesn't eat much. Mom says we don't have room in the car with all our other things. He was the best Christmas present I got

ever. I taught Buster to sit. He likes to be petted and
hugged.

Tommy R.

Just watching Cal read the simple words that carried a
world of heartbreak along with them brought the sting of
tears to her eyes. She blinked them back.

His expression never changing, Cal slowly folded the
paper. His hands were big and work roughened, but while
one held the folder, he used the other to slide the paper
back into the envelope without a hitch.

He'd fastened the equipment on this horse with the same
dexterity. And she knew the power of his hands from New
Year's Eve when they'd held her.

She jerked her mind away from contemplating the skill
of Cal Ruskoff's hands.

"Well?" she prodded when he made no comment on the
letter.

"I thought the dog learned Sit awfully fast."

No one could be that immune to the child's pain that
came through so clearly in that sad note. "Is that all you
have to say?"

"I'm not calling him Buster."

"That's not the issue. Haven't you known times when
money was so tight that you had to give up something you
loved, maybe a lot of things you loved?"

"Can't say I have. You know the phrase 'filthy rich'? It
was meant for my family. Rich. And filthy."

For an instant she was simply stunned that he'd told her
something about himself—he'd *volunteered* it. Adding to
her shock was the fact that what he'd volunteered contra-
dicted what she'd supposed was a deprived background for
him.

The next instant she realized he'd sacrificed that bit of
information about himself to throw her off the topic of the
emotions of the boy Tommy. The realization pushed her to
bluntness.

"Being brought up filthy rich doesn't exempt you from saying something about this note."

"What do you want me to say?"

Not even a crack showed in his indifference. She wished she could shake him.

"You've got the puppy that a little boy loved, even though you tried your best to avoid it. If we could reunite Tommy and his Buster that would be one thing, but we can't. Sheriff Kuerton said he'd put out a call, but he doubted the family could be found with the little we know. Even if the family wasn't just passing through and is long gone, the way the sheriff thinks, I don't know what kind of work we could find the family, or if even having a job would be enough to let Tommy keep his puppy."

With regret and realism, she shrugged away all the half-formed ideas she'd hatched for finding and helping Tommy, along with the reasons that had forced her at last to see they were impractical.

"And now, this puppy is getting attached to you. So you've got a responsibility, a duty—a moral obligation—to love this puppy as much as that little boy did. If you don't, you're taking away one more thing from Tommy, even though he'll never know it. The love a child has for a dog is—oh, hell!"

She spun away, pressing her fingertips to her eyes in vain hopes of holding in the tears before they could trickle down her cheeks where he would see them.

"Hey…hey…" The soft words were almost a croon as he circled around her, and Cal's hands were gentle as they kneaded her shoulders. They exerted only enough pressure to start her turning toward him. She continued the motion on her own, dropping her hands to her sides.

But she squeezed her eyelids tight, partly to hold back any more tears, mostly to avoid looking temptation in the face.

It didn't matter. Temptation whispered to her in the continued kneading of his hands, in the deepening unevenness of his breathing.

Temptation urged her to draw in smells of hay and horse and dog forming a warm island within the ocean of cold outside, then to breathe in even deeper to capture the scent of the man who brought the warmth closer. Right inside her.

Temptation stroked her skin as his lips touched her eyelids, first one, then the other, absorbing her tears into his heat.

She opened her eyes—slowly, because her lashes fluttered against his lingering mouth. Temptation added another sound to the array of assaults on her senses when Cal groaned, low in his throat.

He shifted, wrapping his arms around her, drawing her into him and bringing his mouth down on hers with power. Temptation won the battle.

Chapter Four

Wishing the bulky coats could melt away, Taylor slid her arms around his neck. At least she could thread her fingers into his hair, find with her fingertips the narrow, vulnerable strip of skin below his hair and above his collar and imprint the texture of his skin on her nerve endings.

She knew it wasn't wise. She knew the regrets and doubts that had followed her since New Year's would surely gain bigger and badder siblings. But for this one slice of time she didn't care. Temptation had won and it deserved the spoils of battle.

Deserved the thrust of his tongue into her mouth, its message clearer than words... He changed the angle of the kiss, stroking, seeking. Her tongue met his, a friction glide of desire.

Deserved the pleasurable bind of being caught between his unyielding chest and his insistent arms... He advanced one leg between hers, pressing her back, slow and relentless. Once, twice, three times. Until her back connected with something even more solid than his arms. This time when he pressed his thigh high between hers there was no way to retreat from the pleasure.

Deserved the frustration, torment and joy of his unmistakable arousal... He rocked against her. Somehow her coat had come open, and the side of his duster, designed to swing wide over a horse and saddle, more than accommodated his motion as he fit his hips against her, their bodies straining for what should have been impossible, considering the circumstances and layers of clothes.

Cal rested his forehead against hers. His chest rose and fell against her breasts and his breath puffed across her wet lips. The twin sensations spotlighted the yawning need he'd stirred in her.

Temptation dug another barb into her: if circumstances had been a shade less impossible, or even if there had been a layer or two less of clothes, would she be feeling something entirely different, her need filled to completion? The barb wrung another tear from her.

He straightened, cursed, then gruffly ordered, "Don't cry, Taylor."

For a second she thought he was going to kiss this moisture away, too. Instead he wiped it away with the side of his thumb.

"Don't cry."

She fought against the weighted sensation of her eyelids to lift them. She saw heat in his eyes, and something gentler. She touched the grooves in his cheek, drawing her fingertips down from the smoothness to the bristle of whiskers.

The heat leaped to a flame. And just as quickly it was masked. Coated over and pushed down by the same expression she'd seen New Year's Eve—indifference honed to a painful edge.

She tried to reach past it.

"You can be so kind, Cal. I know you care."

"Goes against common sense to cry over a kid you'll never know, Taylor. Anyway, it's better for him to learn now that *love*—" his mouth twisted with the word "—doesn't do him any good."

His words were like being plunged into an ice bath, and she surfaced from it sputtering angry.

With both hands to his chest, she shoved. Aided by the element of surprise, she made him stumble back several steps. Which would have been more satisfying if he'd released his hold on her. Instead, she was forced to stumble along with him.

"What was that for?"

"Just trying to make things easier for you, Ruskoff. If you're going to retreat into your shell again, you might as well have some breathing room to do it."

"I don't know what you're talking about." But his arms dropped from around her.

"I'm talking about that hard shell of yours. The one you construct of cynicism and rudeness and distance. The one you retreated to at Matty and Dave's party New Year's Eve—then and any other time you've come anywhere close to me."

"That's something you'll have to blame on biology. Or yourself. Holding you like that, hard's just a fact of nature."

He gave her a lopsided grin that was part leer and part endearing. She didn't doubt for a second that he'd intended the leer and that the endearing was entirely accidental, which was all the more infuriating.

"You know damn right well that's not the *hard* I'm talking about. It's that damn shell of yours."

He threw up his hands and gave a snort of disgust, turning away. Every atom of his stiff posture proclaimed that his protective covering had snapped firmly back in place. And even though she knew it was not only futile, but could ricochet back to hurt her in the end, she couldn't stop herself from pounding on it with balled-up fists of words.

"You carry it around all the time, and the rare times you come out, it's not for long. The real man behind that shell is like the pea in the shell game hustlers play on city streets. Now you see him, now you don't. And with Cal Ruskoff, it's mostly now you don't."

Something had flickered across his face, but it was safely hidden once more.

"Shell game? Hustler?" His low voice was mocking. "Sounds like a dangerous kind of person to be around. If that's the way you see me, you better run, lady lawyer. Run fast."

He was right. He was dangerous—to the curb on her tongue. And maybe to something else in her. He could only hurt her. And she couldn't help him. Because he didn't want to be helped. He wanted to stay inside that shell. And he wouldn't come out, not all the way, not even for the fierce desire she'd felt so strongly from him.

"I'm going, Cal." She had her control back, and her voice steadied. "I won't bother you again. It's obvious Sin—Sincere—will get plenty of food and water. I only hope you can shed that shell enough to give him some love. Goodbye."

As she walked to her car without looking back, she tried to decide if it had been her imagination or if she really had heard Cal Ruskoff say softly, "Run fast. And run far."

Operating on automatic pilot, she brushed the accumulated snow off the car and started slowly down the drift-covered gravel road that led to the county highway.

Only when the car's rear end slid unexpectedly to the right did her full attention shift from the exasperating man she'd left behind to the road conditions she faced ahead.

She eased off the accelerator even more. That didn't

eliminate the sliding incidents, but she could control them. Surely it would be okay once she hit the highway.

The car's low speed and the slickness combined to get her stuck in a depression that would never cause a problem in other circumstances. She calmly alternated reverse and forward gears to rock the car out, and continued on her way.

"Ha! I told him I could drive in snow."

The smug mutter was barely out when the right front tire hit another depression at the same time the rear end of the car went into a skid to the left. She tried to steer out of the skid, but with the right front headed downhill, the rest of the car followed, sliding in seeming slow motion off the road to end up angled nose down in the ditch beside it.

After four slow, calming breaths, she tried rocking the car out of this predicament, too. It not only didn't budge, but she heard the tires spinning, declaring they were simply digging deeper into the snow.

With the passenger side angled up and the driver's side down, she could only open her door partway. Climbing out was a struggle. Her efforts were rewarded by stepping into a drift of snow that went over her shoes, and sifted down inside them. But that discomfort faded compared to the realization that she would definitely need help to get the car out of the ditch. She would need *Cal's* help. *Oh, hell.*

Head down against the wind-driven snow, arms wrapped around herself to try to ward off some of the chill, she walked the half mile back to the heart of the Flying W.

She pushed open the same barn door she'd used before and stood there, breathing heavily, grateful to be out of the wind.

"Hello?" she called out when she had the breath for it.

Although several horses were there, the one Cal had been saddling was gone, and no human voice or dog's bark answered her call.

She pounded on the front door of the foreman's frame house. No answer.

No Cal and no puppy. Where could he be? Where could *they* be?

Taylor reversed her circuit, calling, then listening. Nothing.

If he was out on the horse she'd seen before, maybe he would see her car. But it would take at least two people to get it out, one to push and one to steer and feed it gas. So it did no good for her to be here.

On her way back to the car, she tried to squint into the distance to search for any sign of Cal. Only there wasn't any distance to see. All she could see was two feet in front of her, and that was all white.

Entirely white. With no sign of her green car. But surely this was where she'd left it, right after the curve to the right, with a gnarled tree standing stark sentinel. That was the tree—she was sure of it—even though it now resembled a ghost more than a skeleton. So that would make her car that big white lump.

She used her hands and arms to sweep as much of the snow off the trunk as she could in order to get out the brush she'd left there, then used that to clear wherever she could reach. It would be visible for a little while, anyhow. She tied her red scarf to the radio antenna. Then, ignoring the tingle that prickled her fingers through her too thin gloves, she carefully cleared away a drift piling up around the exhaust pipe.

By the time she got back to the car, her feet were numb. She turned the ignition key. Nothing. She tried it again. Still nothing. The third time, the engine turned over and she whispered a prayer of thanks as she turned on the heat.

She turned the heater on full blast, letting it melt the snowflakes that had stuck to her eyelashes, then moderated it. She would allow herself only enough heat to defrost the worst of her chill before she turned off the engine.

About a third of a tank left.

When that ran out, her best bet would probably be the barn. Although she wasn't looking forward to the return trip.

She was trying to calculate how long the gas might last and how long it would take her to warm up enough that she could turn off the engine for a while, when a knock against the driver's window jolted her straight up out of the seat with a scream.

She jumped so hard she banged her head on the ceiling and her knee on the steering wheel. It took her a couple seconds to twist around to look out the snow-encrusted window.

"Taylor! Are you all right?"

Even muffled, she recognized Cal's voice. With a gush of relief she rolled down the window. And found herself looking at a man's cowboy boot stuck in a stirrup, with a horse's side immediately beyond it. She suspected the boot, rather than a hand, had rapped on the window.

"Are you all right, Taylor?"

"Yes." *Now.* But she wasn't going to say that. She no longer entertained any reluctance to take his help, but that didn't mean she had to throw herself into his arms—again.

She craned her head out of the window, blinking against the swirl of snow, to see Cal sitting atop the horse, bundled in a jacket topped by the slicker whose long tails split over the back of his saddle. His hat was tied down with a muffler, and he wore thick gloves. Something squirmed at the front of his saddle, and it took her another instant of blinking concentration to realize it was the puppy, mostly hidden by the slicker and being carried crossways like she'd seen sick calves carried by cowboys on horseback.

"What the hell happened?"

"The car skidded off the road." It dented her pride, but what was the use of trying to hide an obvious fact? "I went looking for you. I thought, hoped, you could give me a push.''

"No."

Before she could do more than blink, he said, "Only a fool would stay here trying to dig this thing out of the ditch. Gather anything you need from the car." Then he snapped out a final order. "And close that damned window."

There wasn't anything to gather from the car except her purse, so after rolling up the window, she turned off the engine, put the keys in her purse and slung the strap across her body.

She pushed the door open. The snow was noticeably deeper despite having been tramped down by her previous comings and goings.

"Why is Sin—?"

The blast of the wind took the rest of her words off to another county, but apparently he'd caught enough.

"Because he has no more sense than you do about staying out of a storm. Give me that thing." He gestured for her purse and she handed it up to him, then slid to the edge of the seat to start the awkward maneuver of getting out of the slanted car. She'd been in Wyoming long enough to know he wouldn't dismount unless he had to, because that increased the risk of the horse bolting, and having a horse in a situation like this was vital.

"Is he—?"

"He'll be fine." Holding Sin with his left arm, he leaned sideways from the saddle and stretched out his right arm. "Take my arm."

"It's okay, I can do it. I don't want to risk pulling you off." Her left foot slid, but she caught herself against the frame of the door. Maybe she kept asking questions to distract him from watching her flounder around. "Where were you before? I went to the barn, but nobody was there."

"Moving stock. Take my arm. You're not going to pull me off."

"Why were you moving stock?"

"A few could calf early, and I want 'em someplace I can get to. Now quit asking questions and take my arm, dammit!"

She clasped his forearm, while he did the same to her. One smooth motion, and he had her out of the car and upright enough to find her footing on the sloped side of the ditch.

"I was worried about you two." The words helped her not think about the odd sensation that had taken hold in the pit of her stomach.

"You were worried about *us?* Are you—no! Don't lock it. If it freezes it'll be harder to get open later. And I doubt anybody's going to steal it."

She'd started the motion automatically, but what he said made sense. He just didn't have to be so sarcastic about it. She closed the door and moved to the level road while he turned his horse around.

"Take him," he ordered, putting Sin in her arms. "And don't let him go. I'm not chasing him in a damned blizzard."

Sin showed no sign of trying to get away, burrowing against the front of her jacket with a slight shiver when another blast of wind came at them.

Cal dismounted. Holding firmly to the reins, he shrugged out of the slicker one arm at a time, then put it around her shoulders.

"I don't need—"

"Yes, you do. And your arguing is just slowing us down."

With his having to keep hold of the reins with one hand, her arms full of puppy, and the wind trying to snatch the slicker away from them, getting it on her took concentration and cooperation. The cooperation carried over as he took Sin from her while she mounted, then handed the puppy back. Both of them arranged the long flaps of the slicker to cover both her and the dog as much as possible.

"Bend low over the horse's neck and it'll cut the wind," he instructed.

He moved to the horse's head.

"Cal! Aren't you going to ride?"

"No. I don't want Reve worn out."

As they struggled through the world of white and cold, she recognized how wise he was to not use up all the horse's reserves. If she'd had on clothing and boots better suited to the weather, she would have walked, too. As it was, her legs were rapidly following her hands and feet in complete numbness. Sin shivered against her lap.

If she'd followed her plan to stay in the car until the gas ran out, then tried to walk back here, she probably wouldn't have made it—a humbling admission, even if made only to herself.

Twice, Cal stopped their progression, as if trying to get his bearings. She didn't know how he could know where they were headed, because even when the stinging wind allowed her to open her eyes wide enough to look around, she saw only a curtain of white. The third time, she saw a fence post, coated on one side by snow, but still showing dark and upright on the other, and realized Cal was following the fence line.

How long had they been struggling against the storm? She had no idea. They had always been in this white void and they always would be.

"Okay! We'll have to walk around to the back," Cal shouted.

It took Taylor a moment to make sense of the words pulled apart by the wind. They'd reached the foreman's cabin, at the side of the front porch, and he was tying the reins to the corner post. The front of the cabin was taking the brunt of the storm, with deep drifts piling up against the door.

She handed Sin to him, then nearly fell when she tried to get down. Still holding Sin, Cal partially wedged her between himself and the horse's side.

"I'm okay," she said when she thought she had a chance of staying upright on her own.

"Stay right behind me, and hold on," he instructed over the howl of the wind, indicating she should grab the back of his jacket. "Try to step in my footprints. It'll be easier."

She knew he was right, but it sure didn't seem easier. The wind not only presented a wall to break through, but then it whipped around and slapped at her side, nearly knocking her down. And it added the continuous insult to these injuries by hurling stinging points of snow into her face.

She was huffing and puffing when he stopped. Over his shoulder, he said, "Halfway there. One-minute breather."

After gulping in some air, he added, "You should have come back here as soon as you got stuck."

"I did. I checked the house and barn and other buildings. You weren't there, so I went back to my car."

"Why the hell didn't you go in the house where it's warm? It's open."

"I didn't want to intrude on your privacy," she said stiffly. Actually, everything she said right now was stiff, because her lips were numb.

"How could you intrude on my privacy when I wasn't *there?*"

"Thank you for pointing that out." Her brittle mood broke in a burst of honesty. "All right, it was stupid. I should have barged into your house and taken over. Is that what you want to hear? I already feel like an idiot for driving the car into a ditch, okay?"

"Could've happened to anybody."

If that wasn't just like Cal Ruskoff—giving her grief for what she thought was being considerate of him, then excusing her act that was entirely open to ridicule.

Apparently he expected no response to his abrupt switch in attitude, because he turned around and resumed their plodding journey. She kept her head down, and concentrated on following the snow-encrusted hems of his jeans.

She stumbled against something hard, almost going down. Suddenly a hand wrapped around her arm and hauled her up. It took her a moment to realize they'd reached the porch and Cal had dragged her up the steps, which she'd blundered into. Sin was standing outside the door, shaking snow from his coat...unless he was shivering that hard.

With one motion, Cal opened the door and bundled her through. Sin trotted in behind her, and Cal yanked the heavy wood door closed behind them. They were in a small space between that door and a windowed door leading into the house.

Her ears roared with the cessation of the wind and her lungs drank in the air that didn't freeze her insides with every breath. She didn't know how long she simply stood there, too numb, too tired to even lean against the wall, before she looked up into Cal's blue-eyed stare.

The phone started ringing that same instant.

Cal held the stare during the silence that followed. But with the second ring, he swung around, took an old towel off the line of hooks by the door, draped it over the dog at the same time ordering him to stay, opened the interior door, then strode across the plank floor, yanking off his gloves as he went.

"Flying W," he said into the receiver. "Yeah, she's here.... No. She's not going anywhere." He sounded decidedly grim saying those words. "Not the way it's going out there now.... I just rode in from doing that.... Yeah...uh-huh...uh-huh...no. Yeah, you too, Matty. One more thing. How'd you know she was here?"

He listened for a long time, a frown growing. "Yeah, I'll do that."

He hung up the receiver, grabbed a chair from the nearby

table, lifting it by its back, and strode to where she still stood.

He tugged her inside by her sleeve. He put another towel down just inside for Sin and closed the door to the porch. "This stays closed or we lose too much heat."

"What did Matty say?"

"Sit." He plunked the chair down. "Take your gloves off. And your shoes."

She started her numbed fingers tugging at her gloves, but obviously wasn't fast enough to suit him. He put one hand on her shoulder, pushed her into the chair and crouched down in front of her, yanking at her shoes and socks. He had them off and a towel wrapped around them by the time she had the gloves off. Using another towel, he started rubbing her hands.

"Can you feel anything?"

The nerves in her hands seemed to burn and sputter, but that discomfort didn't have her full attention. His big hands wrapped the towel around hers, his bent head showed her the thickness and texture of his hair, his upper chest nearly rubbed her knees with his movement.

"Yes, I can feel."

His head came up and his gaze met hers. His hands stilled. Neither moved, and Taylor held her breath to see which came into his eyes, the heat or the indifference. Before that question could be answered, his gaze dropped to her mouth, and then he abruptly stood and walked across to a counter that divided the open area where the table sat from the kitchen.

"No sign of frostbite." Did his voice sound lower than usual?

"Good. What did Matty say?"

He leaned back against the counter, crossing his arms over his chest. "Matty says you're not to try to leave here. They've closed the highway. You couldn't get into town even if we could get your car out."

"Oh."

"Matty also says that you can explain to me what brought you all the way out here in that tin can you drive in this storm."

"It was hardly snowing at all when I started...." She trailed off under his stare. But then she rallied. She'd had a reason for being here. An unselfish reason. Just because it now looked stupid didn't change that her motives had been good.

"Matty called and said you were fed up with Sin and didn't know what you'd do if one of us didn't come take him off your hands right away." Her righteousness hadn't lasted past the half-dozen words. Now her nerve was starting to fray under that unwavering glare. "Matty's truck wouldn't start, and since she and I are responsible for him... You know how Matty can be. She was very, uh, persuasive. And she really sounded worried, so I said I'd come out here and, uh, check on things."

He just kept looking at her.

"Well, dammit, say something, Ruskoff."

"You believed her?"

"Why shouldn't I? Matty had no reason to lie." That drew another of those snorts. "You weren't exactly overjoyed to take him in the first place. It wasn't unreasonable. And he's my responsibility—mine and Matty's."

"So you thought I'd open the door and drop-kick him out into a blizzard?"

"It wasn't sno—"

"Oh, yeah, I forgot. It wasn't snowing yet." He turned away, grumbling under his breath. Curses, she suspected. "Well, it sure as hell is snowing now. And it's going to keep snowing. So you're not going anywhere anytime soon. And let's get one thing straight—Sin isn't going anywhere at all. I'm responsible for him from now on. Understand?"

"Yes."

"Good. I'm going to take care of my horse and the rest

of them in the barn. Then I'll come back. You stay put. Understand?''

As if she intended to go out for a stroll. But all she said was, ''Yes.''

She was in the lion's den.

Or the hermit's cave, she thought, remembering Matty's comment. Or maybe the hermit crab's shell.

''That's the one that fits,'' she told Sin as she used the towel to pull out lumps of snow matting his coat. ''Because he's a hermit, and he's definitely a crab.''

Leaving her coat on to fight the chill that had surely attached itself to her bones, she sat on one towel, wrapped another around her feet and got to work on the puppy's snow-crusted back.

''A hermit and a crab,'' she repeated. The puppy didn't respond, busy lapping up a morsel of snow that had fallen to the floor.

What did a hermit crab do to an intruder who ventured into his shell? She had a good idea of what a lion did. It wasn't a pleasant thought.

That had always been an element of her response to Cal Ruskoff. His No Trespassing signs were clear and stark. And she'd never been one who'd flouted the law—or common sense—by ignoring such postings.

Not only was there no telling what the person behind those signs might do to a trespasser, but part of her figured he'd have some right, since he'd gone to such trouble to make it clear outsiders weren't welcome.

She'd let Matty see only that commonsense element. Because if she ever let Matty know different, Matty would never let go.

But she didn't lie to herself. There were definitely other elements to her response.

Desire was a major ingredient. She'd felt a jolt of attraction when they'd met. She'd thought there'd been an answering spark from him. But as time went by she'd decided she'd been wrong.

Then came New Year's Eve. Talk about mixed signals!

She couldn't mistake his physical response. It was blunt and potent. And it was seductive to be wanted that way.

But her ability to read people had been a valuable asset when she started her law career. Even in her low-key practice here in Knighton, it came in handy. And her reading of Cal Ruskoff on New Year's Eve had been that he hadn't liked wanting her one bit.

"That doesn't exactly warm a girl's heart," she informed Sin.

Especially when that girl's hormones, respiratory system, bloodstream and all her other little parts were standing up and screaming, "Let's go!"

It made her feel as if she knew that a chocolate brownie she really, really wanted to eat could make her desperately ill.

She turned away from the brownie, but that didn't mean she didn't still want it.

So she had these two sides of her reaction to Cal Ruskoff—the chocolate brownie of desire and the desperate illness of his attitude.

And then there was a third side.

Perhaps the most dangerous.

He's a good man, but he keeps such a high wall between himself and the world, it's like he lives in a…cave. And I think you're the one who could bring him out. You two have a…a connection.

Ah, Matty Brennan Currick didn't play fair.

Because that was the tease of the third element. That Cal Ruskoff needed healing, and she could do it.

The door lurched open on a gust, swirling in cold and bitter air, along with a man. He glared at her even before he started unwinding the muffler that had held down his hat.

So much for healing. Maybe it wasn't the air that was cold and bitter, but just the company.

"What are you doing?" he demanded.

"The snow's clumped to the ends of his fur." She was determined to be reasonable. "It's like snowballs hanging there. I didn't think you'd want them melting all over your house, so I'm removing them."

"You're removing his snowballs."

His tone was so neutral it took her an extra beat to catch the double meaning he'd discovered in her words. Even then she wasn't sure, so she looked up into his face.

Mistake.

His expression gave *almost* nothing away. Deep in his eyes, and in the fan of lines at their corners, though, she saw both humor and heightened attention.

Then he started railing at her again.

"You better remember this day the next time you think you need to check up on some dog. Remember it, and count yourself damned lucky. Do you have any idea how dangerous a storm like this is? It's damn near whiteout conditions. What the hell did you think you were doing, coming out here with a blizzard coming? No—don't answer. You might want to stand here jabbering, but I don't want to listen until I've warmed up."

That struck her as unfair, since he was the one jabbering. But she held her peace. Not that it earned her any credit with him. In fact, his frown deepened.

"Why're you still wearing your coat?"

"Because I am still cold," she answered reasonably. Also because she'd been leery of pushing any deeper into the lion's den, but he didn't need to know that.

"Why the hell didn't you get out of those wet clothes, then?"

"And get into what? Nothing?"

Another mistake. A big one. She saw her question create

the image in his mind, and across three feet of distance she felt the heat of it.

"I'll find something. I'll be damned if I let you die of pneumonia after all the trouble it was to save you."

Chapter Five

"And be sure the latch catches when you close the door," he instructed as he added a bath towel to the pile of quickly gathered clean clothes he handed to Taylor. He jerked his head toward the bathroom off the bedroom.

"Is that all? Any more orders?" Taylor asked in a falsely sweet voice.

He frowned at her. He'd simply told her she needed to get out of those cold, wet clothes, take a shower, warming up gradually, and being sure to rub her hands and feet briskly with a cloth. That was just good sense after being out in the cold. And the fact that he'd insisted she go first made sense, too. He was bigger and more accustomed to the cold. The instructions on turning on the shower were necessary with an old, tricky mechanism.

As for the caution about the door, that was necessary, too.

"It doesn't catch all the time, and Sin likes opening doors. Unless you'd like to risk a sudden blast of cold air?"

"No, thank you. I will bolt the door."

"There's no bolt—"

"Metaphorically speaking," she said, sweeping into the bathroom with the stack of clothes and towels.

He waited until he heard the firm click of the latch sliding home, then returned to the main room. Sin, looking disappointed but philosophical, followed.

There was no way Taylor was getting out of here tonight. And the highway being closed didn't make tomorrow look good.

What the hell was he going to do with her?

Despite his chilled state, his body gave a clear indication of what he would like to do with her.

For starters, he'd like to be the bar of soap she was using right now. To glide over and around all of her, to surround her with himself the way his hands had surrounded hers.

His body temperature edged up several notches.

If he could get the furnace in the main house stoked up enough to make it comfortable, she could go over there and he could stay here.

He dismissed that idea. It would take all night, and only a fool would risk using up fuel oil like that. This storm had already proved highly unpredictable. Until they had a better idea of how long they might be stuck here, it was much smarter to conserve fuel by staying together in the smaller, already heated place.

A faint clunk echoed over the sound of running water coming from the bathroom, and he guessed the bar of soap had slipped. She'd be bending over to pick it up. Warm now. Water-slick. Suds running down her sleek legs—

Damn!

Fuel conservation. Survival. That's what he needed to be thinking about. Anything other than *her.*

He jerked his coat off the peg again and, with a terse "Stay" to Sin, slammed out the two doors off the kitchen area that led to the lean-to where he stored firewood.

By the time the bathroom door clicked open, he had brought in a stack of logs that should last into morning, and had laid a good-sized fire. He knew from experience that a fire helped fill the gap if they had to rely on the backup generator.

He didn't turn his head when he heard Taylor crossing the bedroom to the open double doors to the main room.

"You were right, Cal. The shower felt terrific. Thanks."

He turned then, leaving his forearm against the simple wood mantel. The sweatpants he'd shrunk in the dryer last fall bagged around her legs and folded over themselves at the top of her feet, which were covered in his thick white socks. His sweater, once a deep navy, now as faded as old jeans, hung from her shoulders and the cuffs were doubled back a couple times. The bottom of her hair was damp dark, but everywhere else, the curls were wilder than ever.

She looked like a kid, except she didn't look at all like a kid. He was glad he'd added a cotton undershirt to the stack of clothes he'd given her, because the sweater's V neck would have been scandalous on her without something under it.

At least part of him was glad.

"Welcome," he muttered.

"I feel like myself again. I want to say I'm sorry—for doubting you about Sin, I mean. I should have known better. I have no idea what got into Matty, or why she…"

She let that fade off. They probably both had a good idea of what Matty was up to. And when he got a chance to give her a piece of his mind, Matty would know she'd crossed a line that an employer, even one who was a friend, shouldn't cross.

"I'm sorry for imposing on you this way. You were right that I shouldn't have waited so long. If I'd turned around as soon as I saw Sin—"

"You would have been stuck on the highway." He'd had to interrupt. Next she'd be talking about what had occupied their time in the barn. Not the arguing, because that memory posed no danger. No, it was the sensation of her lips against his, the velvet warmth of her mouth, the response of her tongue, the— "You could be freezing to death right now. Better you're here."

She looked up at him, then away. "Yes, well…"

"I'm gonna take a shower. Make yourself at home."

"Oh. Okay. Thank you. Is there anything I can do for you while—"

"No. Just make yourself at home."

He closed both bedroom doors behind him before he crossed to the bathroom. A billow of warm, fragrant air met him at the threshold. Before he could stop himself, he drew in a deep, eye-closed lungful.

She'd used his water, his soap, his towel and she wore his clothes, but somehow the air still managed to smell like Taylor.

He opened his eyes to find, neatly hanging over a hanger that was dangling from the window lock, a pair of freshly washed panties and a white bra with some sort of silky material on the bottom half, and lace on the top half. He could see through the lace.

That stopped his breathing entirely.

If she were wearing it, what would he see through that lace?

The thought ran through his head and kicked a higher dosage of heat to his groin.

If she were wearing it… but she wasn't. She was wearing nothing under the clothes he'd seen—*his* clothes. Nothing.

The words coming from the direction of the bathroom were muffled behind the bedroom doors he'd closed so firmly, but the tenor of Cal's mood was obvious, not only to her, but to Sin, who sat erect with his head tipped and his ears flicking up and down. Cal was cursing.

Could she have used all the hot water?

Possibly, except he hadn't turned the water on yet, so that couldn't be it. And she'd carefully hung all her wet clothes to dry out of his way.

"Is he always this grouchy?"

The puppy looked around at her, then stretched long and hard, with his hind end in the air and front paws extended, before shaking himself and trotting off.

"You've got the right attitude, Sin. Shake it off. Don't let him get to you. That's what I've been telling myself for the past half hour in the bathroom, too."

Now all she had to do was put that plan into action. They were stuck here together for an unspecified amount of time, that was obvious. And Cal Ruskoff had made it equally clear that he had no intention of letting any cracks show in his shell. So, reminding herself that beating her head against a brick wall was not her favorite sport, she'd decided she might as well make this episode as pleasant as possible. That meant allowing only the commonsense aspect of her response to Cal to rule her actions.

"So, let's see what we have here," she murmured to herself, starting an exploration of the main room.

Sin followed her to the kitchen area, which stretched along the narrow north wall. The countertop was uncluttered, the appliances about two decades old, but clean and neat.

"Nothing very interesting here," Taylor said.

Sin gave his food dish a hopeful bump with his nose as if to disagree. Taylor smiled but said, "I don't dare risk feeding you. It might be upsetting some rule set by the Great Dictator."

The windowed door off the long end of the kitchen's U was where they had come in. It opened onto a protected utility area she had barely noticed when they had passed through it earlier. A second door opened onto the porch whose steps she'd tripped on. The wind blustered against the outer door, and she suppressed a shiver.

A square wooden table with four chairs, including the one he'd had her sit on, occupied the area between the outside door and the kitchen. On the wall directly across from that chair hung a large oil painting.

Taylor's gaze started to skim over the painting, then came back to it. A seascape. A quite good seascape, catching the roll and pitch of a restless ocean as it pounded against a sand-dune and sea-grass shore. And where sea met sky, was the glimpse of a while sail, far enough out to feel free.

''Interesting,'' she informed Sin.

She passed the closed double doors that separated the main room from the bedroom, and came to two sets of shelves that stood nearly as tall as she did. The ones on the bottom were covered by doors that swung up and slid back into the shelves. Barrister cases. She had some very similar in her office. They were tempting, very tempting, but she didn't even consider opening them.

However, the uncovered shelves were fair game. She scanned the diverse titles, a good number of thrillers, with classics and several nonfiction hardcovers whose titles promised information on horses, cattle and ranching. But what caught her attention was a model that sat atop the right-hand shelves, back in the corner as if the shadow might hide it. A sailboat.

''Very interesting.''

Sin gave a sort of rumbling assent from the spot he'd taken on the woven rug in front of the fireplace.

Above the mantel was a framed western print by Charlie Russell of a cowboy and his horse temporarily losing the fight with a steer. A solid couch in a faded brown plaid faced the fireplace, with a high-backed wing chair to one side, angled toward the small TV, and a battered coffee table.

The wing chair's partner sat by the front window, accompanied by a small table. The chairs' fabric was good, but worn; the lines refined but solid.

Beyond the window, the storm whirled white and gray, with no sky or ground distinguishable in the mix. The front porch was not only covered, but its shape was masked in the wind-driven drifts. There was no hope of seeing anything beyond it. And even though it was still early afternoon, the light was fading noticeably.

Only when she turned from the window did she notice two more small seascapes hung on the wall where someone seated in the chair could see them, yet they would not be obvious from anywhere else in the room.

"A ranch hand in Wyoming with a yen for the sea," Taylor murmured to herself.

She ran her hands over the fabric of the wing chair and considered the room from this vantage point. The two chairs, the bookcases and their contents and the seascapes—all easily packed in the bed of a pickup—were his. The rest had come with the house. She wondered if he had any idea how obvious that was. She suspected he didn't, or he'd have worked harder to mask it.

It's the one thing that's familiar to him.

Those had been Matty's words about the towel belonging to the puppy, but might the same theory apply to Cal's belongings?

Her eyes suddenly prickled.

He'd been wrong before. If she'd come in here after the car got stuck, she *would* have intruded on his privacy. As little as his home told, it was much more than he'd ever said himself. It might have taken the deviousness of Matty Currick and the ferocity of a Wyoming blizzard, but he'd let Taylor inside his world. At least a little.

The realization made the harsh, arrogant man suddenly seem vulnerable.

She made a point of being in the wing chair close to the

couch, reading a collection of articles by John McPhee
when the shower turned off.

The changing sounds from the bedroom apparently
roused Sin from his nap. He got up, stretched and padded
off in the direction of the closed doors.

A soft bump, followed immediately by a faint squeak,
made Taylor look up from the book—and straight at a
nearly naked Cal Ruskoff.

The left-hand door to the bedroom had swung open—
Sin's wagging tail, as he stepped into the room, told the
story of how that had happened. Cal had apparently been
crossing from the bathroom toward the dresser on the opposite wall of the bedroom when Sin performed his door
trick.

He wore a towel. Only a towel. And not a very large
towel. Wrapped around his waist, with the loose ends not
quite meeting, leaving a slit all the way up his muscled
thigh and smooth hip.

His abdomen was faintly rippled and still carried some
summer bronze. A line of glinting hair bisected his chest,
disappearing under the towel. His shoulders were as broad
as she'd known they would be. His face was set and concentrated.

Their eyes met. She stopped breathing. He stood stock-
still.

No, not quite stock-still. The towel was moving. Shifting...

Taylor's gaze snapped back to his face. And a heated
shiver tingled through her, tightening her breasts, clamping
the base of her stomach.

Then he moved, in a blur of a grabbing hand, a slipping
towel, a hard male haunch and a wagging tail.

"No, Sin. No! Sit."

Cal and the puppy had disappeared from view, toward
the closet. The door remained open, he couldn't get to it to
close it without providing another inadvertent peep show.

Under no circumstances would he want to do that, of course. He hadn't wanted to the first time. It had been the result of a puppy's prank.

Except...

No, no. They were too far apart, the light was too dim for her to put any credence in what she thought she'd seen in his face.

She mustn't read anything into something that was, after all, simply an accident. More embarrassing than anything else. And only mildly embarrassing between two reasonable adults.

That interpretation seemed even more likely when he reappeared in old jeans, a flannel shirt over a black T-shirt and sneakers, and said casually, "Sorry. I told you Sin likes to open doors."

The culprit came prancing by her chair, as if looking for praise.

"I'll keep that in mind." She smiled, hoping she sounded as offhand as he did. "What other tricks does he do?"

"Well, he retrieves socks. Clean ones only, of course. And only when you want them left where they were."

She chuckled and busied herself with petting the puppy, glad it gave her an excuse to keep her head down.

Cal Ruskoff, with a smile playing around his lips and his eyes relaxed, was not only an unusual sight, but a potent one. Almost as potent as Cal Ruskoff in a towel...or not in a towel.

"Cal, please, let me help."

"No need. Go back to your book."

They'd had this exchange four times already, and he didn't think it would be the last one.

He'd refused her help bringing in more firewood. He'd refused her help fixing a dinner that mostly went from the freezer to the microwave to the table. And now he'd refused her help with the minimal cleaning up.

He didn't mind her doing things on her own, like closing the drapes over the front window or hanging up their outer clothes. But having her help him, with the conversation it would start and the nearness it would require was not a good idea.

Dinner hadn't been silent, though, because he'd picked up a station on the TV.

The local newscast was full of the blizzard. Warning people not to take chances, listing signs of hypothermia, speculating on losses of livestock, harking back to historical precedents.

Most storms this bad tended to blow through fast, powered by their own winds. But this one had settled over them and wasn't likely to budge for at least the next twenty-four hours—just, the weather forecaster said with grim satisfaction, as he'd forecast on this morning's early show.

Cal felt the flick of Taylor's look toward him but didn't return it. He had a fair idea that Matty had heard that forecast and Taylor hadn't. But if Taylor was worrying that he thought she'd come out despite knowing the storm was coming, maybe she would keep her distance. That would be good, because this was the most dangerous situation he'd ever been in.

And he didn't mean the snow.

Eventually, Cal ran out of things to do—all of them with no assistance from her.

Taylor felt tension radiating from him as he finally picked up the bookmarked Dick Francis mystery from the coffee table and took a seat at the far end of the couch.

Earlier, he'd ordered her to move to the couch to read, because, he said, the lamp on the table behind the couch was the only one fit to read by. She'd moved, because he was right. She wasn't surprised when he took the opposite corner.

She didn't know how much longer she could pretend to read. She ran her finger up and down the edges of the book's pages.

The forecast had left her with too many questions. If the storm was as bad as they were saying, just how long might she have to stay here with him?

Did he think she'd finagled to come out here in hopes of this happening?

Could the tension between them get any worse without one or both of them exploding?

And what, in heaven's name, did he have in mind for their sleeping arrangements?

There was one bed. A double.

With the doors to the bedroom open, she could see it from where she sat. It was covered by a crisp white-and-blue quilt, with four fat pillows in sparkling white cases, suggesting its owner liked to lie back against the plushness. No one encountering Cal elsewhere in his life would guess that.

Another hairline crack in his shell and her calm.

She had no clue to what he might be thinking. He'd presented her with a curious blend of surprising humor, surrounded by stretches of dour silence, laced with unpredictable snatches of sharpness. Somehow the humor made the silence and the sharpness all the harder to accept.

A sensation that had been growing along her left leg suddenly pierced her consciousness. "Oh!"

Sin was doing his best to turn invisible. His creeping efforts had succeeded in getting his front half on the couch cushion next to her; it had been his efforts to introduce his other half that had caught her attention when his back paw scraped against her side.

"Sin. Down."

Cal's deep-voiced command set a low pulse beating deep

inside her, but obviously didn't thrill Sin the same way. The dog gave her a dirty look for giving him away as he dropped all four feet back to the floor.

"I still can't believe you named him Sin." If she could start Cal talking, this might be an opportunity to get some of her questions answered.

She looked at the puppy, who cast her a quick look before starting the circling motion dogs often used before sitting or lying down.

"Don't let him—Sin!"

"Let him, wha—ow!"

Lancing pain in her left foot felt as if it spread all the way to her head.

"Sin. Up." Cal's order came out muffled. If he was even trying to hide his amusement, he wasn't trying hard enough.

The puppy popped up, but the pain waned more slowly.

"He's got—"

"The boniest butt in creation," Cal concluded for her. "Only dog I've ever encountered whose butt is sharper than his teeth. And you have shoes on. First time—only time— I made the mistake of letting him do that to me, I only had socks on."

"Really?"

"You don't have to look so pleased. I thought I'd have to go for stitches."

She was able to chuckle, now that some of the nerves in her feet were recovering. She toed off her shoe and drew her knee up to the cushion to rub her foot.

"Hey."

She looked up, surprised and something more by the change in his tone. He was leaning toward her, his hand near her face. She felt the brush of his fingertips across her lower lashes, and knew they'd come away wet.

"It stung." Meaning the words to come out light, they instead emerged husky and breathless.

"Didn't know lawyers could be such soft touches." The

fleeting stroke across her cheek with the back of his fingers gave the expression a different meaning entirely.

He eased back so three inches separated his hand from her cheek, then he stopped.

Although she stared directly into his eyes, she could not read their intent. If her life had depended on it, she couldn't have decided which was more likely—his continuing to retreat or his return to touching her. Her emotions were equally jumbled. But her body was united, from the urge to sweep her tongue across her lips, to the tingling in her cheek, to the shouting of her arm muscles to reach for him, to the thrumming low in her belly.

They held there, suspended, not touching physically, but with the desire to touch and the memory of touch so strong they seemed to form a new reality.

The light flickered. Its unsteadiness gave him the appearance of motion, and for an instant Taylor thought she felt his hand on her face once more, his palm gliding across her cheek, preparing to cup the back of her head to draw her near enough that his lips could...

The light steadied, and he was no closer and no farther away than before.

Laughter that might have sounded crazed threatened to bubble up. She couldn't deal with illusions; the reality was tricky enough.

Unable to stem the urge any longer, she started the tip of her tongue across her dry lips.

With the first motion, his gaze dropped to her mouth. She withdrew her tongue and swallowed. He lifted his gaze, and what she saw in his eyes made her lips part once more in a faint indrawn breath.

The lights went out.

She felt like a statue, afraid that moving a fraction of an inch in any direction might set off shock waves whose result no one could predict. This time the darkness remained.

"C-Cal?" The faint stutter came from saying his name,

with the darkness and his nearness bringing thoughts of an intimacy they didn't share. But she understood why he interpreted in another way.

"It's all right."

She felt his touch then. His hand unerringly covered hers where it massaged her foot. And his voice held none of its usual harshness.

"The backup generator will kick on in a minute, and that'll keep the furnace going. We won't freeze."

She heard a faint mechanical sound at a different pitch from the storm's groans.

But they remained in the dark.

"Stay here," he ordered. "You, too, Sin. Stay."

She felt around to find the dog's collar and held on, as Cal made his way across the inky room. Slight sounds gave her clues, but only the scratch of the match, an instant before the flare of light, told her for sure that he was lighting the fire he'd laid earlier.

"This'll give us enough light to find the candles and lanterns. And this room doesn't get as much heat on the backup system."

"The lights won't come on?"

If she sounded shaky, she had good reason. Cal in broad daylight was already too much temptation. In the dark? Well, common sense seldom thrived in the dark.

"No." He didn't turn around, concentrating on the fire. "Backup system feeds some power to the barn and garage shed, too. Keeps the animals' water from freezing solid, and keeps a couple vehicles charged. Keeps the heating system running, hot water, stove and refrigerator. It doesn't have enough juice for lights, too."

The fire fully caught hold, brightening the area where she still sat. He looked back over his shoulder at her, but she couldn't see his expression against the dazzle of firelight.

"Stay put."

He disappeared into the wavering darkness beyond the living room. From the sounds, he was in the same utility closet that held the washer and dryer. After a couple of pulls to try to follow Cal, the puppy subsided, leaning back against Taylor's shins and absorbing her slow petting.

"These'll give us enough light to get around," Cal announced, bringing back two lanterns that he lit with a stick from the fireplace. "Might as well go to bed now. Light's not good enough to read by."

Panic pushed words out of her mouth before she considered how inane they might sound. "Firelight worked fine for Abe Lincoln to read by. Did all his homework in front of the fire using a piece of coal on an old board. Haven't you heard that story?"

He studied her, and she could only hope the uneven light left him at as much a disadvantage reading her expression as she was reading his.

"You put in a hard day wandering around in a blizzard, and it'll be a hard job getting you out of here tomorrow. You need your rest. And so do I."

Her lips parted, but she said nothing. He'd heard that TV forecast, the same as she had—there would be no getting out tomorrow. He must want to be rid of her to even hold out that possibility.

And that pricked enough at something she'd like to think was ego, that she managed to ask what had been on her mind since she'd first realized she would be staying overnight in Cal's tiny house.

"Cal, where…where am I going to sleep tonight?"

"In the bed."

Chapter Six

In the bed.

His own words hung out there like a heat-seeking missile hunting around for a target, and Cal knew damn right well where it would explode—in his gut. At least he hadn't said *In my bed.*

"You've only got one bed."

His body was fully aware of that fact, fully being the operative word. "I'm taking the couch."

"Oh, no. I couldn't put you out like that." Her brows dropped in a frown, but he heard a relief that made her voice almost giddy. "I'll take the couch."

"No." It came out sharp and short. What did she think, that he'd force her?

"I'm shorter and smaller." She sounded almost cheerful now. "It only makes sense for you to keep the bed and I'll sleep on the couch."

He doubted he'd sleep much no matter where he spent this night. Not with Taylor Anne Larsen under the same roof. Not with her scent being drawn into his lungs. Not with her skin an arm's reach away. Not with her hair spread out across his pillow.

"I'm taking the couch."

"Cal—"

"You'd better quit arguing, or I'll think you're angling for me to share the bed with you."

That snapped her mouth shut and brought color up her throat and into her cheeks that he could see even in this light.

So he was satisfied, he told himself as he instructed her on turning down the lantern and how to relight it if she needed it during the night. It didn't bother him that what had shut her up tighter than a drum was the prospect of sharing a bed with him. Didn't bother him at all.

Cal had his hands cupped behind his head, staring at the ceiling, trying to force his brain to plot spring planting. But instead of a field of alfalfa, the image that kept forming in his mind's eye was light red hair on a white pillowcase, the old quilt conforming to trim curves, rising and dipping in the most interesting ways. A hand reaching out from under the covers, reaching to him. And a smile welcoming him, beckoning him to—

The sound jerked him upright. Something had hit the house hard, possibly hard enough to do damage. And damage could let in potentially deadly cold.

He checked the front window as the most vulnerable spot, even though he hadn't heard glass breaking. Beneath the drapes Taylor had drawn against the cold air that seeped through, the window was intact. The moving dark beyond it showed the storm hadn't let up one bit.

In quick order, he inspected the rest of that wall, the fireplace wall, the fireplace itself and the small kitchen. Looking out the window in the interior door, he could see that the back door and mudroom were undamaged.

That left the bedroom.

He stopped near the kitchen table, undecided.

Then the right-hand door of the double doors to his bedroom opened and an apparition floated out, carrying a candlestick with a tiny, weak flame.

It was an apparition wearing an oversize sweatshirt that reached halfway down her thighs and thick socks that reached halfway up her calves, with nothing but long, curved leg in between.

And nothing underneath? Were those bits of white still where he'd seen them in the bathroom?

She never glanced in his direction, but crossed silently toward the couch. At the last instant, she went around the far side of the coffee table instead of in the narrow space between it and the couch.

If she hadn't, and if he'd been lying on the couch as she obviously expected, that bare knee would have been about even with his eyes. If he'd put his hand out to touch her knee, then let his palm run up the outside of her thigh, his hand slipping under the bottom edge of that sweatshirt and—

''Oh.''

He knew she'd realized he wasn't on the couch.

She paused, looking up, listening, her eyes widened, her lips parted in an attitude of alertness but not fear. She held the candlestick with the handle that looped off its base— one of his great-aunt's precious chamber sticks—in her right hand, with her left hand cupped around the flame.

She should have been wearing flowing lace or an old-fashioned nightgown with a high, delicate collar, instead of one of his sweatshirts. He was achingly aware of the curve of her thigh dipping in to the back of her knee, then flowing into the line of her calf before disappearing into the bulk of his socks. He'd had an art teacher in high school who used to talk about how the absolute rightness of the perfect curve could sing in the blood and flood the brain, and for the first time, all these years later, Cal knew what Mr. Bred-haus meant.

But beyond the awareness of Taylor by all the senses he could name, Cal somehow knew—even as he scoffed at himself for knowing it—that he would remember this moment. That it meant something to him. Taylor holding a candle in one hand, the other hand protecting its flame.

He jerked his shoulders away from the wall and stepped forward fast enough that the air current caused by his movement made the flame dip sideways, and her left hand shifted to buffer it.

"Cal?"

It was more a confirmation than a question, but he chose to interpret it as the question.

"Expecting somebody else? A ghost maybe."

"I heard a noise."

"That was no ghost. Something hit the house. Can't see that it hurt anything."

"I used to love ghost stories as a girl. And it's that sort of night, isn't it? Wild and dark."

It could be.

If he hadn't been watching her hands so closely—it kept him from looking at the rest of her too closely—he would have missed the twitch of her right thumb when the hot wax dripped on it.

"What the hell are you doing?"

"I heard that noise."

"Not that. Look at this—"

"Wha-at?"

"You're letting yourself get burned! Of all the damned fool things to do."

"It's okay. The sound, was it—?"

"Something got blown up against the house. No damage so far. I have to check the bedroom. But this is not okay. Why aren't you using the lantern?"

He took the candlestick from her with little regard for

the flame, and it writhed in apparent death throes. Impatiently he thunked the candlestick on the nearest flat surface, which happened to be the mantel, and took her hand in both of his.

"I saw it on the bedside table before I went to sleep—"

Sure, she'd had no trouble sleeping.

"—and it was so beautiful. I thought of it first when the noise woke me. It had a candle in it."

Wax showed in splatters and splotches across the back of her hand, concentrated near her thumb. The biggest one was an irregular-shaped blob at the base of her thumb.

"Beautiful." He snorted. "The lantern wouldn't have burned your hand."

She tried to tug her hand loose. When he didn't release it, she reached over with her free hand and slid a nail under a small blotch.

"See, it comes right off."

"Yeah, and it's red underneath, because it's burned." He touched the largest section of wax and found it still warm. With the edge of his thumb he gently rolled the pliable material away from her skin, revealing a red mark. He flicked the wax away, then bent his head and placed his lips to the spot.

No thought preceded the action. It was instinct. Not any different from innumerable times since babyhood when he'd burned or banged or bruised his own hand, and sucked on it to ease the sting.

The hell it wasn't different.

The scent of softness, of her skin and the dark, clashed with the sharp smell of smoke and desire. He eased his lips across the tender skin again and heard her breathing hitch then escape in a stream. His tongue skimmed across her skin, picking up the faint saltiness and tickled by fine, silky hairs, then meeting the slick surface of wax. He moved back for another taste of her.

She pulled her hand free and put it behind her.

They stood like that for long enough that his words came out raspy.

"You'd best put antiseptic on those burns. It's in the cabinet in the bathroom."

"They'd don't need—"

"Do it."

Her lips parted as if she might dispute his order, but then she spun on her heel and headed toward the bathroom, into the dark.

How the hell she was going to find the antiseptic in the dark, he didn't know, but he wasn't going to ask either.

Not when he felt like he was the one who'd just been burned inside and out.

Breakfast had been silent.

She'd tried to make conversation, chatting about Sin's eating habits, the weather, the eggs and toast he'd fixed. He returned grunts when she'd asked direct questions, and remained silent at the rest, until she'd given up.

Now he was cleaning up; when she'd started to get up from the table he'd told her to stay put and to stay out of his way. She'd gotten up without another word and gone into the bedroom, closing the door behind her.

He'd breathed a little easier until he remembered that the bedroom was the one place he'd never checked for potential damage from whatever had hit the house last night. If it had been something big, she'd have noticed and mentioned it. But it could've been something she wouldn't notice right off.

He put the last dish in the drainer to dry, strode across the floor and knocked sharply.

"Come in, Cal."

He hesitated and that made him mad. He yanked the doors apart and strode in. It was his bedroom, after all.

She was finishing up making the bed. Bent over on the far side of the double bed, sliding her hands up to smooth the quilt so it would be all the more comfortable to slide into.

Looking up as she plumped the pillow on that side, she said, "Cal? Did you want something?"

Only then did he realize he'd stopped dead at the threshold, staring at her.

"Never checked for damage in here," he growled, crossing to the nearest outside wall, starting a close survey.

"Oh, of course. Our ghost." Even with his back turned, he could hear the smile in her voice. "You said something about that last night."

"And didn't do it—so sue me for dereliction of duty."

Silence greeted his comment, though Taylor remained where she was.

The silence endured as he worked his way methodically around the two exterior walls, and even into the closet. She stepped aside as he neared her spot beside the bed, but he was fully aware that she remained in the bedroom, not a yard away from the wide, welcoming expanse of the neat bed.

He didn't look at her as he continued his examination into the bathroom, though he'd already checked it this morning.

When he would have walked past Taylor and through the open doorway to the main room, she stepped into his path.

"I won't ask you what's made you so cranky, because you'll tell me nothing."

"I'm not *cranky*." He twisted the word into mockery.

"Besides," she continued smoothly, giving no indication of having heard him, "I figure it's cabin fever. For someone like you, who's used to such an active lifestyle—"

"Lifestyle," he snorted.

"—cabin fever is bound to set in fast. What we should do, as long as we're going to be stuck in here is to do exercises several times a day to burn off some energy. Even simple jumping jacks would help.''

Oh, he could think of exercise that would burn off energy all right, and it wasn't jumping jacks. More like jumping Taylor.

"That's horse manure.'' He pulled back from a more earthy description, but still figured she would pout or withdraw, or both. Any of the above would do.

She gave him a level, considering look. It had no pouting in it. No anger, either. So he was caught completely off guard when she drew back her fist and punched him in the arm.

"Hey!'' He rubbed his arm with his opposite hand.

And damned if she wasn't preparing for another swing. He pivoted around to get behind her, catching her arms above the elbows and pulling them back so he could slide his right arm between her bent elbow and her back and grab her other arm with his hand. The grip wouldn't hurt her, but it kept her immobilized while freeing his left hand.

And he needed that left hand to hold off Sin, who was jumping on Cal's side, pulling at his shirt and jeans, and barking at fever pitch.

"Quiet, Sin. Sit.''

The puppy wasn't buying it. Cal grabbed his collar with the next leap and held the dog, with his front paws extended against Cal's leg.

"Hey, you didn't bother trying to come to *my* rescue,'' he muttered, making eye contact with the animal.

"He has a sense of justice.'' Taylor's words sounded as if they came through gritted teeth. She pulled against his hold but made no progress.

He ignored her, concentrating on the dog. "Sin, I'm not hurting her. Now, get down.'' He released the collar. Sin looked from Taylor to him, then dropped to all four feet. "Sit.''

The puppy complied, but with an intensity in his stare

and a tension in his body that indicated he remained vigilant.

Cal lifted his head from watching the dog, and found his mouth bare inches from Taylor's profile as she looked over her shoulder toward Sin.

Desire punched low and hard in his gut, and there was no dodging this blow, or stopping it from hitting again. That much he'd learned from being around her. And now they were stuck here for who knew how long. How long could he hold out against wanting her? How long should he even try?

"Taylor..."

His murmur stirred the hair near her ear. He felt the tremor that passed through her. Looking over her shoulder to her breasts thrust forward by his hold on her arms, he could see the taut points poking at the material of her blouse. He could cup his free hand over her breast, take the weight of it in his palm, feel that point against his skin...in his mouth...

She felt the desire, too. He hadn't really doubted that, not since New Year's Eve. But even without knowing the whole story, Taylor clearly had more resistance to Cal Ruskoff than he had to her.

She turned her head straight ahead, and her voice was determined. "Let go of me."

"Are you done getting your exercise by beating on me?" He returned her tone the best he could, since the coolness of reason had not yet made much of a dent on the heat in his blood.

"I didn't beat on you."

"As long as that's what you think, I'm holding on. I don't want to *not* get beat on again by you."

"All right, I shouldn't have punched you and I apologize—" he released her immediately, and she pivoted around to face him "—but it was provoked. You always do that—turn things aside by being rude."

"I thought I got into a shell," he sneered, because that would put more space between them.

It didn't cool her head of steam. "You do—rude *and* too chicken to come out of your shell! I don't know why I even try to make conversation, why I even think I'd *want* to know what you're thinking, even if I could ever get you to be that honest."

"You want to know what I'm thinking?"

He saw that she recognized the challenge, and the danger. He also saw she wasn't going to back down.

"I said I did, didn't I?"

So he told her, knowing it would make her keep wide of him—as wide as she could get in this small house. He told her that when she said they needed exercise, he'd been thinking of a very particular kind of exercise sure to get their heart rates up, and definitely using certain muscles. He was explicit and direct.

Her cheeks looked like the wind had slapped them again. But she didn't look away and she didn't try to interrupt. In the end, he had to stop because the images his own words painted had gained the force of pain.

"So now you know what I was thinking."

"Oh."

"Is that all you have to say?"

"At least you've told me the truth." She had the clearest eyes he'd ever seen in another human being. So clear that he saw the doubt hit them. Then he saw the speculation as she considered possibilities. "If that *is* the truth, and not just…"

"It's the truth." He stepped away, dragging open a drawer as an excuse to turn his back. "But no need for you to worry. I'm going out to the barn now, so I'll be getting all the exercise I need."

When he turned back, holding a turtleneck to add between his T-shirt and his flannel shirt, she was still standing where he'd left her, but both the anger and the wariness were gone from her expression, replaced by worry.

"The barn? Do you think you should do that? There's so much more snow since yesterday, and the storm's still so bad. It's too dangerous. If you lose your way…"

"I set up the guide rope before the storm hit. I've done this before."

"But—"

"I'm going."

Do you think you should do that?

He not only thought he should, he knew he damn well needed to—and fast.

As Taylor surveyed the kitchen, forced to acknowledge that her keep-busy task was as completed as it could be until Cal returned, Sin got up from where he'd finally settled after Cal left, went to the back door, circled around twice and gave two high-pitched whines. Sin had strenuously objected to being left behind when Cal went out, and now he was probably worried about Cal, or at least missing him.

"Me, too," Taylor murmured without thinking.

She'd been doing entirely too much without thinking these past twenty-four hours. Falling for Matty's ploy, for heaven's sake. Getting into a discussion about the boy who'd given up Sin. Then kissing Cal in the barn.

Sensations swept across her like echoes of the originals, and she shook her head, wishing the motion would dislodge a few memories.

Sternly she returned to her catalogue of errors as she took a seat at the table. The book lying open there was her sop to pretending she was doing something other than brooding over her mistakes. Letting the car run off the road. Failing to rescue herself before Cal arrived. Drinking in the sight of him wearing only a towel, instead of looking away.

Coming out of the bedroom last night to find out about the noise.

Well, in fairness, she had thought about that before she'd done it. The noise had startled her from a light doze to heart-pounding wakefulness. She'd lain there, listening for a repeat of the sound, or movement from beyond the double doors. She'd heard nothing more. But something had awakened her. Maybe Cal was hurt—

That was the thought that had driven her out of the warm bed. She'd considered putting on the sweatpants she'd folded across the end of the bed, but by that time she had the stub of a candle lit, and not knowing how long it might last, she'd hurried out as quietly as she could—torn between the twin fears that Cal might be hurt and that she might wake him from a peaceful sleep over nothing.

Letting him fuss over the wax dripping on her hand— *that* she hadn't thought through. Especially when he removed the wax, then bent his head and touched his lips to her hand. Her other hand had lifted, her muscles following the urgent message of her desire to stroke his hair, to complete the circle of touch.

There, she *had* thought before she acted, and so the gesture remained uncompleted. She'd pulled her hand away, and she'd retreated. With dignity, she hoped, but a retreat nonetheless.

The retreat being so fresh might have been what triggered her confronting him despite the "do not approach" flags he'd hoisted by way of his surliness this morning. When he'd started to retreat into the deepest regions of his cave, she had punched him.

She couldn't remember punching anyone since the second grade, when Troy Robell had bustled over to her as soon as her report on butterflies was posted in the weekly place of honor, to tell her that she had misspelled a word. Long ago, she'd figured out Troy had needed to point out her error—and burst her bubble of joy—to make himself feel better because his report had not been chosen.

Too bad Cal Ruskoff wasn't a second-grader with self-esteem issues.

At least with Troy, punching him had made her feel a little better...until her mother heard about the incident.

With Cal, the urge to punch was born of frustration. At that point it had seemed entirely plausible that emphatic physical contact, which sounded so much better than a punch, could jolt him out of his shell, something words had completely failed to do.

What she hadn't stopped to consider were the unintended consequences.

She'd totally missed the possibility that he would wrap her up in such a way that she couldn't move and couldn't see him, while both his powerful presence behind her and the warmth of his breath against her ear made her fully aware of the tightening of her breasts and a corresponding coiling heat low inside her.

And it had made her angry, because she didn't want to feel that for him. She didn't want to feel as if her bones were evaporating when he kissed her. She didn't want to remember the way her body had fit against his in the barn. She didn't want to imagine his hands on her.

And then he'd told her what he was thinking.

Oh, my.

Never had words alone affected her so strongly. They certainly hadn't been romantic, sugarcoated words, and that was part of their effect. The stark, raw power behind his action verbs had revealed more than he could ever have intended. Nothing he'd described could be done from inside a shell.

Clearly he'd intended the words to make her scurry as far from him as possible. Putting it bluntly, he'd intended to scare her.

What he hadn't intended was for her to realize he was

frightened, and what frightened him was a stark, raw desire
that matched his words, power for power.

His desire for her.

And that *did* scare her.

The stakes were no longer kisses. The stakes were exactly what he'd said in earthy, unvarnished detail.

He'd set them out clearly. If she didn't stay away from
him, this was what he was thinking about. It had nothing
to do with emotion or caring about each other, and if she
mixed those elements in, she did it at her own peril.

Sin jumped up and barked, his tail wagging at high
speed. In another moment, Taylor heard muffled treads on
the porch, then the outside door opening.

She drew in a long breath of relief at Cal's safe return,
and let out a short one of exasperation for worrying about
him. He'd said he'd be fine; he wasn't a man who indulged
in braggadocio.

As Taylor went over to him, Sin swiped a paw at the
still-closed door.

"Sorry, Sin, if I open this door before he closes the other
one I'll get yelled at for letting out some of our precious
warm air. But as soon as..." The outside door thunked
closed, and Taylor swung wide the inside door, letting Sin
bolt through. The snow-encrusted form in front of her
looked up. Even his eyebrows and eyelashes were rimmed
by snow, despite the protection of his hat.

"Are you okay?" She couldn't stop herself from asking.

He grunted an affirmative. His lips were tinged toward
blue.

"Everything okay in the barn?"

"Good enough."

"I made hot chocolate. I'll turn the burner up and by the
time you get out of those wet overclothes, it should be
heated through."

His gaze followed her as she went to the kitchen. How
she knew that with her back turned was a matter she wasn't

prepared to examine. She hoped the hot chocolate was decent, considering the tin she'd found looked as if it might have been young when Matty's ancestors homesteaded this ranch in the late 1800s.

"Don't knock me over," Cal muttered from the entryway.

She turned to see Sin jumping around him, whining again.

"Poor Sin, he's been whining like that for a while."

In the act of shrugging off his jacket, Cal groaned, pulled it back on and reached for the snowy slicker.

"What are you doing?"

"He has to go out."

Laughter bubbled up and out of her.

"What's so funny?" He growled the words, but she could see the grooves in his cheek deepening as he fought a grin.

"I thought he was whining because you were gone. I thought he was pining for you."

Like I was.

She didn't speak the words, but they still had enough impact to dim her laughter.

"Well, he was pining for something," Cal said. He dipped his head. "C'mon, Sin."

Had he really been smiling? A genuine smile, with no sneer, no twist, no irony.

Taylor went to the sink, pulled the curtain back from the window, propped her hands on the edge of the counter and leaned forward to look to the right. Through the swirl of wind-driven snow, she could make out the form of a man with his back to the storm, holding the sides of his slicker wide to give the dog a protected area just beyond the back steps.

She straightened, smiling broadly.

Forget Sir Walter Raleigh putting his cape over a mud puddle for Queen Elizabeth. *This* was true chivalry.

Chapter Seven

Curled up on a couch, with a fire in the fireplace, an afghan to snuggle under, a good book, and a sexy man nearby. All the elements of Taylor's idea of heaven.

She was miserable.

The fire, the afghan and the book were all fine. It was the two other elements that had her restless.

The couch was old, but that wasn't the cause of her discomfort. No, the cause was an entirely juvenile and idiotic preoccupation with the fact that she was sitting where Cal had slept last night.

Not, of course, that she'd seen him stretched out on the couch, except in her mind's eye. But she had seen, when she'd come into the living room last night, that his pillow had been at this end. Once her eyes had adjusted, she'd seen the dent left by his head on the unoccupied pillow, and the way the blankets were thrown back by his impatient hand. In the wrinkles and creases, exaggerated by the firelight, she could almost imagine a pattern left by his body.

What would he look like asleep? Would it soften his features? Lower his guard? Make him look boyish?

As for the man himself being nearby…

She darted a look at him.

"Better use the light while we have it," Cal said without looking up from his book.

She jolted, and her book tumbled onto the floor. He picked it up and handed it to her with slightly raised brows.

"You okay?"

"I'm fine. Just, uh, a little tired of reading, I guess."

"Cabin fever?" he asked, deadpan.

"Maybe I should try one of your murder mysteries." She cocked her head and opened her eyes wide at him, suppressing an evil grin. "I bet they're full of good ideas for getting rid of irritations."

A startled expression crossed his face. Although he quickly masked it, she felt a surge of triumph at surprising the unflappable Cal Ruskoff.

His voice was dry once more when he said, "Remember, they all get caught."

"I suppose so." Her theatrical sigh relinquished the notion with regret. In her normal voice, she added, "You like murder mysteries, don't you."

"Yeah."

"Have you read them long?"

"Yeah."

So much for trying to draw him out with general questions. She might as well go for the direct.

"Did you always want to be a cattle rancher?"

"I'm not a rancher. Matty is. Dave is. I'm a hand."

"Okay, did you always want to be a cowhand?"

"No. Just happened. Did you always want to be a lawyer?"

"Not always. By high school I knew." In the hopes of showing him how it was done, she answered as if he'd asked out of interest instead of an obvious effort to turn the tables. "I like the idea of setting things right and law—at its best—can do that."

He made a sound of skepticism if not outright disbelief, but he said nothing she could argue with. Nor did he follow up on her answer. So much for setting a good example.

But she did not give up so easily. "So working here wasn't the fulfillment of a dream to discover the Wild West."

"Working here was the fulfillment of a dream to not be where I used to be."

"Where was that?"

"East of here."

"That leaves a lot of territory."

"Yeah, it does."

"So you left your family and friends behind, and drifted this way."

"Yup."

"Don't you ever think about going back? Don't you miss your family?"

"No. Do you miss Ohio?"

This question was clearly to divert her from his flat, all-encompassing negative answer. He never thought about going back to where he'd come from. He never missed his family. Taylor felt a shiver at the coldness that lay at the heart of those negatives. It seemed so raw a loneliness that the desire to know what caused it was offset by the unwillingness to probe at his pain.

"I do miss Ohio sometimes, and my family a lot. But this is my home now. I can't imagine leaving it. Besides, I couldn't leave my practice. People count on me."

"I suppose you decided you wanted to become a lawyer from watching 'Perry Mason' reruns on late night TV or was it 'L.A. Law'? Wanted all that courtroom drama, and pulling out the case for the client after the last commercial." He didn't quite sneer, but he came close.

"No."

"Perry Mason wasn't your hero?"

"No." *Let's see how he likes having his method turned back on him.*

He stared toward the fireplace for a dozen heartbeats, but then his gaze came back to her. "Who was your hero?"

"Atticus Finch."

"Who?"

"From *To Kill a Mockingbird.* Gregory Peck in the movie."

"Why him?"

Pleasure filtered through her. Now he was asking because he was really interested, not to mock what she had to say.

"Because he believed in justice. He believed in having the law serve justice. He stood up for what he believed in, and he tried to get others to see justice. He was disappointed, but he was never bitter." Did she imagine that he flinched at that final word? "Also, because he loved his children, he had humor and he was kind to Boo Radley."

The silence stretched long enough for Sin to stand up, curve his body in the opposite direction, circle three times and drop again to the rug in front of the fire, sighing deeply.

"That's an awful lot to live up to."

"Yes, it is. Sometimes I feel as if I'll never achieve any of it."

"Not even loving your children?"

It was so unexpected. Of all the things she'd mentioned, for him to focus on that one…their eyes locked.

"I hope to someday."

"That sort of thing can't wait forever."

"What are you? The alarm for my biological clock?" His grin flitted into view at that. "I've still got time. At this point, I'd prefer to have a husband involved in the scenario as the father."

The humor in his expression stepped back and something fiercer took its place. If she didn't know better…but, no. At most, it was his contemplation of the mechanics of how babies got started, harking back to his rough words that morning.

The memory fanned an ever-present ember in her, stirring a heat that put the fireplace to shame.

"So how did Atticus Finch come to be in Knighton, Wyoming?" Cal asked.

"By way of a major detour to Dallas."

"Dallas? You said you were from Ohio."

"Grew up in Ohio, went to school in North Carolina, law school in Virginia. The best job offer took me to Dallas. I hadn't intended to work in corporate law, but I figured I could learn a lot, maybe put aside some money, then..."

"Didn't work out that way?"

She chuckled, and was pleased that she could now. "Well, I did put away some money. And I learned a lot. Maybe too much. Especially about myself. But I didn't realize that until—"

A log on the fire shifted as its support burned through, dropping down, noisily disrupting its fellows and sending a spray of sparks out.

"You didn't realize what you'd learned until you had an epiphany," he stated in a gentle prod.

"That's an awfully dramatic word for what happened."

"What happened?"

"I was home in Ohio for the holidays—just Christmas, actually. Had to fly back to Dallas the next day to depose a witness. I was reading my five-year-old nephew a book he'd received as a present. A story about a boy, his neighbor, named Mama Abedelia and his pet frog, and how he learned the difference between right and wrong."

She remembered the scene vividly. The soft light, the hum of the household muted beyond this cozy room, the Christmas smells of pine and cookies and turkey faintly permeating the air, the warm, sleepy solidity of her nephew against her side as he cuddled to see the pictures while she turned the pages and read. Only the strangest thing happened, the boy she read to in her vision no longer had her nephew's curly auburn hair and warm brown eyes, but straight, sandy hair with blue eyes that weren't guarded at all, but wide and open—

"How did it end?"

She jerked at Cal's voice interrupting her odd vision.

"The Mama Abedelia story? I don't really remember." Still uneasy at the drift of her thoughts, she produced a smile to mask her reaction. "Happily, I'm sure."

"Your epiphany. How does that end?"

"Oh. Of course, sorry. I was reading the story and I found myself telling this five-year-old that it really wasn't as simple as Mama Abedelia made it sound. That there were circumstances and obligations that could complicate right and wrong tremendously, and that gray was the only universal color. It's a good thing my sister-in-law came in then or I probably would have been lecturing the kid on statutes and interpretations in a few minutes. Sally gently took the book from me, and said, 'It's as simple as you make it,' then finished reading the story to Mikey herself. And I stood there with that phrase going through my head over and over. *It's as simple as you make it.*"

"That was it? That was your epiphany? *It's as simple as you make it?*"

"Basically, yes. I told you *epiphany* was too dramatic a word. Although it did lead to some big changes. When I returned to Dallas, it was as if I'd taken a giant step back and I could see things clearly for the first time. Like I'd been a member of a sort of cult, and now I was outside it, and I could see how strange and destructive and...*weird* it was."

"So you quit."

"Not right away. I had cases I was working on, and even if the firm and the clients were... Well, I still had obligations. But I started looking. And when I saw an ad in a trade journal about a small office in Knighton, Wyoming, for sale, I took it. I wasn't fully aware at the time of quite how small, small was," she added ruefully, "so it was a good thing I had that money put aside."

"No regrets? No fast-track-to-partner twinges? No nostalgia for astronomic billable hours."

She noted his familiarity with that terminology, surprising for a rootless ranch hand. "None. That kind of law had nothing to do with justice. It was a game of trying to get the client off no matter what. A kind of con game of working around the truth. Sometimes letting the audience glimpse it, more often hiding it, like some kind of cheap shel—"

She bit off the word too late.

"Shell game," he finished flatly. "Like you say I play."

"I didn't mean it the same way."

"Didn't you?"

"No. The shell game I was just talking about is meant to deceive people, or to deceive justice. You're right that I think you're hiding things. But maybe you have your reasons. There's a reason in nature for creatures to have shells—protection."

He shrugged. "I'm going to read more before the light goes."

And that was that.

Except, when he put the book down and stood, apparently in preparation for fixing supper, he paused a moment, staring at something over her shoulder. She twisted around—he was staring at the seascape painting with the sailboat.

"My great-aunt Eva introduced me to mysteries. She loved to try to figure them out. But the red herrings would always catch her."

Tears stung at Taylor's eyes as he went to the kitchen without once looking at her. They could have been from the sadness that underpinned his unemotional words. Or they could have been from the knowledge that he had given her a gift. A small, precious part of himself.

The light wasn't good enough to read by after a supper of tomato soup and grilled cheese sandwiches, and cleanup hadn't taken much time at all.

Maybe he should consider trying some of the elaborate dishes in the cookbook he'd picked up last summer at the library's used book sale. If he used more pots, cleanup would take longer, Cal told himself as he spread the dish towel on the counter to dry.

And there'd be less time when he no longer had a reason to delay going into the living room where Taylor sat, and this time with no book to hide behind.

He tuned in the battery-powered radio to the weather forecast. It confirmed what he'd already suspected—the storm was beginning to wind down, but nobody was going to be going anywhere for a while yet.

He turned the radio off, put it away, and then there was nothing left to do.

On his way into the living room, he picked up an arm-load of logs and added two to the fire before taking a seat on the couch.

Taylor was sitting on the floor, her back against the edge of the wing chair, her bent legs crossed at the ankles and Sin curled up in the circle her legs formed, with his head propped up on one knee. She was using a brush from the tote bag on his fur.

As Cal passed them to get to the couch, Sin raised his head a moment, gave the man a definitely gloating "I'm here and you're not" look, then dropped his head back in blissful satisfaction.

Yeah, but she gave me hot chocolate.

How was that for pathetic? Comparing indulgences handed out by Taylor—with a dog? And all in his own head, no less. Nearly as pathetic as the warm contentment he'd felt sitting at the table and letting her ply him with hot chocolate and the last of the chocolate cookies from his cupboard.

He couldn't remember the last time he'd had hot chocolate. He was as close to certain as he cared to be that the woman who'd made it for him had been his great-aunt.

"He had some tangles in his coat. Hope you don't mind," Taylor said.

"Why should I?"

"He's your dog."

Cal snorted.

"He is," she insisted. "And I'm afraid I'm getting dog hair on your sweatshirt."

"It'll come off."

He'd meant the hair on his sweatshirt that she'd put on over her blouse, but the color rising up her neck brought another, and more appealing, interpretation to mind.

"When I was a kid," she said in a hurry, "we had an Irish setter named Murphy. I used to love to brush him. And I used to wish on every star and at any wishing well I came across that my hair would turn the same color as his."

"You didn't like the color of your hair?"

She grimaced. "Being called Carrot Top? There might be more blonde jokes, but being a redhead definitely has more nicknames. Besides, the slightest thing anyone said to me turned into a blush. Even now—" She bit that off, with her teeth clamping down on her bottom lip. "No, I didn't like it when I was a kid. The only thing that helped was that having three brothers—two older and one younger—meant if anybody picked on me I had a champion. Unless, of course, it was one of *them* picking on me."

She grinned, inviting him to share her amusement. He was half tempted, even though he knew nothing about the code of siblings.

"You know how it is with brothers and sisters," she added.

"Only by observation," he heard himself saying.

"Ah, you're an only child."

"What does that mean?"

"It explains a lot."

"Like?" He heard the undercurrent of menace in his own voice. He'd intended it, yet her grin widened a moment before her mouth dropped to a straight line.

"Like your solitariness."

"I don't mind solitude."

"Guess that's a good thing in this line of business." Her gaze shifted to the corner of the room that held his bookcases, then came back to him. "And other pursuits."

"Doesn't sound like you would have had much solitude." He could have stopped the conversation cold. He'd honed the skill to a knife's edge these past years. Only reason he could think of that he'd passed up the option was that getting her talking passed the time.

She talked about her brothers and sister, her mother and father, her childhood neighborhood teeming with children, and the scrapes and excitements they got into.

He listened, feeling a warmth inside him that couldn't be explained away as the physical reaction to imbibing hot chocolate. And while he listened, another part of his attention debated whether he'd rather kiss her when she was grinning or when her mouth went straight and she got that intent, solemn expression.

No wraith in the night, holding up a candle, with a hand cupped to protect its flame, appeared tonight.

His disappointment was a sure sign of danger—as if he needed more signs.

He wanted her. That was a danger in itself. Letting himself think about wanting her and how close she was upped the ante, as well as his body temperature.

Hell, he'd even been disappointed when he took a shower before bed to find none of her things hanging in the bathroom.

And there was another danger sign. She'd started him thinking about the past, and he'd told her too much about himself.

When had he started blabbing about Aunt Eva and her mysteries? About being an only child.

On the estate where he'd been raised, there'd been few other children. He remembered playing with one boy, they'd been four or five at the time. But then Scott had disappeared from his life. Much later he found out his father, upon discovering that his son was spending time with a gardener's son, fired the father. Subsequent hires had no resident children who might try to mingle with the son and heir of the household.

Give the old bastard his due. He was consistent.

The last time Cal had been in his father's office, the week before he'd left for good, his father had called him in and dressed him down for playing softball on a team with some of his subordinates. Cal hadn't taken the lecture silently.

So, let me get this straight: it's okay to screw employees, but not to play softball with them. That's screw *in the sexual sense. I know you approve of screwing them and everyone else in the other sense.*

You and your smug superiority. You're useless. I'd hoped to have a son who would follow in my footsteps.

I try to avoid stepping in—

Christina—his father's wife—had come sailing in then, fresh from some luncheon, and he'd made his escape.

The next week he'd made his escape for good, starting the journey that had brought him here to the Flying W.

For good. Was that true? Would it turn out that way? Or would the information he'd unearthed at the library mean an end to his time here?

Cal turned on his side, staring at the fire, burning low but steadily, exactly the way he'd planned it.

Too bad he couldn't make the thoughts keeping him from sleep cooperate as well. The thoughts about how his past might be butting into his future. And thoughts about the woman in the next room.

Taylor opened the bedroom doors the next morning, expecting Sin to come bounding over to her as he had the previous day. Instead, he obviously had more important things on his mind.

Cal was bending over to place something in the licked-clean dog dish. Neither dog nor man seemed aware of her.

"Stay," he said to Sin.

The puppy quivered but kept his bony butt in contact with the floor.

"Okay."

Sin popped up like a jack-in-the-box and stuck his nose in the dish. But instead of eating what was there, he spun around and trotted to where Cal had sat on a kitchen chair, and stared pointedly from Cal's closed hand to his face and back.

Cal laughed.

Tears rushed so fast and so hard to Taylor's eyes that she had to blink like someone coming out of a dark hole into sunlight to keep them at bay. Because that was exactly what Cal reminded her of in the moment of seeing him laugh. A man coming out of a dark place where he never let himself be free enough to laugh.

And the sound was so genuine, warm and deep, she had to clasp her top teeth over her bottom lip to keep from laughing with him.

"You're a smart little dickens," he said to the dog, still chuckling.

Cal stood and started toward the bowl, then caught sight of her.

He erased the laughter from his expression faster than she could have thought possible. What replaced it, though, wasn't quite the blankness he so often hid behind. Instead, she recognized a faint wariness.

"Good morning. What's Sin up to?" She purposely focused her gaze on the puppy, but was still aware of the man's movement as if he'd just relaxed clenched muscles.

"I give him a biscuit after his breakfast. This time, I gave him half, thinking he couldn't know the difference. But he didn't fall for it for a second."

He bent over and placed the other half biscuit in the bowl, a quick bunching and flexing of muscles, displayed by the tightened fabric of his jeans, that turned Taylor's mouth dry.

She passed him to go into the kitchen. Pouring herself a glass of water, she recognized that Cal had already fixed and cleaned up his breakfast.

"You've eaten?"

"Yeah." He didn't look at her, assuming great interest in Sin's attack on the biscuit. "You weren't stirring so I let you sleep in."

She'd slept in because she'd had so much trouble falling asleep. She'd assured herself, as she stared at the ceiling, that it was simply because it had been an inactive day, without any kind of...*exercise.*

Trying to stop her thought before it reached that word was like trying to stop an eighteen-wheeler with no brakes going down Mount Everest.

And once *exercise* crashed into her consciousness, it dragged with it all the things Cal had said to her in describing his idea of exercise. As it had in the morning, her body responded immediately.

Sleep had been a long time coming.

Cal's voice broke in. "I saved a plate for you. It's in the oven."

"Oh, uh, thank you. I'm surprised you were up so early, since you don't have your regular chores to do."

"My body clock's tuned to ranch hours. Besides, I do have chores. I was about ready to head out to the barn."

"Again?"

"Animals need checking."

"What would happen if you couldn't get to the barn?"

"They'd do the best they could, I suppose. But I *can* get there. It's stopped snowing."

She looked out the small center portion of the kitchen window that wasn't either frosted over or lined with snow. The sky was leaden gray, leaving even the drifts below it looking dull. The wind was whipping streamers of snow through the air and forming drifts on the ground.

"How can you tell it's stopped snowing? Besides, I'm sure Matty wouldn't expect you to go out in this."

"I expect it of myself."

"You must really like this job to go out in this stuff."

"I like open space."

"Like sailing."

His eyes narrowed at her, but she thought it was mostly trying to puzzle out what she'd said.

"You could say that," he said slowly. "I've heard the plains likened to the ocean. I don't know about this country. What made you think of that?"

She busied herself getting the plate out of the warm oven. The only logical thing to do next was to take it to the table where he'd set a place for her and sit down near him.

She managed that maneuver without being too obvious that she was avoiding eye contact.

"What made you think of that?" he repeated. It had no edge to it, but his words didn't need an edge to convince her he wouldn't give up until he had an answer.

"Oh, it just occurred to me that a man on a horse alone out on the range might feel similar to a man in a sailboat alone out on water."

Perhaps she overplayed the airiness, because despite her apparent devoted attention to her plate, she saw his gaze shift to the model atop his bookcase, and stay there.

"Could be," he said without inflection. "They probably both have the illusion that they're not in danger of drowning, when, in fact, they could capsize any moment."

Sin, having scarfed up both halves of the biscuit and subjected the mat under his dish to a near-vacuuming for any stray tidbit, now trotted over to Cal and stuck his nose at the hand that had previously hidden the half biscuit.

"No more," Cal told him.

Sin poked him in the leg with his nose, then went back to the hand.

Taylor chuckled. "He figures if you've tried to trick him once, you might try again, so he's checking you out. This puppy isn't going to believe that what you tell him is necessarily the whole truth and nothing but the truth. He *is* smart."

Standing, Cal ignored her comment and the dog.

"I'm taking him with me. He can get some exer—run around in the barn."

If Taylor hadn't known better, she would have said Cal was flustered by the reminder of his words yesterday.

Taylor had seen the ingredients for chocolate chip cookies when she was digging around in the cupboards for the makings for hot chocolate yesterday. She set to work as soon as she'd washed up her breakfast things, dried them and the other items Cal had left in the drainer, and put everything away.

By the time Cal and Sin returned from the barn, she was checking the first few in the oven. Few, because she hadn't been able to find a cookie sheet. She made do with a rectangular pan, which held about eight cookies at a time.

She heard them in the area between the doors. Cal was talking to the dog—grumbling, from the sound of it. Still,

Cal seemed to voluntarily talk to Sin more than anyone else.

Maybe she hadn't been giving Matty enough credit. Matty had said Cal needed a dog, and Taylor would certainly agree the dog was good for him, opening him up, getting him talking, even if it was basically to himself, and laughing—laughing!

The interior door opened to reveal Cal, out of his slicker and jacket, rubbing Sin's snow-matted fur with what looked like the remnants of a blanket. The puppy, spotting Taylor, made a dash toward her. Cal caught him with a big hand to each hip.

"Stay!" Sin subsided slightly. "If you hadn't gone chasing after a twig, you wouldn't have fallen into that snowbank and we wouldn't have to do this. That's the last time I let you loose in the snow."

Without changing his position, Cal looked up at her. "Go ahead and say it, I shouldn't have let him loose on the way back. Report me to the Rescue League and give me demerits, or whatever you have to do."

"No demerits. Looks to me like you're learning your lesson all on your own."

"Nothing like removing snowballs from an antsy dog to…" Cal's voice trailed off and his head came up as if scenting the air. He stood transfixed. "What are you doing?"

"Baking cookies. I had to do something while you were gone, and I thought you might enjoy them."

He said nothing for a few minutes more while he finished toweling off Sin. As he made his way toward the kitchen, though, she heard him sniffing, before he said in a hopeful tone, "Cookies?"

"Chocolate chip cookies," she elaborated, checking the pan again. This time they were the perfect golden brown. She pulled the pan out of the oven. "We finished off your store-bought cookies yesterday. When I found chips in the cabinet, I thought I'd replenish the cookie supply. And since you had all the other ingredients—''

"Did I?"

"You didn't know?" She lifted the first cookie from the pan and transferred it to a waiting plate. Her search had failed to turn up anything close to a cooling rack. "I thought when I found the chips that maybe you made them for yourself."

He shook his head. "Matty must have brought the chips when she picked up supplies. They smell great."

"Not yet!" She protested futilely as he plucked a cookie from the baking pan.

Hands on her hips, she watched him juggle the cookie from one hand to the other, leaving melting chocolate behind, and paying the price for snitching. But he obviously hadn't learned this lesson, because to her jaw-dropping amazement, he popped the whole cookie into his mouth.

"Mmm. Good," he said with his mouth full, his lips closed and his eyes watering. A moment later, he added more intelligibly, "Hot."

"Of course it's hot, you idiot, you saw me take it out of the oven!"

"I thought you made them for me."

He gave a half grin as he spoke, no doubt to convey that he meant the words as a joke. But she saw more than the grin, and she heard more than his words. *I thought you made them for me.* Spoken by a man who hadn't had cookies made for him, and who remembered a boy who hadn't, either. The same boy who'd never had a dog before.

"I did."

Pleasure made the blue of his eyes seem almost a different color. Or maybe it was more than the color of his eyes. Maybe it was his face. Or his heart.

"Then why can't I eat 'em?"

He feinted a movement toward the pan and she shook the spatula at him.

"Don't you try it, buster." She battled her grin with a frown, at the same time bittersweet moisture gathered in her eyes. Every child should have chocolate chip cookies made for him. Why hadn't Cal Ruskoff? Was the answer connected to why he stayed inside that shell?

You know the phrase "filthy rich"? It was meant for my family. Rich. And filthy.

That's what he'd said when she'd said something about his understanding the boy's feelings about giving up Sin.

Rich, but not in the way that counted—in support and love and having someone to fix a broken bike or make cookies for them, even having a dog in the family to love. When Taylor got back to her apartment, the first thing she was going to do was call her parents and tell them she loved them.

"Aw, c'mon," he wheedled.

"No. You'll get burned a whole lot worse than I ever did from some candle wax."

Mistake, mistake, mistake. Talking without thinking again, and then as soon as the words were out of her mouth, knowing she would suffer the penalty.

Should she be grateful or terrified that she wasn't the only one suffering that penalty?

An arc of heat flowed from him to her like a bolt of lightning. And, reflected in his eyes, she saw his head bowed over her hand and felt the intense jolt of desire once more with the remembered sensation of his lips on her hand, his tongue touching her flesh.

She turned away and scooped another cookie out of the pan and onto the plate. It was either that or throw her arms around his neck and beg.

"Tell you what," she proposed, her voice admirably normal, considering. "I was going to save these for dessert tonight, but if you help me clean up, we can have some now."

She transferred the last baked cookie from the pan and started spooning the next one in.

"I thought they were for me, so I should get to decide."

"They're *for* you, but they're not yours." Was that her mother's voice coming out of her mouth? She might have giggled if Cal hadn't still been staying bare inches from her elbow, making her blood run hotter and faster. "Sounds like if I gave them to you outright, you'd eat them all and ruin your dinner."

"I ruin my dinner by cooking it. Eating cookies ahead of time could only help."

Now she did giggle.

"Your cooking's not that bad. So, c'mon, do we have a deal? Help clean up, then we can eat some cookies."

"Who said anything about letting you have any," he grumbled, even as he started running water in the sink.

"Cook's privilege. That's what my Mom always said when we'd catch her dipping her finger in the frosting while she was making a cake, or swiping some batter."

She slid her finger around the rim of the bowl, gathering a dollop of batter, and popped it in her mouth, closing her eyes and smiling at the wickedness.

When she opened her eyes, her finger still between her lips, she faced another—and much more powerful—kind of wickedness. Cal was watching her, intent on her mouth, as she licked the last remnant of batter from her finger.

Taylor felt as if she'd been popped into the hottest oven possible. Her lungs burned and her insides melted.

He hooked his fingers around her palm and drew her hand free, his gaze never wavering.

"Cook's privilege?" he murmured, low and dark. "I'm the one who's been cooking the meals."

She could feel the warmth of his breath on her finger as he brought it to his mouth. His tongue touched the base, far below where any batter might have strayed. That didn't stop his thoroughness as he laved up to the knuckle, around it, then started to climb once more.

Clunk-clank!

Taylor's jolt at the noise jerked her hand from Cal's hold, emphasizing that she could have withdrawn at any time.

Cal spun around and turned off the faucet with a mild oath. The water had not only filled the sink, but had floated the metal measuring cups she'd used over the top of the divider and into the other side of the double stainless steel sink.

She laughed a little shakily, wiping her finger. Saved by the rising tide, when a different rising tide had threatened to carry her right over the edge.

"My two older brothers flooded the kitchen one Mother's Day in an attempt to wash the dishes," she said lightly as she put the pan in the oven.

From then on, as she helped him clean, in between emptying then refilling the baking pan, she kept up a running account of Larsen family stories and events. From the darting glances she sent his way, he wasn't frowning one of his ferocious frowns, and he didn't object. In fact, he said nothing.

With the last cookies now cooling on the plate, she was washing the pan and spatula, and telling him about her mother baking her chocolate cookies the day her supposed best friend turned six and didn't invite her to the party.

"I was so unhappy, and Mom managed to turn that all around with some flour and eggs and chocolate chips." She was smiling, lost in the memory. Six years old once more, and awash in her mother's love. "I always associate chocolate chip cookies with—"

In the next second, she was aware with every fiber of her being of the man who was reaching over her shoulder to put measuring cups away in the cupboard. And she felt nothing like six. If she turned around, she could press her lips to the open V of his collar, taste the warm skin and feel the hammering pulse of life in his throat.

"What do you associate them with?"

Stretched as he was, he was looking down at her even more than usual, his face as full of challenge as his voice had been devoid of emotion.

"I always associate chocolate chip cookies with love." It came out blessedly calm.

He released his stretch, moving farther to her side before turning and propping his hips against the counter beside her, dropping his chin to look at her over the end of his shoulder. "Yeah?" he drawled. "You don't mind crumbs between the sheets?"

She felt heat rising up her chest and into her neck as she rinsed the pan and spatula.

She truly hadn't been thinking of love, as in the act of making love. She hadn't even been thinking of romantic love. And he knew it.

She dried the pan with more energy than it required, then gave the spatula the same treatment.

He'd managed fine with the carnal looks they been sharing, and with the heated touch of his tongue to her finger, but just now she'd been talking about home and family, and he'd responded like Pavlov's dogs. Mention home and family, and Cal Ruskoff automatically pushed her away or crawled back into his shell.

Well, she wasn't going to be pushed this time.

She put the pan and spatula away before she turned to him. "I meant the emotion of love, not the act."

"Love's a load of—"

He pushed off from the counter. Instead of heading out of the kitchen, though, he went to the refrigerator, grabbing a milk jug. This might be an opportunity to get to know the man behind the shell—a rare opportunity—and she wasn't going to waste it. She regarded him steadily.

"You don't think Matty loves you?"

He delivered a scathing look as he returned the milk to the refrigerator.

"You and I both know Dave's the only one she's got eyes for, even when it was clear as day at their wedding that they weren't so sure."

She picked up the plate of cookies and followed him to the couch, remembering that wedding.

There were so many currents running between Matty and Dave that she hadn't understood at the time, but Cal was right: she'd had no doubt that they loved each other when they made those pledges.

She also remembered an instant after the judge said "You may kiss the bride," and Dave complied with great enthusiasm. With Dave and Matty still kissing and the judge starting to chuckle, Taylor's gaze had slid to the other witness standing across from her. Cal.

Was that the first time she'd spied the man hiding behind the shell?

She'd certainly noticed his good looks before, but she hadn't been able to read the emotions in his eyes, even though she had seen the power of those emotions and had recognized how hard he worked to keep them dammed up.

She settled into the opposite corner of the couch from where he'd sat, pulling her feet up to the cushion, with her chin on her knees, while he took a cookie and washed it down with a third of a glass of milk.

At the wedding, the attention had been on Matty and Dave, so she'd had plenty of time to regain her poise. Of course, she also hadn't had any experience with the passion that could flare between her and Cal.

Now she did. That wasn't conducive to poise.

So she had only her own willpower, and the desire to explore some of his hidden emotions to keep her from melting into a puddle of blithering desire.

"*Got eyes for?*" she challenged as he took two cookies

from the plate she'd set on the coffee table. "You mean Matty *loves* Dave. And Dave loves Matty."

"Call it what you want," he allowed with ill grace. At the same time, his stern expression relaxed into something close to ecstasy when he bit off half of another cookie.

"So you think that what they feel for each other is a load of...?" She filled in the question with a shrug.

"That's between the two of them."

Ah, he was hedging now. "I'm asking your opinion."

"None of my business."

"But you don't rule out the possibility that love might exist between them, no matter what your experience might have told you."

"This has nothing to do with my experience."

"Yes it does."

Too close. Taylor saw she'd edged too close to whatever kept him in that shell. The deepening of the grooves in his cheek provided the warning. She backed away. Not completely. Just enough to keep the conversation going and the entrance to his cave open.

"But there are many different kinds of love," she continued smoothly. "And Matty does love you, and trusts you. And you trust her."

He flicked a look at her, noting she hadn't repeated her assertion that he loved Matty. But whether he fully realized it or not, the tenor of that look also had acknowledged that he trusted Matty Brennan Currick, and that was a major concession.

"She's my boss."

"You're sidestepping the question."

"Don't cross-examine me."

She opened her eyes wide. "I was simply applying logic."

His answering growl held some amusement, but she wasn't entirely surprised when he changed the subject with all the finesse of a sledgehammer.

"Let's play cards."

"Cards?"

"Yeah, you know, deck of fifty-two, aces, spades, diamonds and hearts."

"Okay," she agreed. At least he'd suggested something interactive. "What game?"

Their repertoire of card games provided little overlap until they had reached far back into their childhoods.

"Can't believe I'm playing this," he grumbled, not for the first time. "Can't believe a grown woman doesn't know poker. Any sixes?"

"No. Go Fish. I can't believe a grown man doesn't know pinochle. Now, it's my turn to ask—do you have any nines?"

"No. Go Fish. Didn't your brothers teach you anything? Do you have any queens?"

"My brothers taught me lots, but my grandfather taught me pinochle."

"Fascinating, but about those queens…?"

"Yes, darn you!"

She handed over two. "Do you have any tens?"

"Nope. Go Fish—last card."

She picked it up, heaved a sigh that indicated it hadn't helped in the least, then started to lay out her cards.

"I win," Cal declared—again—as he compared his neatly grouped cards with hers. Then something caught her eye.

"Wait just a minute. I asked if you had nines a couple turns ago and you said no."

He looked up, his mouth straight, but the grooves in his cheek cut deeper and his eyes were alight with so much deviltry that she nearly gasped.

She wished she could take a picture of him in that moment, then hand it to him whenever he dropped his barriers back in place, and say, *Here, this is what life can be like when you leave your cave.*

She wished she could take his face in her hands and kiss him.

Instead, she kept her face solemn and pushed accusation into her voice. "You cheated!"

"Yup. I cheat." He sounded about eight years old and very proud of himself. Then all that was gone from his voice as he added, "That's something I learned from my father."

Direct questions wouldn't do, not if she didn't want him retreating again.

"This whole game is built on trust."

"Yeah. That's why it's a stupid game. Besides, I'd expect a lawyer to know better."

"Know better? You mean know better than to trust you?"

"Know better than to trust anyone. You lawyers are supposed to know the truth about people and be absolute cynics."

"We lawyers come in all shapes, sizes, genders, ethnic backgrounds and degrees of cynicism. I happen to be one who believes that being cautious is wise, but being cynical is counterproductive."

"Counterproductive?" One side of his mouth lifted.

"Yes."

Flat and calm, she left it there to work its way up under his skin, and she took great delight in seeing that it did just that. "Counterproductive to what?" He did a fair job of keeping his question as flat and calm as her single word had been, but she caught the telltale tightening of the creases at the corners of his eyes.

He was truly interested. Cal Ruskoff was definitely slipping.

"To living, especially living a happy life. And to being open to the potential of love."

Without turning his head, he slanted a narrowed-eye look at her, and she felt a little like she had when she'd been

putting new wires on her stereo speakers. Her brother Mike
had assured her by long-distance instruction that all she had
to do was scrape some of the plastic protection off the wire,
wrap the bare wire around the screws and screw them in.
He failed to mention a couple steps. When she called and
complained about that failure, he'd told her with astonishment that *everybody* knew to unplug the stereo first and
never, ever to touch the wires.

Not everybody, she'd told Mike with some asperity, and
she had the memory of that distinct tingling, jangling sensation up her arm and through her body to prove it.

Now that memory was the closest thing she could liken
to her response to the charge in Cal's look.

"Another game?" she asked to break the silence.

"Your shuffle."

She leaned over to shuffle on the coffee table, grasping
half of the deck in each hand. But instead of alternating
neatly, then meshing together, the edges of the leading
cards butted up against each other, like kissers bumping
noses. Only kissers could shift and try again...and again.
The cards fountained up, then spewed over the table and
down to the floor.

"Oh!"

She surged forward, tried to grab the cards in midair,
missed and followed them down with her outreached hands.
Cal was already there, leaning over to pick the cards up off
the floor before the last ones landed. Her arms tangled with
his. Already off balance, she tried to gain traction by planting her right foot. Her sock-covered foot encountered something slippery, and her foot shot out from under her, top-
pling her onto Cal's knees.

Before she could slide off them onto the floor, he gripped
her upper arms, setting her up on the sofa cushion like a
rag doll.

And that was exactly how she felt as their positions
brought them face-to-face.

Blue blazed at her from his eyes. No coolness anywhere. And yet he was backing away, contradicting everything she saw in his face, everything she felt in her blood.

She might have made a sound. But it was definitely his move that stopped his retreat and brought them together.

His mouth on hers brought tears to her eyes. Tears of relief, maybe. Tears of rightness, certainly.

She met his tongue, swept her own into his mouth, tasting the chocolate there, and the hunger.

His rumbled growl of pleasure brought a shiver that tightened her breasts and pulsed at her core.

Her fingertips traced his jaw, then moved to map the grooves she'd so often watched. He shifted purposefully, one arm going around her back. His other hand unerringly found her breast, cupping it so softly through the material of her clothes that she could almost think she'd imagined the touch, except her body knew better, filling and tightening, as if straining to deepen the contact.

Another sound came from him, and his hand was under the hem of her sweater climbing her ribs, and covering her breast with only the material of her bra separating flesh from flesh. He swept his thumb across the hardened tip, bringing her back off the cushion as she tightened her arms around his shoulders.

An intimacy, a definitely erotic touch, though far from the most intimate of embraces. Yet Taylor knew in that moment there would be no turning back. Nor would there be a gradual acceleration of embraces, a gradual deepening of intimacies. This was the moment with Cal—the moment they crossed a one-way bridge.

And then he drew back.

Chapter Eight

Taylor reached for him, stifling the cry that rose to her throat.

He held her off by her shoulders, breathing hard, his mouth a stern, determined line, but his eyes still hot and hungry.

"If we do that again—ever again—it won't be the end."

"I know."

Her calmness surprised him. He stared at her, and she knew he was looking for a sign of hesitation, of doubt. She raised no barriers, she simply let him see.

He started to move closer again, though the unwillingness remained. He could have been a bull with its feet planted against the rope drawing him in a direction he didn't want to go, except Cal was also the one pulling the rope.

"Taylor." It was a plea. A plea to stop him, and simultaneously a plea to meet him. She did neither. She held absolutely still.

"I know, Cal."

She knew the turmoil inside him from needs and urges pulling him in opposite directions. She didn't know the reasons for them, but she didn't need to. Not yet.

He released her shoulders.

For the first time in her life she understood how women could wail at the loss of a loved one, at the denial of love. She didn't make a sound.

But instead of retreating, he tunneled his spread fingers into her hair, so she felt them and his long palms molding against her skull. And he kissed her.

Slow, thorough, lips to lips, but no more.

And yet so much more.

The restraint, almost an unwillingness, she had sensed the other times they'd kissed was gone.

His hand at the hem of her sweater once more had her anticipating his touch against her skin...but not that he would simply pull it over her head, so her choices were to become entangled in it or to lift her arms in cooperation. Cooperation, definitely cooperation.

"I'd wondered."

Since he was looking at her exposed body, the words lit a fuse on her insecurity. Yet, his voicing of them sent a warm breath across her skin that would need to heat up a good deal to match his tone.

"Wondered?" she managed.

"How much the lace showed." His fingertip traced the pattern of lace over her nipple, and her back came up off the cushion. She reached for him to steady herself, and grasped his open collar.

That was convenient, because she'd wondered, too.

Working down from the collar, she quickly reversed the status of his shirt's buttoned buttons. Cal gave her a lopsided grin when she gave a disgruntled sound as she discovered he wore an undershirt. But he did his bit for cooperation and the end of wondering by tugging off both layers in short order.

His chest still held faint remnants of summer's gold, though the pattern of hair down the center was a shade darker than his head from not being exposed to the weather year-round. The rigors of his work showed in muscles roped across his shoulders and ribs, and bunched at his arms. It also showed in the darker V at the top of his chest, where open collars exposed that skin more often to the elements. And in a fading red mark shaped like a comet over his heart, with its tail stretched almost to the opposite nipple.

It was nearly healed, surely no longer painful, yet Taylor couldn't stop herself from bending to press her lips to its starting point. If she could soothe his pain retroactively, she would.

The hammer of his heartbeat picked up speed as she gently licked the spot, then kissed it again. Kiss by kiss, she followed the mark's path across his chest, to its nearly invisible conclusion, then put her mouth over the flat brown disk so temptingly close, and felt its response against her lips.

"Never thought I'd be grateful to a stubborn piece of fence."

He cupped the back of her head, urging her up toward another involved kiss, then met her more than halfway as they slid deeper into the cushions.

When the mundane necessity of breathing forced an end to that kiss, Cal looked down, to where her breasts were pressed against his chest.

"This thing doesn't show enough, not nearly enough."

Her fogged brain might have taken a while to make sense of that, except that he slid one bra strap low off her shoulder, exposing the top of her breast to his heated kisses at the same time he reached behind her and undid the hooks in one smooth motion.

She smiled to herself. She'd known his hands would be skilled.

And she had further proof as he shifted their positions slightly, his guiding hand running down her leg until he found the thick sock over her ankle and pulled that free, duplicating the move with her left side.

He settled his lower body between her thighs, and even separated by layers of clothing, the first touch of his hardness against her made her gasp. The gasp deepened and lengthened into a moan when Cal's lips covered her nipple.

The sensation there became a tug that wound all through her. She lifted her hips against him. He met the motion and returned it. A rocking rhythm that reached higher and hotter with each repeat, as he sucked at her other nipple.

Cal lifted his head, then began kissing up her throat, seeking her mouth. A second ago she had thought the loss of his mouth on her breast unbearable, but the press of his chest against her taut nipples sated them, and she found more than compensation in the increased pressure of his body at the juncture of her thighs.

He slid one hand between them, cupping her and bringing her hips off the cushion when he pressed one finger deeper through the fabric.

"Taylor..." The sound of his harsh breathing gave her more pleasure than the most beautiful music.

"Hmm."

"Are you on birth control?"

"Oh. I...no."

He stilled for an instant, releasing a single, heartfelt curse.

He sat, letting the cool air rush in across her heated flesh. He bundled up what clothes he could reach. "Hold these," he ordered, as he set them in her arms. He stood, bent down and picked her up.

"Cal!"

Her arms went around his neck instinctively, adding stability. But it also added something else, as the side of her breast pressed against the hard warmth of his bare chest.

"I have condoms in the bedroom. This is the fastest way."

She wasn't going to argue with whatever got them there fastest, even though she did enjoy the short ride into his bedroom.

"Get the quilt," he ordered, dipping his knees beside the bed. She grabbed the corner and held it as he brought them both down to the mattress, with her holding the quilt up like a tent over them.

They were a tangle of arms, legs, clothes on and clothes off. It was ridiculous. And it was erotic.

Cal kissed her, sucking her bottom lip into his mouth, sliding his tongue over it, then returning to the corner of her mouth.

"Oh...wait," she protested at the sensation of compression against her ribs.

He grunted, rolling back onto one hip to grab the wad her sweater had formed and toss it over his shoulder out of the bed. He started to roll back, but encountered one of the buttons from his shirtsleeve. He tugged at it, and material kept coming and coming like a scarf out of a magician's hat—first one cuff, then the sleeve, then a shoulder, the back. By the time he'd freed the second sleeve, she was giggling.

"You think this is funny, do you?" he demanded, but the deepened grooves and his eyes gave him away.

"Yes."

He threw back the quilt, rolled her to one side to free the rest of the shirt, and tossed it to join her sweater. Socks followed, her bra, and his undershirt. All urges to giggle evaporated as he stepped off the bed, unhooked his belt buckle, unsnapped his jeans and slid down the zipper. One motion, and he'd slid off jeans and briefs, shucking them into the same pile.

He saw her watching him as he returned to the bed, and his already swollen erection stiffened more. Holding her gaze, he knelt beside her, his hands going to the waist of her sweats and catching the top elastic of her panties as well, but instead of stripping them off in one quick motion as he had with his jeans, he drew them down slowly, the backs of his fingers stroking over her waist, then the point of her hips.

She lifted her hips off the mattress to let him draw them lower. He paused, kissing her waist, then her belly button before brushing his mouth lightly over her damp curls. Her hips arched higher, and he made a sound blended of satisfaction and torment.

Nothing had ever made Taylor feel more desirable than that sound torn from Cal Ruskoff.

But he didn't hurry as he slowly stroked down her legs, carrying the material of the sweatpants with his touch, even stroking her feet as he pulled them free of the material. He never took his eyes off her as he dropped the pants over the side of the bed.

Torn between the urge to haul the quilt over her nakedness and the desire to stretch and arch under the provocation of his regard, she remained still, watching him watch her, and gaining pleasure from it.

Finally, with a hand at each ankle, he gently parted her legs, moving to kneel between her calves, then stroking the tense muscles of her thighs before moving up higher, spreading her legs wider.

It was too much. Too exposed. She reached for the quilt. But he caught her hand, held it in his.

"Touch me."

He didn't force her, he didn't even guide her to him. He waited.

She touched him. The smooth, hard heat against her fingertips and palm communicated itself to her, coursing

through her. This was what she had needed. To touch, no
simply to be looked at.

And in the pleasure-tensed planes of his face, she knew
this was what he needed, as well.

"Cal...now."

She urged him toward her. His hands covered hers, still-
ing her, though he had no such control over the pulse o
desire his flesh enclosed by her hands gave.

"Let me get..."

Balancing on one stiffened arm, he reached across her to
the drawer of the tiny bedside table, yanking it open at a
awkward angle. He didn't seem to notice as he dragged ou
a foil packet. With only one hand free, he was clearly prepared to rip it open with his teeth.

"Let me." She took the packet and opened it readily
despite the tremors in her fingers. "Let me," she repeated
but with a hint of a question in her voice, as she caugh
and held his gaze.

He answered with a quick, jerked nod.

She doubted he would have agreed if he'd known he
inexperience at this task. It required fumbling, stretching
stroking, rubbing concentration. In the end, she had he
reward in the hissed breath he released, and the head-back
eyes-closed, jaw-clenched groan that preceded a growled
"Enough."

He shifted away from her, made a slight adjustment, the
came back between her legs, high and tight, the tip of hin
pressing against her. He framed her face in his hands and
kissed her.

"Now, Taylor."

"Yes, now."

He stroked into her partway, retreated almost to with
drawal, stroked again, retreated again. The third stroke
powerful and sure, brought the knowledge that she had
wanted this through all the weeks of telling herself and

Matty and anyone else that it was impossible—all that time she had wanted *this*. This man, above her, inside her.

She met the fourth stroke, fully, completely, wrapping her legs around him, wrapping *herself* around him. And there was no more counting.

They found their rhythm, or it found them. Beating with the life that pulsed in each of them and with the life that pulsed between them. Hard and driving and inexorable. A pounding climb to the summit. Heart hammering, body straining with the rarefied air, but so close to being able to open her mouth and just swallow a star...so very close...if she could just reach a little higher. Could she?

"Yes." He panted, as if he'd heard her question. "Taylor."

Higher...higher...and—yes, she had the star, swallowing it into herself, its power bowing her back, throwing her head back, shooting rays to her toes and fingers and everywhere in between.

"Cal—Cal!"

His response wasn't a word but a sound.

"Yes," she told him, as he'd told her.

His muscles clenched, turning to granite under the pressure in seconds instead of the eons geology demanded. His head went back, and only the pulse of him inside her defied his stillness.

With a murmur of her name, he dropped down to her, wrapping her in his arms.

Cal came back from the bathroom, donned another condom and returned to her, exactly as he had been before, and she opened her arms to welcome his weight.

But instead of simply lying in each other's arms, he began pressing slowly inside her. Not as fully as before, but effectively—definitely effectively, as her inner muscles clenched around him.

"Cal? Already?"

"Apparently." Behind the laconic drawl was the hint of a cocky grin.

It changed to intensity as he slid deeper, then stilled.

Supporting himself on his elbows, he put his fingers through her hair, holding her head in his hands as he had before. He brushed kisses at her hairline, from her temple to her ear, then back. The other side. Her forehead. And started all over.

She accepted the sensation of those kisses, as her palms stroked lightly, absorbing the texture of the bones of his shoulders, tendons of his neck, muscles of his back and the flesh of his throat. Over and over, his lips touched her, and her hands touched him. Until they had set up a new motion, rocking against each other, for each other,

Rocking between the friction of his body against hers with the prickly hairs on his chest rubbing her nipples to hardened tenderness, and the softness of his kisses and her touches.

She held on to that rhythm until she couldn't live another second without digging her fingers into the hard flesh of his buttocks, urging him. He filled her, harder and deeper, yet with the same slow tempo they'd created. She locked her legs around him, her movements also blending with the tempo. Even her breathing and her heartbeat had found that same rhythm, consistent, relentless, exhilarating.

And in the next pulse of her blood, she was over the edge, exploding in tremors that arched her off the bed. Cal growled low in his throat, then stiffened. Taut.

"Taylor."

Her eyes filled with tears, though she smiled as he collapsed against her once more.

Her tears had dried to faint tracks, and she still had no will to move when Cal shifted, rearranging their positions with a murmur about not wanting to crush her.

Too late. She was already pulverized. Exploded into dust that would never reform in quite the same order.

She rested her head where his shoulder met his chest, and knew that making love with Cal had reordered her. Like the cards she'd tried to shuffle, the pieces of what she wanted and what she expected and what she hoped for had fountained up into the air, then fallen back to earth. All the same elements were there, but in an entirely different configuration.

Taylor's hair was spread across his pillow.

It was also spread across the bare arm he had under her neck. It tickled with any move she made. Between the tickling and the cool air beyond the quilt pulled up to their chins, goose bumps had bloomed across his arm. He didn't move it.

Words—sometimes whole words, sometimes fragments—bubbled into his head. Before they could threaten to bubble out of his mouth, he snatched at something else to say. Something neutral. Safe.

"Is everybody in your family a redhead?"

She blushed as, under the quilt, he brushed his hand lightly over the proof that her red hair came from nature. Though why she would blush at that gesture, he couldn't imagine when he had touched her there more intimately— *deeper*. The thought stirred a tightening in his groin.

"More or less. My sister's hair is lighter, one brother has more brown in it."

"What's the order of the kids in your family?" he asked to distract himself from other thoughts. This must be what an addiction felt like.

He wanted to mock himself—carrying a woman to bed for heaven's sake. It was like getting in a taxi and saying, "Follow that car." Something you'd always heard about but never expected to do in your life.

Now he'd done one of them, and had no inclination to

apologize for it. He'd certainly had no inclination to regret it when he'd followed her down to the bed. Not then, not the second time, and not the third time, when need had awakened him sometime after sunset, and he had set about the enjoyable task of waking need in her.

"Three older—two brothers and a sister—and a younger brother, and I love them all dearly. They're great people. You'd love them, too. Everybody does."

Now she'd caught his genuine attention. "Why'd you say it like that then?"

"Like what?"

"With a sigh."

"Oh, nothing, really."

"For a lawyer, you're not much of a liar."

She chuckled. "I don't know if I should feel insulted over your opinion of my profession, complimented that you don't think I'm a good liar, or insulted that you don't think I have the requisite skills for my profession!"

"Tell me."

She turned on her side, resting one hand on his chest. Could she feel the hammering of his heart? Did she know how much he wanted her again, right now?

"It's not them. Truly," she said. "They are great, and I do love them. It's me. I just don't have a niche like the rest of them. My sister is the brain, winning all the academic prizes and getting straight A's. My oldest brother is the financial whiz. My next older brother is the people person, able to connect with everybody and a leader of everything. And my younger brother is the jock—played every sport, and in great physical shape. So what was left for me?"

"All of that."

Her lashes swept up as her eyes opened wide. "Me? No. I'm the ordinary one among the extraordinary Larsen kids." The smile left her voice as she added, "I think that's part of why—"

"Why you got sucked into high-powered lawyering."

"Sucked into it makes it sound like I had no hand in it, Cal. I'm responsible for that period of my life. I embraced it. I wanted that kind of success at that time. And, yes, I suppose some of it was trying to prove to my family that I was as good as them. Or maybe to myself—until I realized the cost."

"Or maybe by then you'd proved you were as good as or better than your sister and brothers." Her lips parted, but he gave her no time to get words out. "You're smart— gotta be, or you never would have succeeded in that big law firm. You're enough of a financial whiz to have your own practice. You're good with people—I don't know about in your other job, but I've seen you come into an area like this that isn't used to outsiders and turns to its own first, and you've won these people over. Folks in Knighton are crazy about you."

"People have been very warm and welcoming, and—"

"They aren't that way to me."

"They could be if you let them."

"I'm not complaining," he said dryly. "It's better this way. I like it like this. And you just proved my point that folks are warm and welcoming to you because of who you are. They're reacting to you. And as for being in great physical shape, I can testify to that."

She blushed. Not just her cheeks, but her throat and shoulders and breasts. He suspected he would never see her blush again without wanting to kiss every pinkened area.

"You have all your siblings' specialties wrapped up in one. I figure that makes you the most extraordinary Larsen kid."

She stroked his chest, fingering the hair on his chest. "Tell me about your family, Cal."

"Nothing to tell. I don't have one."

"But you said...about being filthy rich. You must have had a family."

"Never was much of a family, and they're all gone now."

"I don't understand. What—"

"You have chocolate at the corner of your mouth."

Chapter Nine

His diversionary tactic was blatant. But if she repeated that she wanted to know about his family—well, he already knew she did. She could say she hoped it would help her understand him. He probably knew that, too, and the odds were even better that he wouldn't like the idea of her understanding him better.

"I do?"

Automatically she reached up, but he wrapped his fingers around her wrist before her hand reached its destination.

"Let me." He closed in.

"It can't be much, if you have to look so clo-ose."

The last word was mangled as his tongue darted out to sweep her skin. He repeated the action, then kissed her almost primly, before returning to the corner of her mouth, teasing it with his teeth, sucking it in between his lips and licking once more, before backing up a good, oh, two inches.

"All gone?" Her question and her smile were breathless.

"No."

"It's still there? But—" She wiped at the corner of her lips, still damp from his exploration.

"No. You don't have chocolate at the corner of your mouth."

"But you said…" And then it clicked. "Did I before?"

"No. It was never there, so it can't be gone." He straightened, then dropped back beside her. "Just like…"

His family.

She held her breath, afraid even that automatic movement might give away how much she wanted him to talk to her, how afraid she was that he would withdraw again.

"If he could have, I think my father would have rolled in money, like Sin does in whatever muck he finds, to get the smell of it deep into his pores." His voice was emotionless. "Of course that wouldn't have been dignified. Instead, he satisfied himself with wallowing in the trappings—cars, houses, boats, servants. And the proper wife. With the proper background and the proper pedigree. No mongrel for him. Only a thoroughbred would do. Then when he had her, she became another trophy for his case. No more valuable than any of the others.

"No, that's not true—she was more trouble than the others, and that made her less valuable. After all, the cars and boats and houses he could hire other people to take care of while he put his energies into what was really important—making more money. But it was harder to do with a wife, not that he didn't try.

"My mother was what the family liked to call delicate. By the time I was old enough to understand, separating cause from effect got tricky. She was on pills a lot. Sometimes she had a private nurse. Even when she didn't, there was almost always someone around murmuring, 'Remember what the doctor says about taking your medication, Janice.' God, I hated those people—the doctors, the nurses, the aides."

With his neck propped up by the pillow, he was staring toward where the wall met the ceiling. She rested her hand on his arm. His stare never wavered, he didn't so much as twitch. She thought he might not even have felt the touch until he spoke again.

"Don't feel too sorry for me. I was insulated from it in a lot of ways. My mother's maiden aunt lived with us—her own wing, actually. She had the bluest blood of the East Coast blue bloods, and not a penny to her name. Family story is that her father considered her too rebellious, so he wrote in his will that he wasn't leaving her anything and no one in the family had better give her any money of her own, but that the family was obligated to take care of her—that would teach her humility, he said. He was a fool. Eva never did learn humility.

"She had a back like a ramrod and face that looked as if she faintly disapproved of everything and everyone around her. But she was one hell of an old broad." His laughter was hoarse but sounded genuine. "God, how she would have hated being called that. I wish I'd thought of it when she was still around."

Even without the laugh, his voice had gentled when he spoke of his aunt. Taylor wondered if he knew that.

"She'd roll up slacks that looked like hand-me-downs from Katharine Hepburn's grandmother and take me on what she called rambles. Climbing over the rocks, going through the woods. Telling me about the ocean and trees and weather and sky—Nature she called it, always with a capital *N*. When I was a little older, she taught me to ride. And she taught me to sail. That was the real escape. Out there on the water. With Aunt Eva, mostly. Sometimes alone. Just a scrap of lumber, a bit of canvas, some ropes and your own skills to eke the most out of the breeze and outwit the ocean."

"You loved it."

"Yeah, I loved it."

His voice had an odd flatness she didn't understand any better than she understood why a man with that kind of feeling for the ocean had landed in landlocked Wyoming.

"Was it always just you and your aunt?"

A flicker crossed his face, as if a pain had clamped down on him.

"No. On her good days, my mother came along. The summer I was eleven was a good one for her. She came along a lot. The end of August, we were out when a storm blew up. It was rough seas and I think all three of us were pretty giddy with just getting back in safely. Mom challenged me to race from the boathouse up to the house through the rain. I won. I went to the closest doors—French doors in from the terrace—and burst in."

He came to a halt, staring unblinkingly, and Taylor waited. If he turned away now, if he dammed it all up again, would he ever break through?

"My father was screwing his assistant on the couch."

Horrified for him, Taylor tried to fathom what an eleven-year-old boy must have felt. All she had to go on was the man before her now, but that told her more than he probably thought. Did he think the uninflected harshness of his words revealed no emotion? To Taylor it screamed of betrayal and anger.

"I tried to block Mother, but she was too close behind me. She stood there, dripping rainwater onto the floor, while Father got up, unhurried, unapologetic. And she said over and over that she didn't understand, because he'd never even liked that upholstery."

His croak of laughter brought tears to Taylor's eyes. She blinked hard. Cal wouldn't like tears, not tears for him.

"She offered him a divorce. It might have saved her, but he wouldn't let her go, and she didn't have the strength to leave without him releasing her. He didn't want a divorce. Why the hell should he? He had things the way he wanted them.

"I was sent off to boarding school that year—two years earlier than planned, and summers I went to camps. The holidays...well, Mother didn't have many good days after that. She died when I was seventeen. Official cause of death was heart failure—guess there's no arguing with that.

"If it hadn't been for Eva, I'd have taken off then. But she didn't have any money and neither did I, except what Father gave me for an allowance. I can't say he was cheap—have to keep up appearances, you know. But it didn't matter. He knew I wouldn't take off without Aunt Eva. I asked her to come. Said I'd get some sort of job to support us—pumping gas, working at a burger joint. Anything. She said no."

"She was protecting you."

"Maybe. I got mad. Said she was like the rest of them, only cared about money. She said she wouldn't dignify that with an answer—she said things like that, and you believed them. I didn't go back to that house for a while. After Eva and I patched it up, it was mostly slipping in to see her. Especially after Father blessed me with a stepmother."

Taylor must have made a sound, because he glanced toward her, his mouth twisted.

"No, not the assistant. Much too low-class for Father. Another blue blood. Only Christina was anything but delicate. Give a wounded man a choice of being in a pool with a shark or being between Christina and something she wants and a smart man would take the shark.

"I'd met Christina at college. Thought I was in love. Got engaged, and took her home to meet Aunt Eva. Christina had other ideas. She zeroed in on my father from the second we walked in the door. Two months later she was my stepmother."

"Your fiancée? Your father married—oh, Cal!" A tear slid down her cheek.

He shook his head without looking at her.

"Better him than me. Didn't take long for me to realize

my ego was a small sacrifice to pay for not being married to her. If I'd had any doubts left, they were answered when Aunt Eva started having strokes. Small ones at first. Then worse.

"Christina wanted her out—had wanted her out before that, but hadn't succeeded in chipping away at Father's attachment to having a real, live blue blood under his roof. For once Father's obsession with appearances paid off. How would it look if he cast off an elderly, infirm relative? That was even more important to him than money, so Aunt Eva wasn't shipped to some nursing home. She needed round-the-clock care, but she got to stay in her haven as she called it.

"But it was provisional. I'd graduated by then, and Father made it clear that I was to join the family corporation—assume my proper role was how he put it. Once I turned twenty-five, I would inherit enough stock from my mother's estate to be a real thorn in his side on the board. It was never stated as an outright threat, but there was always the understanding that if I didn't toe the line, Aunt Eva would be yanked out of the only home she'd known.

"She lived three more years. That last day, she gave me a journal she'd kept. She couldn't talk very well, but she said to read it. After she died, I stayed up all night, reading. One of the last entries, after she'd started having the strokes, she said she was sorry—sorry she hadn't said yes when I wanted to pump gas. She'd been so determined to not run away, because her father had never thought she was tough enough to stick out his punishment, and she'd been determined to show him she was as tough as he was. And in the end he'd won, because she'd stayed in the prison he'd put her in."

Taylor made no effort to check the tears tracking down her cheeks. Cal didn't notice. He was lost in the words he'd never before let out.

"Christina saw the danger right away—they didn't have

a hold on me any longer. She tried to seduce me the night after Aunt Eva had died.'' His smile was stark and pained. ''On the same couch that Father favored for such events. I dumped her on the floor and walked out.

''After the funeral, I walked up to my father, told him I was clearing the books before I closed them, just like he'd always said to do, and I told him what I thought of him. Then I left straight from the cemetery. I sold everything I could lay claim to, right down to the clothes I'd worn to the funeral. I haven't looked back since.

''So that's the story of Cal Ruskoff. Not a pretty story. A grown man, and I ran away from home. I'm not proud of it. If I'd been tougher...''

Taylor leaned forward, resting her hand atop his on the quilt. He flinched and pulled away, but she followed the motion, stretching partially across him. His gaze came to her, and she could see him gradually returning his focus from the past to now.

''You ran to stay out of that prison your aunt wrote about. That took a lot of courage. But you can't keep running, Cal, or the running becomes another kind of prison— that's what your aunt was telling you. Sometime—''

''Hey, you're crying.'' He wiped at her cheek with his fingertips. ''Don't cry, Taylor. I never meant to make you cry.''

She shook her head. ''That doesn't matter. Listen to me, Cal. You can't keep running or hiding out. You have to face those demons from the past. If you went back, faced your father and talked to him—''

''No.''

''Maybe you could never reconcile, but until you resolve the situation with your father—''

''It's never going to happen. I'm not going back there. I'm not going to ever talk to my father again. And I'm done talking *about* him. Understand?''

She understood. He was giving her a choice—no, an ul-

timatum. If she tried to press him on this, he was leaving—
not physically, but emotionally, pulling right back into that
shell.

She couldn't lose him now. Not after their time alone
had stripped the protective layers from around him, so
she'd seen the man inside.

"Yes, I understand."

The wind had scoured an occasional patch clear of snow,
while drifting other areas waist high.

Cal skillfully maneuvered the truck with the plow blade
attached to the front to push the uneven accumulations off
the road, while Taylor contemplated how different this trip
down this snowy route was from their previous one.

She had an urge to smile for no good reason. The sky
was clear and bright. The three of them—Cal, her and
Sin—were snug in the cab of a truck instead of struggling
on horseback. And most significant, she was snuggled close
enough to Cal's side to feel the muscles in his thighs work
as he fed the truck more gas.

Just to emphasize that difference, she placed her gloved
hand on his thigh. When she'd been battling the storm,
she'd regretted wearing these thin gloves. Now she was
glad, as his warmth and movement communicated to her
palm. He glanced down, but didn't say a word. In fact,
something ahead had caught his attention.

Her car.

Only one corner, sticking up at an angle, was uncovered
by snow. She wished the whole thing was invisible. Better
yet, that it had disappeared.

*Oops, can't leave now, Cal, my car's disappeared. Guess
I'll just have to stay here with you forever.*

She waited for him to say something, but Cal drove the
truck past the car. The only sign that he'd noted its exis-
tence was the fact that he'd left no piles of accumulated
snow that would interfere with getting the car out.

He kept plowing, past the main house, to the last big curve before the highway would have come in sight. Then he stopped.

Before them, the wind-frothed snow stretched like a moat surrounding their private world.

"Can't get your car anywhere until we dig it out, anyhow," Cal explained in a mumble when he started backing up the truck.

She didn't say a word. She was too happy.

"Stay here, both of you," he ordered when they'd backed up near her car. "I'm going to see if we can hitch up the car to tow it out."

From inside the truck, which he'd left running with the heater going, she watched him clamber down into the ditch to her car with a shovel. Sin whined a little from her right. After a minute or two she realized she was smiling. Simply from the pleasure of watching Cal.

He wasn't doing anything dramatic. He shoveled enough to find the shape of the car, then concentrated on the area around the rear bumper, pausing to feel under it with his gloved hand. Once in a while, he would step back and consider the car and the ditch and the road.

It didn't matter what he did, it was simply the fact of him—Cal Ruskoff—doing it and her getting to watch him that gave her pleasure.

That pleasure and her happiness were undimmed when he shook his head, frowned and headed back toward the truck.

He climbed in. Before he could close the door, she scooted up against him, took his face between her gloved hands and kissed him, her lips traveling over the cool surface of his before her tongue slipped inside to the warmth awaiting her there. He let go of the door and wrapped his arms around her, drawing her almost into his lap.

Unwilling to relinquish control of this kiss to him, she

tugged back. Sin gave a single bark and jumped to the floor, clear of this human game they kept playing.

Even through jackets and sweaters and jeans, the maneuverings of their bodies against each other set up a friction she relished. She felt him push against her, then heard the driver's door creak fully open before a new layer of cold settled over them.

With a disgusted grunt, Cal sat up, bringing her with him. "Must have kicked it," he grumbled. With one arm around her shoulders, he reached out with the other and yanked the door closed. Then he turned to her. "What was that for?"

"Wanted to warm you up."

"You succeeded."

"I had help." She smiled. A smile that warmed several degrees when she saw the way his gaze went to her mouth.

But he was clearly trying to sound stern when he added, "I've got work to do."

"You're going to tow my car out now?"

Once the car was out, how long would it take him to clear the rest of the way to the highway? Would he expect her to leave right away?

"Can't. This truck would pull the bumper right off that tin can of yours. So we'll have to go the old-fashioned—and slower—route. We'll have to shovel it out and push."

A renewed fondness for her car welled up in Taylor. Tin cans had their upsides.

"I can shovel." Helping would speed the process, but she'd be with him.

"I only have one shovel."

She answered his glower with a smile. "That's okay, I have hands."

"Don't I know it, and they're good for a helluva lot more than shoveling snow." His lips twitched, but he kept his tone dour as he said, "There's another shovel in back."

She laughed, as warmed by his look as by the truck's

heater, and followed him out of the truck, with Sin on their heels.

The first part was tough going, but once they—mostly he—had cleared a starting area, they had somewhere to stand while they dug, lifted and tossed shovelful after shovelful of snow. They'd started back to back, and headed in opposite directions around the car, brushing it off as they went. Now they had nearly met on the far side of it. Even though Cal had shoveled a much wider swath across the back to help form a ramp up toward the road surface, he'd covered more than half of their route. Maybe she hadn't been in much of a rush to get this chore done.

She stretched her back, then leaned on her shovel, watching him methodically attack the snow coming toward her. Absently one hand dug into the pile of snow at her side.

"Don't even consider it." Cal hadn't looked up, and he didn't stop shoveling.

"Consider what?"

"Throwing that snowball."

She looked at the clump of snow in her hand. "This sorry thing? I wouldn't ever throw this poor excuse for a snowball at you. Now this—" in one motion, she had captured a shovelful of snow and was flinging it at him "—is worth throwing."

It cascaded over his head and shoulders, sliding down his slightly bent back.

Before her chuckle had a chance to reach adulthood, he'd dropped his shovel and lunged at her.

"Throw snow at me, will you?"

She squealed, spinning away, but he caught her arm, pulling her back to him, even as he tumbled into the snowbank, with her on top of him. Sin was barking and leaping around, more than willing to aid the cause of chaos.

"Happy now?"

"Extremely, since you're the one in the snow!" To emphasize her point, she levered up and swept more snow onto him.

"Oh, no you don't." He wrapped his arms around her and rolled until she was caught between icy snow below her and heated man above her. "How do you like that?"

"Not as much as this." She'd grabbed a handful of snow during the roll and now released it at the gap between the back of his neck and his clothes.

He yelped, arching his back. It provided no escape from the coldness sliding down it, but pushed the heat of his groin into her, between her parted legs.

Before she could initiate another attack, he captured both her wrists, transferred them to one of his in the snow above her head. With his other hand he scooped up snow.

"Now, what shall I do with this? So many possibilities," he mused with an evil grin. He loosed a plop of snow on her cheek, then followed it with his mouth.

"Here," he murmured, licking the snow and her skin, and replacing the icy moistness with sultry heat.

Sin, bored with their apparent inactivity, wandered off.

"Or here." Another constellation of snowflakes fell on the point of her chin, then slid down its underside, heading for her throat.

He nibbled the snow from her chin, then followed its melting descent, down her throat, pushing aside the scarf that had kept her coat closed around her neck. Eyes closed, she shifted under him, and he rocked against her in response.

"Or here." His voice dropped to midnight velvet.

In the next instant, cold exploded in the hollow at the base of her throat and headed for the valley between her breasts. It brought her off the ground. But that only pressed her harder against Cal, and in that same instant, the heated caress of his mouth touched the same tender hollow.

His tongue flicked against the rise of her breast just

above her bra, but her clothes kept him from going any deeper. And she definitely wanted him to go deeper.

"Cal…"

"Or here?"

Her eyes popped open as the words coincided with something pushing and opening at the closures of her coat. And he still had snow in his hand.

"Cal, you wouldn't—"

He had his snow-holding hand under the bottom edge of her sweater now. She was twisting and writhing beneath him—a vain effort in trying to get away, but quite productive in stoking the heat where their lower bodies met.

"Oh, wouldn't I?"

Cold wetness connected with the sensitive skin of her stomach, and her muscles clenched, trying to escape it.

"Cal!"

She was only vaguely aware he was using his teeth to pull his glove off—a glove no longer needed since its payload was busy freezing her skin. Then, in an almost instantaneous alchemy his hand spread over the cold and turned it sizzling.

The cold, now consisting of air instead of snow, advanced ahead of his touch, up her rib cage, under the edge of her bra, defying gravity to climb the underslope of her breast, then pebble her nipple. And everywhere it was followed by the incredible heat of his touch, feathering across her ribs, stroking her breast, skimming her nipple to rock hardness.

He closed his mouth over her nipple, and rocked against the apex of her thighs.

"Cal…"

Her voice sounded strange to her, though she wasn't interested enough in that to try to pinpoint why. But Cal stilled, then raised his head, meeting her gaze.

He swore, low and heartfelt. Before she could guess what

was coming, much less prepare herself for it, he jackknifed up and away from her.

"What? But..."

"You're shivering." He was pulling her clothes into position, then he was tugging her upright.

She was going to protest, but then a tremor shuddered through her.

He wrapped one arm around her, snagging the two shovels with the other hand and started bundling her up the slope toward the truck. She gave him a half grin.

She tried to say something, but her teeth chattered. "Taylor—"

"It's not that bad, honest, Cal."

"C'mon, Sin!"

He had her in the cab, the heat on full blast, wrapped in a blanket he'd pulled from somewhere faster than she could imagine. With Sin on the floor and the heater fast melting snow from his coat, Cal quickly turned the truck around despite the big plow blade, and headed for his house.

"I—I thought every man wanted to make women tremble."

He looked her over before he answered. Apparently that reassured him, because he relaxed a little.

"Preferably not right before they turned into an icicle."

"A little longer and I'd have been a very satisfied icicle."

He put his arm around her shoulders and dragged her a little closer. "Well, now you've done it, Taylor."

"*I've* done it?" she laughed. "I wasn't alone, you know."

"You're going to freeze if we don't get you into the house where it's warm." A glint lit his eyes even before the heated smile came. "And get you out of those clothes."

Chapter Ten

They didn't get back to her car until midmorning the next day.

By the time they both got into the shower after their roll in the snow yesterday, there'd been more danger of his igniting in spontaneous combustion than of her freezing.

They made it from the shower to the bed, and stayed there until both their stomachs were growling from missing lunch and delaying supper, and Sin was whining to go out.

They made love again in front of the fire, like they would have the first time if he'd had condoms in his pocket.

Except it still wouldn't have been like the first time. This was even better. Slower. Less desperation and more pleasure. Though the desperation came. Yes, it definitely came.

He thought the *even better* should be worrying him. He'd never experienced anything like this before.

Other than his ill-fated engagement, his experience ran more to sex than relationships. Not that this interlude was a relationship. It was the peculiar circumstances that made it seem that way, what with them holed up like this.

Maybe having a craving grow was normal when you were with the same woman so many times in a short stretch.

Maybe it was normal to come in from the barn after caring for the animals first thing this morning, and have her find a piece of hay in his hair, and start laughing about rolls in the hay and rolls in the snow, and end up back in the warm, soft bed he hadn't left long ago judging by the clock, though his body said it had been too long—much, much too long.

Maybe it was normal, a few hours later, to find yourself scanning the sky, thinking another blizzard wouldn't be so bad.

And maybe it wasn't normal at all.

So it was a good thing she'd be leaving soon. A damned good thing. Then things would truly get back to normal.

Before they'd finished the little bit of reshoveling needed because of the wind-drifting, he heard a plow from the direction of the highway.

He saw her turn that way, then dart another of those looks at him. He didn't return it.

He'd put it off longer than he should have, and now the moment was coming toward them in the form of a powerful Slash-C truck outfitted with a top-quality plow. It would break through any minute now.

And then he'd do what he had to do.

"Is everybody okay? Are you hurt, Taylor?" As Matty slammed the door of the Slash-C truck closed behind her, she shifted her questioning to her foreman. "How could you let her try to leave after I told you—"

"It had already happened," Taylor said, cutting off the accusation, "when you called and said the road was closed."

Matty's gaze stayed on her an extra beat before returning to Cal. "But why didn't you tell me her car was in a ditch?"

He shrugged. "What difference did it make? Nobody could do anything about it."

But Taylor had a sudden feeling that there was more to it than that.

I already feel like an idiot for driving the car into a ditch, okay?

Could've happened to anybody.

Cal Ruskoff, of all the people in the world, was protecting her feelings.

She wanted to hug him. But that would bring a barrage of questions and speculations—spoken or unspoken—from Matty that she just wasn't ready to deal with yet. This was too new, too...unformed.

"How're the roads?" Cal asked Dave.

"Not bad. They started on the state roads day before yesterday, and had the county roads pretty well done by last night."

"Everybody else has been out since yesterday afternoon or longer," Matty added. "Even those who were enjoying being snowbound."

Taylor felt her cheeks burning with more than cold and wind. There was no denying she had enjoyed being snowbound with Cal—at least the past forty-eight hours. But Matty was smiling at Dave, and Taylor realized her friend was referring to her own experiences.

"I can't imagine," Matty continued as she turned now to Cal, "why it's taken you two so long."

"Snow's deeper here." Cal gave Matty back look for look, daring her to challenge him.

"It does look deeper." She kept her face straight, but her eyes were dancing. "If I'd known Mother Nature was going to dump so much snow here, of course, I never would have suggested Taylor come out here."

"Well, something's deeper," muttered Dave, with a look at his wife.

Matty looked back at him as if she didn't have the least idea what he was talking about. But everyone else knew. Then Matty's expression changed as she met her husband's gaze, and Taylor looked away.

Was she as transparent as Matty?

She shook her head at herself. It wouldn't matter if she was, because even if everyone could see straight into her, what they'd see would be confusion and uncertainty. Along with a contradictory satiation and growing hunger.

"So, what kind of job does it look like to get this car out, Cal?" Dave asked. "Won't your truck tow it out? Think mine will?"

"That's not the problem," Cal started.

The men lapsed into a technical discussion that came to the same conclusion Cal had drawn yesterday. Trying to tow the car out of the ditch could do considerably more damage to it than it had incurred with its slow, gentle slide in. They finished shoveling, then decided three would push from the front and one would be behind the wheel, feeding the gas as soon as the tires gained traction. Cal insisted Taylor be the driver. "She doesn't have cold-weather gear on and she knows the feel of the car," he explained.

To prevent anyone from having to worry about Sin's whereabouts while they tried to maneuver the car, he got in with Taylor.

Cal and Dave each took a front corner and Matty was in the middle.

They would need coordination, the human force pushing the car toward the road at the same time Taylor fed it gas, then letting it slide downhill a little before they repeated the process. The rocking motion kept the tires from spinning and digging into one spot. Finding the right balance would be difficult.

Maybe so difficult she'd just have to stay till spring.

Sin's bark jolted her out of a reverie brought on by that thought. The pushers were pushing, but she'd missed her cue.

"Now, Taylor!" Dave shouted.

She touched the gas pedal, but the timing was off.

"Sorry!" she called out, as the pushers relaxed for the next attempt.

She met Cal's gaze through the windshield and had the oddest notion that somehow he knew what had distracted her. A new warmth bloomed inside her. Was he wishing she could stay, too?

When the trio began pushing again, Taylor still had her gaze on Cal, and seeing him strain against the weight of the car, she couldn't do anything but her best in trying to get the car out of the ditch.

"All right!" Dave and Matty whooped when the car finally was back on level and plowed road. Sin barked four times in excitement.

Cal, she noticed, was as silent as she.

With Sin pawing at the passenger side door, Dave opened it to let the dog free, bending to ruffle the fur at the top of the puppy's head. Sin licked Dave on the chin in passing as he leaped from the car and cavorted around Dave, then Matty.

Cal opened the driver's door and held out a hand. She needed no help getting out, but she put her hand in his anyway. And it didn't even matter that it was glove to glove, she felt the warmth of connection there.

For an extra beat, their hands remained locked, then he opened his, and she followed suit.

"I think we should get ourselves a dog, Matty," Dave announced, chuckling over Sin's darting charge at a snowbank. "One for the house."

"Sure. That would be great. Maybe the next rescue dog."

Taylor frowned. "I thought you were allergic."

Dave looked around as if to see whom she might be talking to. When he realized she was looking at him, his brows shot up. "Me? No. We always had house dogs when I was growing up. It wasn't until after my folks started their wanderings and I moved in there alone that it didn't seem fair to have a dog. What made you think I was allergic?"

"*Matty* made me think that."

"I must have gotten confused." Matty was a fearless but lousy liar. "What is it you're allergic to? Dogwood trees? Dogtooth violets?"

Shaking his head, Dave looked as if he wanted to laugh, but was restraining himself. "Not that I know of."

"Must be something," Matty insisted. "Well, we better get going now. We've got to pick up supplies in town. Can we get you anything, Cal?"

"No thanks."

"Okay. I'll come over in the morning if you need any help around the place."

With waves and smiles, Matty and Dave got back in their truck. While Dave expertly maneuvered it to turn around in the single lane that was plowed, Cal and Taylor stood side by side, silently watching, not touching.

Only after the truck had disappeared from view did Taylor turn to him and put her hand on his arm.

"Cal, I didn't know. Truly, I didn't know Dave wasn't really allergic. I wouldn't lie to you. I wouldn't have tried to trick you into taking Sin."

He put his gloved hand over hers. "I know."

Relief swept through her, quickly joined by sensations familiar from the past two days as he kissed her. He ended the kiss while she was still sinking into those sensations, leaving her feeling as if she'd just had a rug pulled out from under her.

Cal had been used by so many people, perhaps it was natural that his first thought was always that someone was trying to manipulate or use him. But as long as his second thought told him that she wouldn't do that, perhaps they...no, she wouldn't put it into words even in her own head. She'd simply leave it as *perhaps*.

"You better go. Daylight won't last long."

"Yes, you're right." She got into the car, thinking there should be something else to say, some way to wrap up the past few days into a string of words that would let him see what they meant to her, what she felt—and what she thought she might be on the verge of feeling—without his shell dropping down around him.

She rolled the driver's window halfway down, fiddled with the keys, let the engine warm up, checked the windshield wipers, adjusted the rearview mirrors. She knew she was stalling, giving Cal time.

Time to ask to see her again. Time to say he'd call her. Time to say anything to indicate this wasn't an end.

Standing beside the car door, looking in at her with his face impassive, he said nothing. But silence now didn't mean there wouldn't be more between them, just as his saying something wouldn't have guaranteed there *would* be more between them. She could only wait and see what happened.

She produced a smile and a would-be jaunty wave as she put the car in Drive and pulled away.

The road was probably easy going for one of the big ranch trucks, but with her small car she had to concentrate on her driving. Still, in the moment before a curve would cut off her view, she looked into the rearview mirror.

Cal was standing just where she'd left him, utterly alone in a landscape of stark white except for the truck in the background and the brown-and-white dog sitting next to him.

"Take care of him, Sin."

* * *

Motionless, Cal watched the smudge of green that was Taylor's car turn to the right, onto the highway, heading for Knighton. Back to ordinary life. *Real* life.

He gave himself until the green was swallowed between the whiteness around it and the blazing blue above it. Then he pivoted away, a jerky motion from standing too long in the cold, and headed for the truck. Back to the life he'd led before Taylor.

For how much longer?

Could he hold off his past and the people who would be looking for him harder than ever now?

What was that old expression about where there was a will there was a way? Well, there sure as hell was a will, and it essentially turned him into the quarry in an old-style fox hunt.

And that might not even be the worst danger to his sanctuary.

The worst danger was Taylor. Hell, be fair, it wasn't Taylor as much as his weakness for her.

I know.

They'd been the topper on all those words that had come since he'd spotted her car in the ditch and felt as if his guts were being squeezed in a vise. What had possessed him to tell her so much about his past, about his family? If she worked at it, she might even piece it together.

That would give her one hell of a motive. The kind people didn't pass up.

She'd said she wouldn't have lied to him, wouldn't have tried to trick him, and he'd said he believed her.

It even made sense in a way to believe her about that, since he'd heard her surprise when Dave said he wasn't allergic to dogs, and he'd seen Matty's guilt.

I know.

He'd seen the relief cross Taylor's face that he'd accepted what she'd said. Relief and something else. Did it mean that much to her that he'd said he believed her?

He hadn't had cause to doubt either Matty or Dave Currick on the important things to this point. So maybe some people could be trusted on some matters. If Taylor was one of those people, maybe—

Or maybe she was smart enough to know trust was a step toward a much more powerful weapon. A weapon that could destroy a lot more than an identity he'd come to enjoy. A weapon he'd seen destroy hearts and souls and the will to live.

He'd vowed to never give that weapon to another creature on this earth, and that rule had stood him in good stead these past years.

Taylor must have used every weapon she could while climbing the ladder at her high-powered law firm. That wasn't the sort of skill someone forgot. And the fact that he was letting himself wonder about trusting showed exactly how dangerous she was.

Well, he just wouldn't see her anymore. He wouldn't call. If she called, he wouldn't return the call. He'd avoid town for a few weeks, which wouldn't be hard with spring chores around the corner. They were hardly likely to get snowbound again, no matter what Matty said or did. If the temptation of Taylor was out of his way...

Barely remembering how he'd gotten back in the house, he stared at the opposite corner of the couch from where he sat. It was as if she was sitting there. His old sweatshirt trying to slide off one shoulder, her hair bright in the firelight, legs drawn up, her arms wrapped around the excess fabric of socks and sweatpants cushioning her ankles, her chin on her knees, and her eyes on him. She was smiling.

And he was hard.

He wanted to hear her and taste her and smell her. He wanted to be inside her, and then to lie beside her.

She hadn't been gone an hour and he was ready to cave from just the memories of her sitting on the damned couch. What would he do when he tried to sleep in the bed where they'd—

He stopped that thought with a sound that brought Sin's head up off the rug.

Determination had gotten him through a lot of situations, but he was afraid it wasn't going to be enough this time.

He needed something more than his own willpower to keep him away from the danger named Taylor Anne Larsen.

"Cal?"

Taylor's heart lurched at the sight of him. It had only been a day, but there'd been something about that kiss before she drove off that had unsettled her. She'd spent yesterday afternoon on the phone to her family telling them about her adventure without telling them the whole story. The past three hours she'd been sorting out the work she needed to catch up on and pushing down the thought that the kiss had tasted of the New Year's Eve not-wanting-to-want-her Cal.

Smiling, she stood and started around the desk to him.

His posture went stiff and he gave his head a slight shake. Lisa was closing the door, her gaze going from one to the other of them. Was that why he'd reacted that way?

But the door closed and he sat in the client's chair across from her desk, leaving her standing in the strained limbo of uncertainty.

"What's wrong, Cal?"

"Nothing's wrong. I'm here to give you more business. To consult you in your professional capacity. I'd think you'd consider that good news."

He was in trouble, and he'd come to her.

The warmth of that hopeful interpretation didn't stand up to the coolness in his voice and eyes. Whatever he was here for, all her instincts said it wasn't good news. "Business?"

"I want to hire you."

"Cal, you don't have to hire me. If there's something I can—"

"I want this official. What's your usual retainer?"

And there it was—the shell, the wall, the cave—whatever name she called it. He'd retreated once more, and he was pulling boulders up over the entryway as fast as he could. Leaving her outside.

"I might not be your best choice for representation, Cal," she said as calmly as she could. "The appearance of impropriety can—"

"I know you won't do anything improper."

In fact, she understood in a flash, he was counting on it. It was one of his boulders.

"Since we have a personal relationship, it could be awkward." If he tried to deny they had a relationship, the fight would be in the open. That would be something. "You could ask Dave—"

"I want you."

Half a heartbeat after the words left his lips, a flare that should have been visible at the Canadian border heated his eyes. He did want her. In the carnal, primitive way that bypassed whatever was tangling up his mind and his heart.

"You have a personal relationship with Matty and you've done fine by her. That's good enough for me. Will you be my attorney?"

She looked away because it hurt too much to see the flare ruthlessly brought under control, especially now that she knew how it felt when he let the flare become a flame.

Business. Professional. Attorney. Retainer. All the words he used to close off the real Cal Ruskoff. He'd ventured out, or he'd let her in these past few days, and now he was letting her know that was over. He meant things to return to the way they were before the blizzard. Just as after New Year's Eve, when he'd done everything to avoid her.

But he wasn't avoiding her this time. He'd left a crack open between the boulders.

Her gaze snapped to his face, then away. If he didn't realize what he was doing but read it in her face, she'd lose even this opportunity.

"Yes, I'll be your attorney."

As his attorney she would have reasons to talk to him. As her client he would have to see her. The crack would remain open, and the fire would stay stoked.

He hesitated, and she held her breath. He could say he'd changed his mind, that he wanted to see what might happen between them if they gave this relationship a chance. He could say he'd changed his mind, that he wanted no connection with her, even as her client.

He said, "How much do you want as a retainer?"

"What sort of a matter do you want me to handle?"

"I don't think I can afford what it would cost me if you based your charge on that."

He shifted onto his left hip to reach into his right back pocket, and her gaze followed the motion as he drew out his wallet. Cal had shifted nearly that way in a prelude to covering her body with his own. Her hand had slid over the sleek power there, unfettered by clothing.

"Taylor—did you hear me?"

She blinked, feeling her cheeks heat. "I'm sorry. What?"

"I said, I'd give two hundred dollars now so I'm officially your client and attorney-client privilege applies, and then we can work out compensation when you know what you're dealing with." He counted out twenties and laid the neat stack on her desk.

"Two hundred? You don't have to give me that much."

"Take it. I want this official."

Representing him was almost certainly her only opportunity to keep a connection to him, yet she paused before she pulled the stack to her side of the desk.

"You've now officially retained me."

His chest rose, then fell slowly—in relief, sorrow, satisfaction, regret? It could have been all or none of those. He was back to being unreadable. Except for the grooves cutting much deeper from his nose to his mouth.

"You can't tell anyone anything I tell you without my permission?"

"That's right. Unless you're about to commit a crime that could endanger someone."

He snorted. "The only danger is to me."

"Cal, what—?"

"Don't worry, the people after me want me alive, not dead. Trouble is, they also want my soul."

She fought down the stream of worried questions brewing in her mind. Letting a client tell the story not only went faster, but it often produced information she wouldn't think to ask for.

"To start, the name on my birth certificate's not Cal Ruskoff. What I didn't tell you about my family is that my mother's maiden name was Bennington. Her family founded a chemical company. My father was Laurance Whitton. That is the first thing I don't want you to go telling anyone."

"Laurance Whitton." She ignored the jab in that last sentence, trying to remember where she'd heard the name. Something recent. But before she could snare that memory, the other name he'd mentioned hit like a hammer blow to her head. "Bennington? *Bennington Chemical?* Janice and Laurance Whitton!"

"Yes. Janice Bennington, heiress to the Bennington fortune, who married ambitious Laurance Whitton, who became chairman of the board of Bennington Chemical, and since my mother's death, the chief stockholder."

"But..." And then she remembered where she'd heard the name recently. "Oh, Cal, I know you haven't been in touch with your family and working such long hours at the Flying W, you might not have heard—"

"Don't worry, you're not breaking the news—I know. The sonuvabitch is dead."

She shouldn't have been surprised, not after what he'd told her, but at some level she was. There would be no chance of a reconciliation now—clearly, to Cal, there never had been.

"I saw it in the paper," he continued. "Would have ticked him off that the *Jefferson Standard* only gave him three lines. I read through the library's *Wall Street Journals* last week for more. That's why I'm here."

She remembered seeing him go into the library. It seemed a hundred years ago. Right now, yesterday seemed like a hundred years ago.

"Because your father passed away?"

"No. His dying doesn't make any difference. Or it wouldn't make any difference if he wasn't trying to control me from the other side of the grave the same way he tried to manipulate me and everybody else this side of it. It's not his death that brought me. I want you to take care of things so people won't look for me anymore."

"What makes you think they'll look for you? The company's run well in your absence all this time. The board of directors can search for a new chairman and—"

He shook his head. "Doesn't matter how well it's run before—they're hamstrung by his will, and I'm the only one who can untie them. The bastard's made me majority owner of the company, and no vote can carry without me."

Taylor couldn't imagine another soul sounding so bitter at being handed what amounted to a fortune. *You know the phrase "filthy rich"? It was meant for my family. Rich. And filthy.*

Cal had seen too much of wealth's destructiveness to take any pleasure in its freedoms. He'd found freedom his own way, and all it had cost him was a hard shell around his heart.

"I don't want to wait until they up the reward to the

point that it'll be a nationwide manhunt. You take control of this. Get me free before they make it impossible to stay here. That's why I need your professional services." His gaze met hers for an instant that chilled her even before the words came. "Your professional expertise."

Her professional expertise—not as a small-town lawyer, helping people through the legal dealings of straightforward lives. But her professional expertise in dealing with corporations like Bennington Chemical. The professional expertise she'd gained before turning in her Shark Lawyers of the World membership card.

"You need a lawyer who's up-to-date on corporate dealings. I've been out of it for several years, and things change quickly."

"I'll take my chances on you."

It was not a vote of confidence.

And she'd been entirely too optimistic in feeling good that he'd trusted her with his family's identity. That was a pawn he was willing to sacrifice in his larger chess game of distrust.

A game he played ruthlessly. She'd confided in him about letting herself get so caught up in her career that she'd lost perspective on her life. And he'd used that confidence to spot a potential weakness.

So now Cal was dangling a return to that world—near the *top* of that world—in front of her like a fresh pack and a book of matches in front of a reformed smoker.

"I lost my taste for that sort of law, Cal. I won't do it." She pushed the money back toward him.

He didn't move, not even his eyes, which bored into her. "Scared?"

Find the opponent's weakness and exploit it—a ploy she'd seen used time and again in corporate law. She'd used it herself. She'd never expected Cal Ruskoff to use it against her.

But then he wasn't Cal Ruskoff.

If she told him no, he would walk away. Maybe that would be best. But whatever his name, she'd seen inside the man inside the shell. Which was the reason he was doing this—and the reason she couldn't say no. She had to try.

"To represent you effectively I'll need to know more details." His gaze following her motions was like a drag on her hand as she took out a fresh yellow legal pad and poised a pen over the first line. "Let's start with why you're so sure they'll look for you rather than try to break your father's will."

"If people weren't smart enough to know he'd make it foolproof they wouldn't be working for him. And if Christina weren't smart enough to know that she'd never have landed him. So they know I'm the key." His mouth twisted in a grimace. "And they'll search for me because they've never quit searching."

"Tell me about that. From the start." She made the order clipped and cool.

"After I left, I caught the first job I could crewing on a boat headed for Florida. By the time we arrived, there was a private detective waiting for me. A fellow crew member heard the owner talking to the detective and warned me. I left on another boat that night. For almost two years, I went from crew to crew. Couldn't stay anywhere because, before too long, another detective would show up."

"Sounds like your fellow crew members helped you."

"That was before Father put a bounty on my head. Oh, it wasn't worded that crassly, but that's what it amounted to—*Information on the whereabouts will be amply rewarded.*

"Never occurred to me that he'd look for me in sailing areas. He'd never noticed my sailing, but Christina had. She had six months of being my fiancée to stockpile knowledge about my ways, and she turned them all around against me.

I had to give up sailing if I wanted to keep them from finding me."

"Because your fellow sailors were giving away your whereabouts?"

She jotted a nonsensical note as an excuse to keep her head down. When the silence stretched, she had to look up. A frown had tucked grooves above his nose, and his eyes had gone unfocused. Then he blinked and met her gaze.

"Only a matter of time," he said with a faint edge. But he'd recognized, maybe for the first time, that some people hadn't betrayed him despite the money offered. "The reward got bigger. Maybe my absence—or the absence of my block of votes being exercised—was making board members nervous."

"So, you left sailing," she prompted.

"I started working for some people running a cattle herd in Florida. I liked the work, but the water was too damned tempting, and I went to the dock one day, got talking to someone who needed crew for a race, and pretty soon I was spending most of my days off there. Until..."

"Until?"

"I ran into a woman who'd been a couple years ahead of me in school. I'd had a crush on her. She said she'd always noticed me. She said my secret was safe with her, because great sex was hard to come by." His mouth twisted. "She sold me out. Guess she figured with the money she could buy great sex elsewhere. By pure luck I heard a stranger asking a waitress in the dock bar if she'd seen me after one race."

"They might have found you another way. How do you know your friend from home—"

"I know. And she wasn't a friend. I couldn't risk going back to my job. Sent the people a message and took off west. Worked cattle a while in Texas, then headed up this way. Met up with Henry Brennan nearly three years ago, and stayed put at the Flying W ever since."

"Okay, now let's go over it again, with the details, especially names and dates."

His brows dropped into the familiar frown, but when she blandly took him back to the start, asking for dates and names, he answered. Briefly, and with no frills, but he did answer.

She wrote what he told her. And when she'd covered the period after he'd left his family, she went back and filled in gaps from his earlier life, and as much as he could tell her about the business. Until she couldn't think of any more questions.

"I'll need a great deal more information on the business, and the will if possible."

"I've told you all I know."

"Then to get the information, I'll need authority—probably a limited power of attorney. I'll look into what form would work best and let you know."

"Power of attorney."

She looked up at the flatness in his tone, and found he was watching her.

If she got caught up in the rush of such an exciting, complicated client, then he'd be completely safe from the greater danger of letting their emotional ties develop.

No way, Cal. You're not safe from me, not yet.

"Yes, power of attorney. Now, if there's nothing else, I would like to make some phone calls to get started." But only after she'd pulled herself together, and she couldn't start on that Herculean task until he was out of her office. "And with the time difference to the East Coast..."

"I'm not done."

She could almost persuade herself that he was unwilling to leave her. Almost. If she didn't have a pad's worth of notes under her elbow.

"What else?"

"A will. A will nobody can break. If I die, I want half of everything that comes to me from my father's will to go to some program that lets poor kids go sailing. Find me a good one, and if you can't find one, put it in the will how to set one up. The other half goes to scholarships for the kids of ranchers. Doesn't matter what school or what they want to study.'' His mouth lifted in a smile that didn't melt a molecule of the blue ice in his eyes. ''Even law school, as long as they have the grades and don't have the money. I want to see how you'd set the programs up.''

''Of course.'' After everything else, did he think a client who wanted to review her work was going to bother her? ''Personal bequests?''

His gaze flickered, but his answer was a solid, ''No.''

''And the shares you inherited from your mother?''

She saw that his first instinct was to disavow that, too. He'd so firmly connected the company with his father, he'd forgotten Janice Bennington Whitton's ties to it.

''Give it to Matty.''

Before she'd done more than write Matty's name on her pad, he spoke again. ''Wait. Give a third to Matty. A third to the Knighton Library—as long as they use some of it for more comfortable chairs. And a third to you.''

''I won't take it, and I won't write a will saying that. It wouldn't be ethical, and I don't want anything from—''

''Fine.'' He stood abruptly. ''Don't take it. Half to Matty and half to the library. It's not like I'm expecting to die soon. I just don't want that damned company dragging me down to hell if I do.''

He'd taken two long strides before she thought of one thing she had to know now. For practical reasons, yes. But that wasn't what pushed her.

''Cal?''

He turned back from the door, and for a heartbeat of hope, the Cal of the snowstorm looked back at her. Then he was gone.

''What is your real name? I'll need it for any legal documents.''

He paused, his reluctance obvious. "Bennington Caldwell Rusk Whitton."

"What did your family and friends call you?"

This hesitation was even longer, and she knew that whatever name he gave, she would never use it, because it wouldn't belong to the man she knew.

"Benning."

He walked out, leaving Taylor to wonder if Bennington Caldwell Rusk Whitton was any easier to figure out than Cal Ruskoff.

Chapter Eleven

"Hello."

"Cal?" He didn't answer the faint questioning in her voice, but she didn't need it answered. Her heart was beating so hard because it had recognized his voice in two ordinary syllables. "This is Taylor, Taylor Larsen."

"I know who it is."

His gruff, low voice should have been cold. But it was too close to the timbre she remembered from the hours in his arms to strike anything but heat and longing deep inside her.

"I have taken the initial steps you requested, but I have some matters I need to go over with you, to determine how you want to proceed. Could you come to my office tomorrow afternoon, say four?" Two weeks of hard work had produced some results, and no peace.

"No."

"Another time, then? Or another day? You can call Lisa and set up an appointment at your conven—"

"No time's convenient. It's calfing season. I can't get away."

"But with the good year the Flying W had last year, Matty's hired more men."

"Doesn't mean I can go off whenever I feel like it. Foreman has to take his turn. Better for morale."

"When do you think you could—"

"Just going to get busier. You come out here."

"Oh, I don't—"

"I'll pay for your time."

"It's not that." But what it was—a fear of memories and longing—was not something she was prepared to discuss. "This is confidential, and with other people around…"

"There're thousands of acres on the Flying W. I don't think we'll have a problem being alone to talk business."

Did he mean that only in the literal sense they'd been talking about? Or did he mean that he would have no problem keeping their time alone together on business? Because he had no interest in being alone with her in any other way. Because he wasn't tempted. Because he didn't care.

"Fine," she said with more snap than she'd intended. "I'll be there at four tomorrow."

"Fine."

This is Taylor, Taylor Larsen.

Like he wouldn't recognize her voice? He heard it damned often enough in his head.

Like the sound of it saying his name hadn't jolted through his bloodstream? His name… *Cal.* Until she'd said it he hadn't known he'd feared she would start calling him Benning.

Call her office manager and set up an appointment? Hell, no, he wasn't going to do that.

So he'd made her come to the Flying W. Maybe that was stupid. Maybe it was even masochistic, having her here where they'd—

But at least it would be as hard on her as it was on him. He hoped so, anyway.

Taylor parked by the barn, well away from the house, and allowed herself only a glance in that direction.

She noticed one of the new hands Matty had hired for the Flying W heading into a metal shed that had recently been reclaimed from near dilapidation. The shed had lights against a gloomy day.

"Let's try there," she said to her passenger, Lisa.

Her office manager nodded. "Looks like a calving shed, so that seems reasonable."

Stepping inside, Taylor spotted Cal at the far end. The new hand was giving him a set of metal chains. She started in that direction, but Lisa stopped her before she'd covered half the distance.

"We better wait here. They're going to pull a calf."

"Pull a calf?"

"When the mother isn't having much luck pushing her calf out, they get in and pull it."

"Pull a calf," Taylor repeated, understanding the phrase now.

Lisa gave her a sympathetic smile. "It can get messy, and neither one of us is dressed for that kind of work."

"No."

But Cal was—with holey tan coveralls that showed his jeans underneath in places, a down vest over a faded blue plaid flannel shirt with sleeves rolled up well above his elbows along with another shirt beneath it, battered work boots and his equally battered brown cowboy hat. Dressed for it and suited to it.

His calm came through in his confident movements and his low, easy voice, sure to be soothing to a mother-to-be cow, even as he gave clipped orders to the two nearby hands. If she didn't know better, she'd think he'd been raised to tend cattle in childbirth.

Taylor couldn't see everything he was doing, but he was at the business end of the standing cow, which had its head secured in what looked like a vertical and modern version of the stocks used for punishment in colonial days.

"He'll reach in to find out how the calf's situated," Lisa said beside her.

"She's nearly ready," Cal said so softly Taylor almost didn't hear him.

"He loops the chain around the calf's front feet and pulls," Lisa explained. "Sometimes that's enough."

Taylor watched the concentration and strain in Cal's face as he braced his feet and pulled. And pulled. She knew nothing about pulling a calf, but she knew from his expression that this effort wouldn't be enough.

"What now?" she asked Lisa in the same low voice.

"They'll use the calf-puller."

"The…?" Her question died out when she saw the metal and leather contraption one of the hands brought to Cal.

The main part was a metal band shaped into a half circle, with a handle attached to the top of its curve. They fit that against the back end of the cow, strapped it in place over her hips, then connected the chains looped over the calf's front feet and used a pulley for greater leverage.

The seconds stretched tense, with only the sound of the chains clinking against metal as the links advanced, and an occasional complaint from the cow.

"There're the shoulders," Cal said. "C'mon, girl—push. If he's not hip-locked, this might—yeah, c'mon, almost there—do it. Here he comes."

Even before the men reacted, Taylor knew the calf had been successfully born by the grin stretching across Cal's face.

"He's alive—and a big one!"

"No wonder she had trouble with a young'un that size."

"Thought for sure we'd have to cut to save this fella."

"You did it, Cal!"

He tamed his grin, then met her eyes, with a look of…of…she didn't know how to describe the look, though it sent a shiver of warmth through her when he continued holding her gaze.

Only when the chatter around him slowly subsided did he turn away, issuing orders about cleaning up the area and releasing the mother cow so she could lick her calf, cleaning and warming it and bonding at the same time.

As he put his arms under the faucet of a deep metal tub, scrubbing up to his folded-back sleeves, and with the men scattering to follow his orders, she finally found the label for his expression.

Satisfaction.

A fierce satisfaction she'd never seen—no, that wasn't true. She had seen an even fiercer satisfaction in his face when they'd made love.

She wanted to laugh at the idea of comparing pulling a calf to their lovemaking. But the lump in her throat made it impossible.

And there *were* connections—the elemental nature of the act, the awe at participating in something that was somehow greater than themselves, the universality and age-old pattern of the acts.

She couldn't begin to fathom what his feelings might be now about their lovemaking, but she was certain that, for Cal Ruskoff, taking his turn at calfing watch had to do with something deeper than his men's morale. The man who worked so hard at being cynical and bitter wanted to see this miracle of birth. Wanted, even more, to make it come out right.

This was the true man inside the shell. This was the man who'd held her and made love to her. This was the man worth fighting for.

She blinked hard and realized Cal was coming toward them, drying his hands and forearms on a towel.

"Oh, there's Troy Dutton. We went to high school together. I've got to say hi." Lisa sounded more like a gushing teenager than her usual self. "I'll be right back."

Cal nodded to Lisa in passing, but never took his eyes off Taylor. She returned his look, not certain if she did so to prove she wasn't afraid to match him look for look or because she *couldn't* look away.

She wanted to talk about the birth. She wanted to ask about the calf. Instead, she retreated to safe ground.

"These are the power of attorney forms for you to sign. And this packet includes copies of your father's will, the past five years' financial statements for Bennington Chemical, and a current management roster. You should read them and—"

He plucked the power of attorney forms from her hand. "Leave the rest on the shelf by the door on your way out."

"Cal..."

But he was already absorbed in the cumbersome prose. He shot her one quick glance—she suspected that was when he reached the provision limiting her authority to matters dealing with assets inherited from his father—then read it a second time more slowly.

"Got a pen?"

"Just a minute. Lisa?" she called.

The other woman gave a wave to the young man she'd been talking to and headed toward them.

"Cal's going to sign this form, and I'd like you to witness it, Lisa."

"Sure."

Cal frowned. "I thought you said this was confidential."

"Lisa needs to know all the ins and outs of this. The same confidentiality that applies to me, applies to her."

Cal obviously had reservations. But instead of studying Lisa, his intent stare was aimed again at Taylor. She returned it coolly. Encountering that frown could frazzle her in a lot of contexts, but they were on her turf now.

After another moment, he signed and dated the two

sheets in rapid order, and handed them to Lisa. She glanced them over—one eyebrow rising as she looked at the signature—then added her signature before handing them to Taylor.

"Is that it?" Cal demanded.

"For now. After you've read this information—" she tapped the packet she still held "—if you have any questions, call me at the office. Lisa or I should be able to explain. And there will be a lot more information later. These represent what's public record. Now that I have power of attorney, we'll be getting more detailed records."

"Fine."

"I'll make sure there's a valuation for tax purposes, but I'd also like another kind of valuation if that's all right with you. It's for—"

"Fine. Do it. Whatever's needed. I've got to get back."

Without another word he walked away.

Aware of Lisa's diplomatically concerned look, Taylor smiled at her. "We've finished our work here. Let's get back to the office.

She paused only to leave the packet of information on the shelf as Cal had instructed.

She made a vow as she drove back to town.

Over the next few weeks, as she did this work for him, she would try to remember the look on Cal's face when that calf was born. Try to use the memory as a counterbalance to what she could already see was going to happen: her frustration building, her patience waning, and her heart breaking.

Taylor Anne Larsen: Seer Into the Future.

That's what it should say on the sign in front of her office, instead of Attorney-at-Law, she decided as she drove back to the Flying W nine days later.

Her vision of frustration and impatience had been right

on the mark. The matter of heartbreak she refused to consider at the moment.

This, after all, was a business meeting. A meeting she'd arranged in the hope that she could pin Cal down better in person than she'd succeeded in doing during brief, unsatisfactory telephone conversations.

Boy, there'd been times in Dallas when she'd have sung hallelujahs for a client who didn't give her any guidance about his wishes. More often, she'd had clients who had all sorts of wishes—many of them conflicting, most of them unreasonable and a few illegal.

Could Cal have somehow known that? Did he think autonomy—*power*—would send her rushing back to big-time corporate law? Was that why he pushed every decision back to her?

On that happy question, she parked her car and headed for the barn, which was where Cal had said he'd be.

She did her best to ignore a swell of longing when she passed the stall where she'd found Cal and Sin the day of the storm. She tracked Cal down at the other end of the building, where he was taking advantage of a recent warm spell by shoeing a horse near the open doors to a corral beyond.

She was pleased when he turned the work over to the man he'd been working with and directed her to sit on a nearby bench. "Thank you for putting aside your work to go over this, Cal."

"I'm not putting it aside. I'm getting out of Sam's way. He was showing me how it's done—he's the expert."

Taylor clenched her teeth. "Fine. Let's get started. Here's the draft of your will with the provisions you requested."

He dropped the envelope beside him without looking at it.

"You need to read that. And here's a list of matters we need to discuss."

At least he held on to this piece of paper, though *discuss* was not a good description for what happened. Only by asking direct, specific and numerous questions, did she draw out more information than she had on the telephone.

"Last item," she said crisply. "The actual running of the company—keeping the business going while the legal machinery turns. Is the management team now in place top-notch?"

"Hell if I know. I haven't been around there in ten years."

"Yes, but would you expect your father's choices to be capable of taking the company through a transition."

"I'd expect him to hire good people and then not give them an inch of latitude or responsibility."

She nodded at the confirmation of what her digging had hinted at. "In that case, you might want to bring in a few handpicked people to loosen everyone up, to let them see that a new management culture is going to—"

"Leave the people in charge in their same positions," Cal said with no interest.

"You mean until you go to Connecticut and can see firsthand—"

"Go? I'm not going there."

"But you've inherited a *company*. A very valuable company that's the livelihood for its employees. There'll be transitions, things to take care of. Even if you leave it running under the same management, the employees will want to know the new owner."

"I want nothing to do with it. That's why I hired you. If somebody has to go to Connecticut, it's going to be you, not me. I'm not going back there."

"Cal, I know there were a lot of reasons for your leaving—"

"There was one reason—I left to have my freedom."

She sat back, studying him, then gave a small sigh.

"You also left to punish your father—oh, I don't blame

you. But who are you punishing now, Cal? The people who work for your family's company? They're all strangers, aren't they? Christina? She treated you horribly, but she's practically a stranger, too. So it comes back to your father and—''

"I'm not punishing anybody, certainly not Christina. Her dumping me for my father was the greatest break of my life. Married to her I don't know if I ever would have escaped."

For someone who spent so much effort at not letting anyone see inside him, sometimes Cal was remarkably transparent. He was dangling his ex-fiancée Christina in front of Taylor now in hopes of distracting her from a discussion of what had happened between him and his father.

She leaned forward, resting one hand above his knee, feeling the solid muscle there.

"Cal, you can't keep trying to punish someone who can't feel it anymore—if he ever could. You'll only hurt yourself."

Two long beats passed. She felt as if she was on the brink of a cliff, fighting to keep her balance.

Then Cal's mouth twisted and, even before he spoke, she felt the stomach-plummeting sensation of falling off a cliff—or being pushed.

"I could've sworn I hired myself a lawyer, not a therapist."

She forced herself to remove her hand slowly, when she wanted to snatch it away. She forced herself to straighten equally slowly, when she wanted to run. It wasn't only pride that wouldn't let her. It was Cal.

If she turned tail and ran, who would fight for him?

"You hired a lawyer, and a good one. So I suggest you listen to me when I say you need to go to Connecticut. No—don't say anything now. Just think about it. I'll be in touch when I have something more to tell you."

* * *

Two weeks later, and Taylor no longer knew if she was fighting for Cal, or merely fighting against him.

She had never been so miserable and confused in her life. Which was exactly what she'd thought he'd intended when he hired her. Or was she personalizing a situation that no longer had anything to do with her? Had he succeeded in restoring his shell so completely that he no longer had feelings for her—if she hadn't imagined his feelings in the first place?

Or was that what he wanted her to think?

All in all, she was in no mood to mince words when she spotted him climbing into an aged Flying W pickup.

"Cal, we need to talk."

He looked through the open window, his face as neutral as ever.

"*We* need to talk? Most people who say that mean they have something to say, and they're not particularly interested in hearing anything the other person might say back. Is that what you mean, Taylor?"

"Yes, I need to say something, and no, I'm not particularly interested in hearing anything you might say."

"Then you better climb in, because I've got a field to check."

Recalling too vividly the last time they'd been together in the cab of a truck, and how hopeful—how foolishly hopeful—she'd been, she hesitated. Until she caught a glint of triumph in his face.

She marched around to the passenger side of the truck, climbed in and slammed the door. "Have you read the draft of the will?"

The thwack-thwack of the windshield wipers countered the light sleet falling from a bleak sky that exactly suited her vision of these past weeks.

"No. Told you, I'm not planning on dying anytime soon."

"Other people might have other plans," she said grimly.

"Do you have something in mind?"

"Don't tempt me. You know the saying about *First, you kill all the lawyers?* Well, the lawyers' version is *First, you kill all the clients.*"

And damned if the man didn't chuckle. Then he stared out the still-open driver's window as if he might be embarrassed.

"Read the draft, Cal," she ordered in a remarkably neutral tone. "Now, what I needed to talk to you about…"

As the truck bounced over the rutted road, she succinctly updated him on her progress, keeping to an absolute minimum her comments about the roadblocks his lack of participation had erected.

"And I've arranged to have a former colleague who's a partner in a firm in Connecticut represent you in contacting the board. He's up on all the latest nuances of business law, and I trust him."

"I told you, no one else—"

"He doesn't know where you are or your Cal Ruskoff identity. He just knows everything has to go through me. If it's the expense you're worried about—"

"Screw the expense. My father hired the best legal talent to ensure he always got what he wanted, so any of his money that goes to lawyers will feel right at home." He stopped the truck, staring through the windshield toward an empty field. "I don't want anyone else to represent me. I hired you to represent me."

She turned to face his profile. Only when he looked her way did she speak.

"You hired me because you could keep me at bay—or keep your feelings for me at bay, but maybe that's flattering myself."

"That's crazy." The challenge in his voice matched his expression when he turned his upper body to face her across the gap of empty seat between them.

"Yes, it is, but that's what you did. You hired me because you figured that my having to look at you as a client would counter what happened between us during the storm.''

"I told you who I am. Doesn't that show I trust you?''

She delivered her opinion of that argument with a humph. ''It was a no-lose situation for you. You said your stepmother and the board wouldn't have rested until they found you, so I likely would have known eventually. And by doing it this way, any feelings for you I might express, you could write off as my being after the money. And, hey, if I got caught up in the rush of a high-profile board fight, all the better—because that would really prove there wasn't anything real—not inside me and not between us.

"I can forgive you being scared, Cal. And I can forgive you not trusting yourself or me. But I opened my deepest closet and showed you my demons, and you used it against me. You used it to keep me from getting too close to your demons—'' she reached across the space to thump him on the chest ''—what's in here.''

His hand immediately covered hers—to stop her motion or to hold it there? She pulled her hand free.

He leaned forward, draping his forearms atop the steering wheel.

"So you're handing me off to this other lawyer and walking away?''

"No. You hired me to do a job and I'll do it. I'll see that you get the best representation possible, and do my utmost to protect your privacy. I'll be your lawyer, and not your lover. So, you've gotten what you wanted, Cal.'' Her voice held no tremor, but she had to swallow before she could finish. ''It would have been so much easier on both of us if you'd just said you didn't want anything to do with me.''

His silence defeated her as completely as the harshest words could have. Her shoulders slumped and she sighed. ''As I was saying, Greg Salisbury, my former colleague, is a partner in a firm in Connecticut. He can deal with things in person if necessary.''

"You can go yourself. I'll pay the expenses.''

And she'd be out of his hair.

"I've involved Greg to protect your privacy. Think about it, Cal. If I go there—a lawyer from small-town Wyoming—how long would it take them to start looking around Knighton for you?''

"Not long,'' he acknowledged.

"Right. So we needed another layer of protection. Consider it a sort of fire wall.''

His grunt gave voice to his skepticism.

"Although I would strongly advise you to plan at some point on going back. Some of the issues should be finalized in person.''

"No.''

"It doesn't have to mean they'd know about your life here.''

"Another of your fire walls?''

"You could call it that.''

He turned the key in the ignition, but instead of turning the truck around, he continued on the way they were headed.

"Cal, I need to get back.''

"Got another field to check.''

Neither of them said more as he steered the truck around hills and between pastures. They had climbed to the rounded top of a hill, when he stopped.

Outside her window, the ground sloped away to a creek bed, then rose toward a neighboring hill. All of it was desolate, with only occasional blackened skeletons of trees remaining to give a clue to what had once been there, and what had happened.

"This is the field you needed to check? There's nothing here.''

"They tried a controlled burn two years ago. Said they

needed to get rid of some of the brush that would've been fuel for the next lightning strike or spark. It got away from them. The firefighters worked like dogs just trying to contain it.

"The Flying W was lucky that only this section burned. I stood right here and watched it coming. You've heard people talk about something spreading like wildfire, but you wouldn't believe it unless you saw it. It's hot and angry and cruel. Consumes everything in its path. There was an old line shack from the early days down there by the creek. It had stood for a hundred years. And it went like that." He snapped his fingers. "Along with trees and grass and brush."

"Why are you telling me this, Cal?"

"This is what happens when a fire wall doesn't work."

Cal spent the afternoon stringing fence. There were other hands to do the chore, unlike his earlier years at the Flying W. But it suited him today—solitary work that could burn off residual anger from this morning's talk with Taylor.

The reason for his anger was hard to pinpoint. Sure, she'd acted distant. She'd yanked her hand away as if it had touched something slimy when he'd put his hand over hers on impulse.

But Taylor feeling that way was all to the good.

Taylor being angry at him should be a hell of a lot easier to keep his hands off than Taylor looking up at him by firelight, her smile warm and her eyes...

He cranked the handle on the wire stretcher taut enough to make the wire sing.

It would have been so much easier on both of us if you'd just said you didn't want anything to do with me.

She'd waited then, as though she expected him to pipe right up with, "You're right, Taylor, I don't want anything to do with you."

He couldn't say that, and he wouldn't say anything else, so he'd said nothing.

When he'd thought she was passing him on to another lawyer, his gut had felt like he'd been gored by a Texas longhorn. What did he care if she hired a string of lawyers every two feet from here to Connecticut and back. As long as she was the one he dealt with. As long as he kept seeing her, and at the same time didn't let himself hope to have her.

When she'd started talking about fire walls, that's what he'd thought about. That was the fire wall that needed to stay intact. Because that was the fire that could burn him to a cinder.

Two days later, Cal waited until Matty had mounted Juno to return to the Slash-C before saying, "One more thing."

They'd crossed paths a half-dozen times during their workday around the Flying W. But he'd chosen now, with daylight waning.

"What?" Matty's readiness to leave for home showed in the way she held Juno in place without calming the mare to a standstill—for a rider and horse so in tune it was the equivalent of an engine left idling, waiting to be revved.

"I've had some news."

He had all her attention now, whether he wanted it or not. "Bet I know what it's about. Dave made me swear I wouldn't bug you or Taylor after the storm, but I could tell when we saw you. I just *knew*—"

"Family news."

Her eyes widened and her mouth closed. He could almost hear her thinking *I never knew you had family.*

"My father's dead."

"Oh. Oh, Cal, I'm sorry." She stilled Juno. "I didn't— I'm so sorry. When did you find out? You take whatever time you need. For the funeral or—"

"Funeral was weeks ago, and I've known for a while."

"Oh."

Of course she didn't understand. How could she? Part of the reason the Flying W was so important to her was the strong family ties it represented.

"He was a sonuvabitch. I couldn't care less that he's dead. The only reason I brought it up is I might have to go handle a few things eventually."

He didn't like that Taylor's opinion on that had started to undermine his absolute certainty that he would never go back. But if there was any chance that he'd need time away to take care of his father's final effort to make him dance to Laurance Whitton's tune, he wanted Matty to have fair warning.

"Of course, anytime you need to go, and for as long as you need. You just let me know. And if there's anything—"

"I won't go if I can help it. But no matter what, I won't be going just yet, especially not with calfing. I told my lawyer to try to make it so I can handle anything from here. But she's not sure she can do that."

"*She?*"

"Taylor."

He saw the questions and speculation crowding into her eyes, but all she got out was an echoing "Taylor?"

"Yeah. She's done a good job for you, so I hired her." He did that well, he told himself, making it sound like a simple recommendation between friends of someone providing professional services. "You better go, you're running out of daylight."

Then he gave Juno a slap on the rump, and he couldn't tell which female was more surprised and irked at him—the horse or his boss.

Taylor's office door burst open, jolting her from a reverie. She didn't mind leaving those particular thoughts, but, recognizing her visitor, she suspected the subject was not going to change much.

"Okay, what in the world is going on?" Matty Brennan Currick demanded as she crossed the threshold.

"Hello, Matty. It's nice to see you, too. How are you this morning? So glad you could stop by, and knock on my door, or let my office assistant announce you."

"Yeah, yeah. Lisa's not out front, and I knew you'd say come in if I knocked, so I saved you the effort." Matty waved off the objection and sat across from Taylor. "What's this business with Cal hiring you?"

"You know I can't discuss a client's business."

"Of course I do, and I'm not talking about what he hired you for—although if you ask me, anybody so sure he doesn't care a bit about his father's death really does care, at least at some level. No, I know—nobody asked me. That's not the point, anyhow. It's the *fact* of his hiring you that I want to talk about, and what it means to what's going on between the two of you."

"Nothing's going on."

"Tell me another one, Taylor. I saw you two when we all dug your car out."

"Which was snowed in because of a certain devious person I know."

"You can thank me later. But you can't tell me there was nothing going on between you. I was really hopeful. Now with this hiring thing, and his father passing away, I don't know what's going on. I'd love to think this was good news—the two of you spending time together over romantic depositions or something. But, knowing Cal, that would be too good to be true. Still, he turned to you, right?"

Taylor sighed. "Have you ever had somebody you thought you were getting closer to? You know, really starting to know them, even though they were the hardest person to get to know you'd ever encountered. And getting to know them seemed almost..." *Against their will.* "Impossible. But it wasn't—impossible, I mean because it started to happen.

"And then they told you something—confided something to you. And you realized that telling you was a way to keep you from getting any closer."

Matty leaned back in the chair for the first time.

"My husband says I jump to conclusions, but I'd say it's about as safe a jump as they come that this mysterious somebody is your friend and mine, Cal. Still, it must mean he trusts you, or he wouldn't have retained you as his lawyer."

"Yes, he would."

Matty studied her. Taylor had always recognized Matty's intelligence. Since she and Dave had settled into married life, Matty's happiness had made her more aware of other people's emotions. Right now, Taylor could have done without that trait in her friend.

"Of course. The skunk. A skunk with a wide streak of yellow down his back."

"Skunks have white streaks. And Cal's not a skunk or yellow."

"Oh, give me a break. He's as chicken as they come. He's retained you as his attorney on something because you came too close—not only a skunk and yellow, but too damned clever for his own good. If he didn't have a good heart under all the armor, he wouldn't be worth all the effort."

Taylor couldn't argue with the last half of that assessment.

"But he does, and he is—so the only answer is to throw yourself at him," Matty said decisively. "It's not the most dignified thing, I'll admit. But when he crumbles like a month-old cookie—and he will—it will be well worth it. Course, you'll have to go out there, because chances are, he'll lie low, since he knows he's in a crumbly stage, too—

otherwise, he wouldn't have pulled this stunt in the first place. So go out there, and remind him what he's missing."

"He's fixed it so I can't."

"Nonsense. Drive out, around sunset—"

"I don't mean I can't go out to the Flying W."

"I know you don't." Matty picked up her plan without missing a beat. "Get there around sunset, when he's coming back in from a long day, so his resistance is low, and—"

"I can't, Matty." The words were harsh enough to draw a searching look. Taylor couldn't reveal the scope of Cal's commission and therefore the temptation it might represent for herself, so she could only make clear one of the obstacles Cal had erected. "He's a client."

"So? That's a great excuse to go out there. Have something legal he has to look at. Then make sure you touch somehow, brush up against him or—"

"No!" Taylor's sharp word stopped Matty in midstream, her mouth open, her eyes wide. "I'm sorry, Matty, but…" *Your words are sparking too many images, too many sensations, too many memories, too many unobtainable wishes.* "You don't understand, Matty. As long as he's a client, we can't be involved. It would be unethical."

"But lawyers are always representing their friends, and—"

"Friends, yes. But not someone you're…intimate with." She hurried past that admission. Matty showed no sign of surprise. "I had a professor who used to say that you should never take on a client if your relationship was going to be another, silent client. Dave hasn't suggested you move your business over to him, has he?" She dredged up a smile. "He would certainly give you a good rate."

"But I like having my own lawyer for my own business dealings…oh, I see what you mean."

Matty ran her fingertips across the edge of the chair's arm, over and over. Taylor, trying to not think about her own situation, watched the other woman's face, and could see her determination welling up.

"That's all well and good, and I understand it for Dave and me with the two ranches going and all, but for you and Cal it's different. You just have to get through this shell of his, and once you do, then you can send him to be Dave's client or something. In the meantime, you'll just have to make an exception. It's not—"

"No, Matty. I won't do it. I won't do it, because I won't be the kind of lawyer—the kind of person—who makes excuses or says 'just this once' or any of that other crap. And I won't do it, because Cal knew that's how I felt and that's why he retained me. He wants this barrier—" *And others.* "—between us. When one barrier came down, he put this one up in its place. He's like a turtle that sheds one shell and grows another."

"That's snakes. Turtles keep the same shell for life."

"It doesn't matter. It still comes down to Cal can't be dragged out of that shell. He has to want to come out. For good."

He has to believe in me and in himself, and what there could be between us. And what's the chance of that?

Chapter Twelve

Taylor would never have believed that only hours later it would be all she could do to curb simultaneous urges to hug and laugh at Cal Ruskoff.

Matty had the idea just before she left Taylor's office. Taylor tried to talk her out of it, but when had anybody succeeded in talking Matty out of something? And maybe part of her didn't want to.

If the man wouldn't come out of the cave, the world would have to barge in.

In the case of Cal, that translated into a caravan of three pickups, a four-wheel drive and Taylor's small car pulling to a stop in front of the Flying W foreman's house.

Cal came out of a shed they used for farming equipment, wiping his hands on a rag. His gaze came to her first. It was a look of pure wariness.

Sin bounded out, rushing up to greet each newcomer, barking and wagging his tail. Nobody seeing the contrast would ever again believe the saying about humans and their animals resembling each other.

"Cal, come here," called Matty. When he was close enough to talk to, she added, "You're done working for today. C'mon. Let us in. You don't mind, do you?"

Since Matty had led the way toward the back porch with Lisa, Ruth and Hugh Moski, Taylor and Dave following her, and she now had her hand firmly around the doorknob, it would have taken an even more antisocial man than Cal to turn her down.

"It's not locked," he muttered, still standing in the yard. With the late afternoon air a throwback to January, his breath sent up a solitary plume of white. "But I've got work to finish."

"No more working today. That's an order. C'mon, everybody."

As they trooped past Cal, Ruth patted his arm and said, "Sorry for your loss, Cal. It's hard when you lose a parent."

Again Cal's gaze came to Taylor, but this time, behind the blue ice she saw a man who'd had his dark suspicions confirmed. And maybe was a little relieved to have it happen.

"Don't blame Taylor," Dave murmured as he passed Cal. "If you can't figure out who's behind this, Ruskoff, you shouldn't be allowed out without a keeper."

Before Dave guided her toward the open door, Taylor caught another glimpse of Cal's expression, and saw astonishment that the other man had read him so easily, followed by uneasiness. Was the uneasiness because Dave had read him, or because of his own misjudgment of her?

She'd tiptoed around him those first few days of the snowstorm. Maybe she should have handled it the way these other people were. Matty was stowing the food they'd brought in the refrigerator. Lisa was putting items out on the kitchen table. Ruth had commandeered the coffeemaker.

Dave was preheating the oven to Matty's specifications. And Hugh was checking the contents of the cooler he'd brought in, taking time to draw out a can of beer.

"You sit down right here, young fella," instructed Hugh, pressing Cal into a kitchen chair.

"We need silverware," Lisa said, looking over the table. "Where—?"

"I'll get it."

Taylor made the offer in order to have something to do. But the flurry of exchanged glances that ricocheted around the room had her cheeks burning.

"I helped with the dishes." She could have bitten her tongue. Explaining made it worse.

"Helped, hell. I made her do all the kitchen work," Cal announced. "No sense having a woman around otherwise."

"Cal Ruskoff, you—"

"What a pig!"

Matty and Lisa had spun around, jumping on his words, then obviously recognized that he was yanking their chains. Did they also recognize that he'd done it to divert attention from Taylor?

"Right, Ruskoff. Tell us another one," Matty said.

Lisa tsked at him and turned away.

Poor Cal. He liked to think he was so impervious to other people seeing inside him. In the space of ten minutes, he'd been found out by Dave, Matty and Lisa.

"Hoo, boy, you're in for it, Cal!" Hugh Moski chuckled. "Better have a beer."

"He's just talking that way to get a rise out of people," Ruth explained to her husband. "Some people react that way to grief."

From the corner of her eye, as she set out forks on the table, Taylor saw Cal's brows crash down in a frown.

Before he could dispute Ruth's statement, however, the older woman was continuing with her own agenda. "As long as we're all here, I had a bit of business—if you don't mind, Cal. It won't take but a minute.''

"Be my guest," he said with a hint of irony.

"Taylor and Lisa, I've already told Dave, but I wanted to let you know I'm leaving in the morning to go to Grand Forks. And if it's all right with the two of you, I sure would appreciate it if Lisa maybe could pitch in a couple hours every other day or so to keep the office from getting totally out of hand.''

"That's entirely up to Lisa. It's fine with me.''

"Of course I will, Ruth. I hope nothing's wrong?''

"Our oldest granddaughter's come down with pneumonia. It was either me going to look after her, or her momma going. And with three more at home, it made more sense for Brenda to stay there.''

"I'm sure your granddaughter will be happy to have you take care of her.''

Ruth sighed. "She'll be chomping at the bit before I know it. Girl's got more go than sense. You know she's in medical school?''

Taylor fought a grin. As if anyone in the region didn't know.

"Trouble is, she's working, too, to put herself through school, and she's just plain wearing herself out. I wish we could make it easier on her, but she won't hear of us dipping into our retirement savings. If it weren't for my working for Dave, we wouldn't have anything to send along to help her. And don't think I don't notice how I suddenly get bonuses when tuition's due," she added with a swat at Dave's arm as if she were scolding him instead of thanking him.

"Hey, I'm just trying to keep you from deciding to quit.''

"I don't know why you don't leave this selfish man high and dry, Ruth," Matty teased. "All he can think about is

his own convenience. And the state of his filing cabinets
You are the most—''

Taylor didn't hear the end of Matty's description of her
husband, because there was a knock at the back door. That
alone wouldn't have diverted her attention, but the hunted
look Cal cast at that rectangle of wood did. He snagged
Sin's collar as the puppy went by in a joyous flight toward
new arrivals. But Ruth ordered Hugh to take over Sin patrol
so Cal could greet his guests.

These arrivals were Reverend Ervin Foley, accompany-
ing a small, white-haired woman who held out a covered
blue plastic cake plate toward Cal. He hesitated before
bowing to the inevitable by taking it, the homey item looking laughably incongruous in his hold.

"I'm so sorry for your loss, young man." The white-
haired woman stretched up one hand and patted his cheek

Taylor was aware of a breath-holding moment in the
room. Without taking her gaze from Cal, she caught Matty
and Dave looking at each other, and Ruth looking up from
her task. They weren't sure how Cal would react, but Taylor was.

"Thank you, ma'am. It's kind of you to come by and
bring me some, uh…"

"Rum cake, of course." She was clearly astonished he
didn't know.

Taylor stepped forward, taking the plate from Cal's un-
resisting hands. She met his eyes for a significant second
then fought to keep her voice casual as she said, "How
nice to see you, Mrs. Brontman. Lisa, is that open spot
available to put the rum cake?"

"Absolutely."

Another knock sounded, and the small house soon filled
to overflowing with the arrival of three neighboring ranchers and their wives, followed by two Flying W hands, and
the Slash-C foreman, Jack Ralston.

The number of people made traffic flow a definite problem. The incoming tide of visitors had carried Taylor to the fireplace. Now she was trying to work her way toward the kitchen to give Lisa a hand. She saw an opening and slipped between Ervin Foley, in deep conversation with Fred Montress, and the bookcase. Only when she cleared the minister did she see Cal dead ahead, sitting astride one of the kitchen chairs, with Sin leaning against his side.

That look they'd shared over the Widow Brontman's rum cake had left her shaken. She was working at accepting Cal's decision that there would be nothing between them— and then he had gone and looked at her like the man who'd rolled her in the snow and heated her shower way past the boiling point.

It wasn't fair, and she wasn't going to put up with it anymore.

Taylor made a sharp left, and barely avoided running directly into Matty, who had appeared out of nowhere. With Cal straight ahead, Matty to her left, and the bookcase to her right, Taylor made one last bid for escape, but Ervin Foley had shifted, blocking her retreat.

"Looks like you and Sin are getting along fine," Matty said to Cal. "And to think you didn't want to take him. Guess you don't always know what's best for you, do you?"

Cal's stroking hand stopped. For an instant Taylor thought he would take his hand away. Instead, he resumed petting the dog, giving Matty a bland look.

"What do you think you're up to, Matty?"

"Not a thing. I simply passed the word to some of your friends that you'd had a bereavement in the family."

"It's no bereavement, and I doubt these people count me as a friend. Hell, I didn't even know Mrs. Brontman's name until the reverend said it."

"Taylor was the one who said it, saving your sorry neck, and you know it. As for knowing the widow, you took her arm and helped her over the rough ground at Great-Uncle Henry's funeral.''

He shifted his shoulders. ''So.''

''She hasn't had the easiest of lives. She remembers kindnesses. When she heard me telling Ervin, she insisted on coming and bringing her rum cake. There hasn't been a decent funeral in this county in forty years that she hasn't brought her rum cake to.''

His fingers burrowed into Sin's fur, kneading the flesh below. ''This is no funeral.''

''No, but it's the way people around here express support. Let your friends extend their condolences the way they know how.''

''I don't want—''

''Too bad, Cal. We're your friends, whether you want us or not.''

Matty walked away, leaving Cal and Taylor face-to-face. Their gazes locked.

His feelings for her—whatever they might be—weren't dead, and she supposed she would have to be grateful for that, only it hurt so much to see the flame surrounded by a ring of ice. He still wanted her, and still didn't want to want her.

They were back where they'd started. No, not where they'd started, because now she knew more of the man behind the shell, and she could no longer pretend she didn't care deeply for him.

Someone called his name, and he turned away. But she was fully aware of where he was as he circulated among the guests. How he nodded at something Ervin said to him. How he gave Hugh another beer. How he thanked Lisa for keeping the food flowing. How he limited his murmurs to ''Yes'm'' as Ruth doled out instructions.

Taylor knew by the fanned creases at the corners of his eyes that he was consciously restraining from making one of his sharply humorous retorts.

Funny how those creases deepened both when he laughed and when he was irked, yet she would never mistake one emotion for the other.

He sat beside the Widow Brontman for a good twenty minutes, listening and nodding and eating another piece of rum cake. Taylor saw the way the men looked Cal in the eyes as each shook his hand and clapped a hand to his upper arm, and she recognized it as a mark of acceptance that had to be earned among these Wyoming men. As much as Cal claimed to be solitary and to like it that way, Matty was right: he had friends here. Not only that, but he was well on his way to accepting that friendship, whether he knew it or not.

So maybe it was only with her that he had such issues over an emotional connection. He had feelings for her, but he'd certainly made it quite clear he didn't believe in love. Yet that was what she'd hoped for. And Cal was too intelligent not to have recognized that.

In that, maybe she wasn't drawing him out of his shell, but keeping him in it.

Suddenly she couldn't be here anymore. Not in the three small rooms that had seemed for such a brief time to be a haven.

She took her jacket from the back of a kitchen chair and headed out. It probably wasn't fair to leave the others with the cleanup, but at the moment a lot of things didn't seem fair.

Taylor was leaving.

"Breeding in some Red Brangus, might cut the dehorning problems if we can—"

"Excuse me."

That was all Cal said as he broke away from the foreman of the Slash-C. He saw Jack follow the direction he was looking, and knew he'd recognized Taylor as she slipped out the back door. He gave Cal a knowing look, a clap on the shoulder and a hearty "Sure."

Cal would have winced if he'd had time, but Taylor was moving fast.

He couldn't let her go. Not stopping to consider that urgency, he followed her.

"Taylor."

She stopped and turned around. He dug his hands in his front jeans pockets and hunched his shoulders slightly against the cold. He should be wearing a coat. "What is it, Cal?"

"You're leaving without saying anything?"

She made no attempt to hide surprise that he was lecturing her on manners. "Yes."

"I thought there might be something legal you wanted to tell me."

"If there had been, I would have called. I'm here for the same reason as everybody else." That clearly made him uncomfortable—tough.

One side of his mouth tilted up, though she wouldn't have called it a grin. "The rum cake?"

"I noticed you had a third slice."

"Couldn't refuse, not with the widow offering it."

"And you couldn't refuse to sit and listen to her talk, either." An elderly, lonely, powerless old woman. Had he seen the link to his aunt as clearly as she had?

"She was talking about Henry Brennan. I think they might have been an item when they were young."

"It was kind of you to let her talk about that."

He closed down.

She watched it happen. She turned before she could give in to the desire to pound on his chest and demand that he let her in.

"Good night, Cal."

She reached the bottom of the steps.

"Taylor."

She stopped again, and waited.

"Sorry."

"For?"

"For thinking you'd told people. I should have known I could...that you would be more professional."

"Yes, you should have. Since you've counted on my professionalism to get you out of the messy possibility of actually letting someone care about you. And if not my professionalism, then my greed and ambition."

His gaze flickered. It couldn't have been with shame...or regret? No, probably discomfort at being found out.

"You're the one who said people need to face their demons. You seemed to consider your past a demon, so you should thank me for letting you face it."

"Oh, I'm facing my demon, all right. I've faced my demon time after time these past weeks, and I'm facing him right this moment. And I most definitely do have you to thank for that."

She saw his understanding that *he* was her demon in the tightening planes of his face in the moment before she turned away.

For a second, when he'd called Taylor's name, he'd thought she might keep going, pretending she hadn't heard him.

She'd followed the porch around the house to the front, stopping where the railing turned to run down alongside the front steps. As she'd faced him, the light outside the barn revealed her face starkly. She looked tired. He didn't remember those shadows under her eyes. He wanted to touch his lips to them. That's when he knew he was in trouble.

Nothing either one of them said made it any better.

Demon.

Taylor's car had been out of view for a while before Cal

turned around and found Dave leaning against the wall behind him.

"Want some advice from someone who's been there?"

"No."

Dave ignored that. "It's scary as hell when you're thinking about jumping, but once you make the leap, you got too much going on to think about how scary it is anymore. At least that's the way it is if you're with a great woman. And Taylor's a great woman. The kind to build a life with."

"You and Matty have always wanted the same thing from life. Taylor and I are going different directions."

"Oh? You planning on leaving?"

"No."

"You can't be thinking Taylor's going." The other man studied him, then slowly shook his head. "But you do, don't you? Why?"

"You know what kind of job she had before she came here?"

"I've got a pretty good idea, yeah."

"And you think somebody like that's going to be satisfied staying? It's different for you and Matty, you were born here, you belong here. But Taylor...she'll go back to that other life. She was too good at it not to."

Dave nodded his head, but Cal wasn't fooled into thinking he was agreeing. "So you think she's using Knighton as a breather between stints of high-powered lawyering? Could be, I suppose. How about you? What are you using Knighton as a breather from?"

"Nothing."

Dave's disbelief was clear, but he didn't pursue it. Not directly, anyway. "People who aren't born here don't usually end up in Knighton by accident."

"I did," Cal argued.

"Not entirely. You must have been looking for this kind of place or you never would have found Henry Brennan's ad. The job at the Flying W fit your needs. Same with Taylor. She was looking for this kind of place, and Knighton fit her needs. But she had to make more of a commitment to being here. She couldn't tell herself she was drifting through, staying here as long as it suited her, then moving on.''

Cal didn't for a second think it was a fluke that the other man had slightly emphasized the pronoun in each of those statements.

''She had to find a spot that could take another lawyer,'' Dave continued, ''then she had to pass the state bar, and brush up on areas of law she hadn't needed with that big Dallas firm. She had to invest in a practice. Money, of course, but more than that. They'd have run her out quick if she hadn't invested in caring about the people, too.''

''All right. Taylor Larsen's a great lawyer and a great person.''

''Yes, she is.'' Dave let that sit a while before adding, ''You know, I seem to remember you asking Matty before she and I got married if she loved me.''

''She didn't answer.''

''No, she didn't. But you felt you could ask because you cared about her, and you were worried about her. I suspect,'' he added in a lazy drawl, ''that's also the reason you gave me that hurt-her-and-you-die look when the judge asked if anyone knew a reason we shouldn't get married.''

Cal said nothing, because the other man was right, and they both knew it.

''So you'll understand how I feel about Taylor. Don't hurt her, Cal.''

Unhurried, Dave Currick turned and walked back into the house.

A song being sung about a fine romance led Taylor through the barn and out the other side before she found Matty pulling a saddle off a black horse in the corral.

"Hey there." Matty waved. "Can you believe this weather? Did you finally come out to take me up on the offer of a ride? I can't go with you myself because I'm heading to an appointment in town, but maybe Cal—"

"I'm here to see Cal on business, Matty."

Matty's grin disappeared. "Oh, you should have called. He rode up to the Three Widows hills a while ago."

"I did call, dammit. And he knew when I was coming and that I have papers he needs to read."

"Oh."

"Yeah, oh. I told him he might as well come into town and look at the papers in my office, since his signature needs to be notarized. But, no, he insists I come out here— again—so he can look them over, and says he'll come into the office later in the week to sign. Which I'll believe when I see it. He keeps dragging me out here, reminding me of—" She reined in her tirade with effort. "Sorry, Matty. I shouldn't spout off to you. I'm just so frustrated."

"On several levels, I suspect. The good news is Cal's sharing your frustration. With the mood he's been in, you'd think the man was raised on sour milk. I wonder what could be making him act that way?" Matty obviously thought she knew exactly what was molding Cal's mood, and didn't await an answer.

"But he's weakening. Otherwise, why would he keep making all this legal work for you to handle. Good heavens, he's got you bringing papers out here more often than a head of state would need. His left hand might be saying he wants a strictly business relationship of lawyer and client, but his right hand keeps dialing the phone to get you out here." Matty looked smug. "Before too much longer, seeing you won't be enough. Mark my words, Taylor."

Since Taylor couldn't tell Matty the whole truth, she couldn't effectively argue.

"Fine, I'll mark your words. And if it turns out you're right, I give you full permission to crow I-told-you-so at me, okay? But right now, I need to get this to him so I can get back and keep my other clients happy.''

Matty gave her directions to the Three Widows hills, and Taylor drove slowly and carefully over the rutted ranch roads that wound up and through the hills, until she came up behind an empty Flying W truck blocking the road. When she got out, she saw Cal down the hillside to the right, astride a horse, talking to a young man on foot. The young man spotted her and tipped his head in her direction.

Cal slowly turned, gave a single nod, then resumed his conversation.

She turned her back to him, leaning against a fence post.

He'd been dealing out power plays ever since he'd hired her, but this was the most blatant. How long did he think she was going to keep doing everything his way?

Or was that the idea—to irk her to the point of quitting.

A short time ago she had thought that all she wanted was a clue to how he felt. After the gathering of his friends and neighbors at his house, she had more than a clue, and it didn't make her feel one bit better or less confused.

His feelings for her—the feelings she'd seen and felt and heard—weren't dead. But would he ever let them live? Was she doing him more harm than good? And how long could she exist in this limbo waiting to find out?

With those thoughts swirling through her head, Taylor had been staring at a hillside to her right for several minutes before what was in front of her rose to her conscious mind.

It was the burned-out ground he'd brought her to earlier this spring when he'd been talking about fire walls.

She'd wondered then just how much it would scare him to know that she'd figured out he wasn't talking about lawyers. After all their talk about shells and caves, didn't he think she could see how ''fire wall'' might apply to the two of them? Didn't he think she could recognize that, when he looked at that burned-out piece of land, that's how he envisioned himself if he ever let himself care?

"Taylor?"

"Hi." She turned with a big smile. He sat astride the same horse he'd ridden the day the snowstorm started. The sky behind him was nearly as blue as his eyes. The strong square lines of his face and his broad shoulders, along with his self-assured ease in the saddle made him look like the epitome of a Westerner.

He studied her an instant, as if to be sure her expression was genuine, then frowned. "I didn't expect you to drive that tin can out here."

"No problem. I made it fine."

"How'd you know where to come?"

Ah, he'd thought that, when she arrived and he wasn't in sight, she'd stay put by the home ranch waiting for him—and stewing, no doubt.

"Matty gave me directions."

His frown deepened with his curt nod. "I had things to clear up with Jason."

He was becoming positively transparent. Now he expected her to be peeved for leaving her waiting after she'd come all the way out here. Of course, she *had* been peeved, but there was no reason for him to know that.

"Uh-huh," she said simply.

"Why are you smiling?" He asked it as if he couldn't stop himself.

"Look over there." She gestured toward the burned field.

"What about it."

"You said the fire took the line shack and the fence and the trees and the grass—nothing survived. But you were wrong. Something's growing there already."

He peered down the slope at what looked like green tufts scattered over the slope. "It's just fireweed."

"Fireweed? That's that tall wildflower with rosy-pink flowers that bloom up a spike like gladiolas, isn't it? I love those."

"All I know is fireweed is a weed. It's no big deal."

"I don't care if it's a weed or not—it *is* a big deal. The fire leaped the fire wall. The field was burned out, and now there's something growing here. It's not dead, Cal. It's growing."

Chapter Thirteen

Matty Brennan Currick glowered at him the whole time he was giving out assignments. So it didn't surprise Cal that when the hands had gone their separate ways she marched up to where he was making notations in the work log.

"I should fire you."

Cal looked up. "What for?"

"For being a jackass."

"In general or something specific."

"Both."

"Start with the specific."

"The way you're treating Taylor. And me, if it comes to that. I know you're in trouble—no, don't look like that, Taylor hasn't said a word. But I do have eyes. So does half the town. They see the thunder on your face, they see the misery in hers, and they can figure it out. Whatever the trouble is, Cal, it'll be less if you share it. Stop trying to be the big brave man who does it all alone. Let us help you.''

"Don't need help with anything."

"Right. That's the reason you've hired Taylor, but run from her all the time. Like yesterday morning, when you knew she was coming."

"Taylor complained about my manners?"

"You know better than that. In fact," she added with emphasis, "if you're doing this to irk her, you're far off the mark. When I saw her in town yesterday afternoon, she was quite cheerful. She told me she was glad she'd gone to the Three Widows hills after you because she got to see the burned-out field with the fireweed starting to grow in it."

He said nothing.

Matty slammed her hands on her hips and glared at him.

"*That's* why you're a jackass, Cal—because you try to close everybody out. Because you think it would make a difference if you didn't carry whatever it is all alone." Matty's eyes narrowed. "Or is it fear that it *wouldn't* a difference to Taylor? Dammit, Cal, let us help you. You can't spend the rest of your life hiding out on the Flying W."

"Are you sending me off your land?"

"Oh, don't be an ass. Of course I'm not. But you can't hide out from the past—or the future."

"'...So I told him not to be an ass and to quit trying to hide out," Matty concluded her tale.

If Dave Currick hadn't seen Cal's hungry gaze following Taylor's car nearly two weeks ago, he would be more pessimistic about the two of them. If he hadn't heard Cal's cold words, he would be more optimistic.

"Dave, maybe if you talked to him..."

"I might just mention that flower shop in Jefferson

where I got your wedding bouquet with the Indian Paintbrush in it.''

He kissed the top of her head, and she snuggled closer.
But her brows knit. ''I don't think Cal's thinking along the
lines of sending Taylor flowers.''

''No, I don't think so, either. But you never know when
it might come in handy…''

Cal would be here soon—after finally agreeing to come
to her office. Taylor straightened the papers into two stacks.
Each represented a task completed to the best of her ability.
The ones he'd instructed her to deal with, and the ones he
hadn't.

Those were the ones she handled almost tenderly. It was
stupid to have put so much of her heart and her hope into
them. But she hadn't been able to help herself. They represented the one way she could think of that he might stay
in Knighton.

''And sign here—the last one.''

He did.

''You're now the majority owner. Since that means your
vote would carry even if all the minority owners banded
together, you're running the show.'' She was proud of her
composure. ''And from what Greg Salisbury tells me,
they're more than a little anxious about their new owner.''

''Let 'em wonder.''

''You…you're not going back? Even now?''

''No.''

''You are one stubborn man, Cal Ruskoff.'' That brought
his head up, and she repeated, ''Cal Ruskoff or Bennington
Caldwell Rusk Whitton, doesn't change a thing—you are
one stubborn man. And it doesn't change that the question
now is, how can you run the company from here?''

''I didn't say I was staying here. But wherever I am, I'm
not going to run that damned company. The old bastard

tried to manipulate me all my life. He's not going to do it from the grave.''

''Are you going to sell it?''

''No. I don't want his money in that form, either.''

She drew out the other folder and put it on the desk.

''I thought you might still feel that way, so I did some research.'' She fought to not put him on the defensive by letting her hopes come through. ''If you don't want to run the company, and you don't want to sell it, you could turn it over to the employees. The other voting stockholders probably won't like it, but if they sue, the precedents favor you. The valuation's being done—you said to go ahead with that, remember? That would speed up the process, though it would take time to sort it out. But I think Bennington Chemical is a good candidate for an employee-run operation. Changing the culture of the company might be the most difficult aspect of the transition. But if you go there and—''

''No.''

''Not permanently, Cal. Just to set things up. Then maybe a time or two—''

''No.''

''But you own a company. What are you going to—?''

''Get rid of it, that's what I'm going to do.''

''You said you didn't want to sell.''

''Not sell it. Disband it, dismantle it, close it down, wipe the thing off the face of the earth.''

''You can't. You have a responsibility to the stockholders and employees—''

''That's why I hired you, to make sure I don't have to have anything to do with that damned company. So your next job is to wipe it off the face of the earth.''

''There are other ways, Cal. These ideas I've been working on—''

''You said I can do what I want with it, that even all the

minority owners together can't outvote me. And what I want is the thing destroyed.''

Taylor stared at him, too heartsick at this moment to even cry.

"You're just like him. You're just like your father."

His head snapped up. She had his complete attention now. "You don't know what you're talking about."

"I know what you've told me, and what I've read. That's enough."

"I'm nothing like him. He wanted power, especially the power that money brought. That company was all he thought about, all he cared about because it brought him that. I want nothing to do with that company."

She shook her head, wishing that could negate the truth she was seeing.

"Your father thought nothing of crushing people to get what he wanted. He rolled over them or used them as it suited his purposes. And that's what you intend to do. Have you given a single thought to how this might affect other people?"

"You're not feeling sorry for my sainted stepmother Christina, are you? His will left plenty for her to get by on, so don't waste your sympathy."

"I'm not. But the fact that she's the only one who comes to mind proves my point. You want to be free of this company because of what it represents from your past. I suppose I can understand that. But how about all the people for whom that company represents their livelihood? They never did anything to you. By dissolving this company, you'll dissolve their lives right out from under them without another thought, simply because it suits your purposes. Isn't that what your father would do?"

She saw the struggle in his eyes, the recognition, the questioning.

"Your father used money and power for destructive purposes, and now you're doing exactly the same thing. Cal, there are ways to make money work, not just for yourself as your father did, but for a lot of people, to help a lot of people.''

And then she saw him lose the struggle. So she should have been prepared for his words. But she wasn't.

''Including you? If I dissolve the company, you lose one hell of a client. You can console yourself by knowing that it'll take a good long while to put all this through. So the money will keep rolling in, and you can use the contacts for getting back into the game you so obviously miss. They'll miss you here in Knighton, but I don't suppose it'll surprise anybody much.''

Every word, every gesture, every touch between them. He'd thrown them all back in her face. The pain was like her insides crumbling to powder.

But the decision of what to do next was easy. And it had nothing to do with her pain or hurt pride. It came from the knowledge that the only way to fight for him now was to make him fight for himself. There was no other choice.

That was the only explanation for her absolute calmness—that and the numbness.

''I quit.''

The silence must have lasted a full minute. She didn't know if he was shocked wordless or waiting for her to say more.

''I told you, there'll still be work—''

''Get someone else to do your dirty work, Ruskoff, or should I call you Whitton. It seems to fit you better these days than Cal Ruskoff, because I'd like to think he wouldn't foist his dirty work off on someone else. But that's what you've been doing all along, isn't it?''

''You're not making sense. I couldn't have done this legal stuff—''

''I'm making perfect sense. You used the work as a shield against me, and you used me as a shield against the outside world. Ensuring that I kept my emotional distance saved you the effort of telling me to get lost. And you knew I would keep my distance, one way or the other. If I fell back into my old ways, then ambition would take precedence over what I might feel for you, and if I didn't, then there were my professional ethics keeping me at a distance. The old shark lawyer in me has to say it was a pretty neat trick while it lasted. But no more. I quit.''

She started to rise, then dropped back to the chair, slapping her palm on the desk.

"No! No, I don't quit—I fire you. Yes, that's much better. You aren't manipulating me anymore, and I fire you!''

She grabbed a legal pad, flipped to a clean sheet, wrote three sentences, then hit the button and said, "Lisa, I need you for a moment, please."

Lisa was in Taylor's office in no time.

"Lisa, I want you to witness my signature and notarize it. It's informal, but it should hold up if there's any question until we can do it officially. Read it first—aloud, please—so we all know what it says."

Lisa accepted the legal pad from her, scanned the lines there, then read aloud, "'I, the undersigned, hereby revoke the power of attorney assigned to me by Bennington Caldwell Rusk Whitton. In addition, I hereby cease representing Bennington Caldwell Rusk Whitton in any capacity whatsoever. Monies received to date constitute payment in full for any services rendered.'''

"Thank you, now give it to me, Lisa." Taylor signed and dated the sheet with a flourish and handed it back. "If you would notarize it at your desk, and have a copy ready for Cal—for Mr. Whitton—when he leaves, that would be great, Lisa. Thank you."

The younger woman gave them each another look, then left.

"So that's it?" Cal's mouth twisted.

"That's it, because that's how you're making it, Cal. I know you don't believe in the power of love—"

"Oh, I believe in its power all right." He rose with slow grace. But his voice was taut and harsh. "I believe in the power of love to make you so vulnerable to another person that they can break you."

"Maybe I can understand, with your history, that you're worried about me doing that to you," she said to his back as he opened the door. "But how do you explain your trying to do it to me?"

Taylor heard the thrum of the truck idling under her apartment window near midnight.

She rose from the easy chair where she'd sat wrapped in her fleece robe and an afghan and went to the door, standing in the open frame, looking toward the dark form of the pickup.

The engine turned off, leaving a yawning silence. Her arm holding the door was trembling when the truck door finally opened, so she propped the door open with her back.

Cal's tread was slow. She didn't move, even when he stopped at the bottom of the stairs up to the narrow porch.

He looked up so slowly that she'd imagined the instant their eyes would meet a half-dozen times before it happened for real. And when it did, she still went breathless.

"I never meant to hurt you."

If he'd used that voice back at the start of this year, she would have thought it was devoid of emotion. No longer. Threads and layers of concern, regret, anger and frustration came through.

"I know."

He came up two stairs, until his eyes were level with hers. He looked at her steadily, the grooves cut deep and his bones stark.

"So you're not my lawyer anymore."

"No."

"Then there's no reason not to do this."

He came up the final step and across the porch in a stride.

That was just enough time to form the thought that she should run, and to know she wouldn't.

He didn't embrace her or hold her, meeting her only mouth to mouth. His mouth on hers was all that she'd been longing for, and all that she'd feared these nearly three months since the snowstorm.

Lips and tongues and teeth rediscovered textures and touches that erupted heat inside her.

She tasted the anger and bitterness in him. But more than that, she tasted the frustration. He'd tried to map their relationship according to the peculiar geography of his background, and she'd tossed in streams and valleys where he'd expected desert, then erected a few mountains where he thought he had the molehills under control.

He pulled away abruptly, his breathing as harsh as her own. His eyes glittered from between narrowed lids. The light behind him showed the tense outline of his shoulders.

She swallowed down the tears, shouts, cries and pleading moans that could have come so easily, and forced herself to return his look. Steady, calm.

"No reason at all not to do that," she confirmed as if the kiss between his words and hers hadn't changed her body from ninety-eight percent water to all steam.

He closed the space between their torsos, without so much as a brush of fabric against skin. Breathing room evaporated, because breathing would have eliminated that infinitesimal gap and, with it, her control. Without that control she would be crying like a banshee, or begging him, or railing at him.

And yet she didn't hesitate.

He was offering her—or requesting from her—a last time. She'd ended his manipulation of her, but that in no way lessened her feelings for him. She would give him every drop of love he would let her give him. As for herself, she would need this to sustain her through the vast expanse of never-again.

She stepped back, letting him in.

* * *

He didn't know what to say to her now that he'd said the words that had driven him here. He hadn't meant to hurt her. It was why he'd tried to keep her away.

He didn't know whether to blame her naiveté or his weakness for the fact that he'd failed.

He'd had no intention of kissing her on the porch. He'd had no intention of coming in. He'd said what he had to say. He should leave. He'd only advanced a few steps—it would take seconds to turn and be out the door, down to his truck—

Then Taylor darted him a glance, and leaving was beyond him.

She wanted him.

Despite everything.

More important, she wanted this. Maybe she even needed it.

That need—her need—pushed him. Two long strides to reach her, one hand hooked around the back of her neck, pushing away the small blanket she'd had around her shoulders, and then his lips were on hers again.

Too long, it had been too damned long since he'd kissed her. Since he'd tasted her and felt her.

It didn't matter that logic told him he'd kissed her just moments ago on her porch—it had been too long.

Two brief kisses, and he was as hot and hard as he'd ever been when they were snowbound. That's when he knew what he'd suspected during those days they'd been together. With Taylor, none of the rules held. Making love with her didn't sate him. Each time just built the hunger, wider and deeper, and harder to fill.

So making love with her now would make it even harder to not have her again. But hard on him didn't matter. Taylor mattered.

He stroked one hand down her throat, into the opening

provided by the crossed-over material of her robe, but she held the lapels together, denying him access.

He was turning her, guiding her toward something he wasn't consciously aware of until the side of his calf came into contact with the corner of her bed. He didn't remember noting the bed when he'd come in the door—he sure as hell hadn't noticed anything else. But some instinct had dropped its location into his subconscious.

He'd warned her at the start that instincts were dangerous. Now they were both about to experience the effects of crossing into danger.

With one knee on the mattress, he started the twisting motion that should carry them to its surface, with him covering her body. But the maneuver required cooperation, and he wasn't getting it. Instead, without breaking the kiss, Taylor knelt on the mattress facing him. She wrapped her arms around his neck and kissed him like this kiss could decide the fate of the world, or of a single heart.

The demands of their lungs ended what should have lasted forever. Their expansion and contraction brushed her breasts against his chest, and even through the thick cloth of her robe he felt the heat and the softness.

Taylor eased back, cupping his face between her hands. Her lips brushed across his, feathery kisses mixed with the sensation of her breath across his skin. He grasped her shoulders, fully intending to take control. But that would have ended this delicate torture, so he simply held her.

The kisses soon took on a weight and substance no feather ever dreamed of. Her tongue lining his lips brought such heat he thought he'd be branded forever. Her teeth gently tugging on his bottom lip brought a surge to his already swollen groin. Her tongue sliding into his mouth brought a need to wipe out the space between them.

He was kneeling on the bed now, too, and he brought their bodies together from knees to shoulders, rubbing with languid movements that produced the hottest friction known to humanity. Her one hand left his face and slid down his back to his waist, then lower. The light stroke had the impact of a diesel engine, rocking him forward against her. Shifting against her, he pressed one knee between hers and rocked again. Her hand flexed into the flesh of his buttock and he surged against her.

He wanted the damned robe gone. He wanted her skin—to see it and touch it and taste it. She'd stopped him once at the neck, so this time he reached to where the material pooled around her bent knees, found the opening and laid his hand against the silky curve of her thigh. Stroking up, his fingertips found the elastic edge of her panties, slid under, and came to her warm, moist center.

She gasped into his mouth and swayed. He held her up by pressing her even tighter against him, slipping his fingers deeper into her. They were both rocking now, trying to find the rhythm even before they'd joined.

And he learned another lesson. His hunger for Taylor didn't just grow from one time with her to the next. It grew from one instant to the next.

He yanked the tie loose and pushed back the robe, leaving her wearing only panties, and those just barely because of his movements. With something like a growl, he bent and took her pointed nipple into his mouth, sucking strongly.

"Cal..." It was half a moan and half a plea.

The sound changed to satisfaction when she discovered the snaps of his shirt opened with a series of short tugs. Fingers spread wide, she placed her hands over his chest before slowly—so slowly—pushing the material back. He had no patience for it, and yanked his arms out of the sleeves, letting it fall.

His urgency had infected her or she'd discovered her own, because her fingers found his belt buckle. The backs of her hand brushed against his abdomen as she worked, and his muscles contracted. Taylor hesitated an instant, then

bent her head, and the next instant, he felt the cool sweet-
ness of her lips at the flesh just above his waist. How such
coolness could ignite pure heat he didn't care. All he knew
was the fire was inside him, and around him, and she was
its cause.

The metallic hiss of the lowering zipper stoked the fire.
When her cool, soft hands slipped inside to cup him, no
fire wall on earth could have contained the blaze. He
dragged jeans and briefs down himself—letting her do it
would have been jumping right into the inferno—balancing
on one knee to yank them off the opposite leg, then switch-
ing. All the while her touches, her nearness, her simply
being threatened his precarious equilibrium.

And then they were pressed together again, knees to
shoulders. Naked flesh to naked flesh. Desire to desire.

Cal recognized his unwillingness to either drop back onto
the mattress, or to use his strength to force Taylor to do
so—recognized it and pushed aside consideration of what
it might mean.

Instead, he carried her down so they were on their sides,
still face-to-face. Hooking one hand under her smooth
thigh, he drew it up over his hip, opening her to him, feeling the heated dampness awaiting him, knowing the tight,
smooth ecstasy that was so near.

Her hips rocked against him, one hand pressing against
his buttocks.

"Wait."

"Oh." Her soft breath of a syllable acknowledged why
he'd stopped. "Hurry."

But he didn't hurry and he didn't reach for his jeans.

He had to slow it down. *Now.* Or it would be way past
the time—or need—for protection. But that wasn't the reason, either. He didn't want to use protection. He wanted to
stroke into her, skin to skin. To let his seed spill into her.
To watch her swell with his baby. To watch their baby
suckle at her breast. To—

"Cal?"

For one fraction of time he met her eyes, and all the fantasies he'd just imagined welled up between them.

He jerked away, swearing short and harsh. Then, shifting around, he reached for the condom in the pocket of the jeans behind him. Still swearing under his breath, he put it on and came back to her.

Tears darkened her eyelashes but didn't fall.

"Taylor?"

If she said no, he'd stop. If it killed him, he'd stop.

She shook her head—two sharp motions. "I want you, Cal." Low and fierce, her voice pushed the fire deeper inside him. "I want you now."

He stroked into her, hearing his own groan at the rightness of finding his place inside her. But just that fast, the pulsing needs of the rhythm rose up with its demands. Her arms and legs wrapped around him.

Each stroke was a force of will to hold back the fire another second, another movement, another lifetime. He wanted, needed, to hear her call out. To have one last memory of her voice as he brought her to the peak.

Her internal muscles clenched around him, and she threw her head back.

"Cal!"

He exploded. Beyond force of will, beyond his experience. Up, hard and fast in a rush of sensation that erased everything before it.

Holding her, feeling her arms around him, he tried to pretend the landscape of his emotions had somehow remained untouched. And especially he tried to pretend that he hadn't needed her not only to call out, but to call out that name—*his* name.

He was a damned liar.

The fact that he'd lied to himself made it worse.

He'd wanted Taylor even more than she'd wanted him.

Cal stuffed a pillow behind his shoulders so he could angle up enough to look at her—her cheek resting against his chest, one arm draped across his waist, one leg hooked over his. Where the drifts of covers receded, her skin glowed pale in the moonlight.

Taylor deserved more than this, more than him.

Taylor deserved someone to love her.

If he'd been standing, the thought would have buckled his knees, like an unexpected punch.

Love? Someone to love her? How could he wish that on her? Someone she would show her generosity and vulnerability to, and then would use it against her?

Like he had?

Maybe I can understand, with your history, that you're worried about me doing that to you. But how do you explain your trying to do it to me?

Because, God help him, he loved her. And that's what love did.

No. God should help Taylor, because even after the lesson at his hands, she still believed in love.

Taylor woke with a start. She hadn't meant to sleep. She hadn't meant to miss even a moment. She hadn't meant to leave him the option of leaving silently.

But he was still here. His arms wrapped around her, his body her pillow. She tipped her head back and met his gaze. For one heartbeat he held her still—a snapshot in her heart of what could be if he'd allow it.

Then he released her and moved away. A powerful shifting of his muscles and he'd rolled out of the bed to stand beside it, reaching for his briefs. Watching his motions brought the familiar thudding heat to her bloodstream, but the tightness in her chest and throat came from the meaning behind his motions.

"You're leaving for good—no, not for good. Forever."

She said it not because she didn't know the answer, but to make him say it.

"I'm doing you a favor."

"You expect me to say thank you?"

With his back still to her, he looked around, pausing in the act of pulling on his jeans. "I can do without a thank-you."

Regret underpinned the starkness of his voice. It made her all the more certain that he was leaving forever.

"There's one thing I do thank you for, Cal." She'd thought yesterday she'd said everything she had to say. She'd been wrong. "Without realizing it, I was afraid I might be tempted back into being that shark lawyer I used to be if I got too close to it again. I'm sure that's part of why I came to Knighton—not much chance of being drawn back into that world here, right?" She tried to smile. "I hadn't counted on you."

Shrugging his shirt into place, he looked at her over his shoulder.

"But now," she went on quickly, before she could beg him to stay and be the man she knew he could be, "thanks to you, I have been exposed to that old life, so my fears and doubts have been tested. And I've come out the other side knowing—no fears, no doubts—that my life here is what I want."

"I'm glad. It should make you understand that's what I'm doing—trying to protect my being able to stay where and what I want to be."

"That's not what you're doing, Cal." She sat up, holding the sheet to her throat, though it offered no protection from the pain. "That's what's so heartbreaking about it. You learned a long time ago where you didn't want to be and what you didn't want to be, but you've been running scared ever since that, if you let yourself get too close to your old life again, it would swallow you up and make you just like your father."

"That's bull." He sat on the farthest corner of the bed from her to pull on his boots.

"It's not. It's…" Understanding produced from a thousand fragments—words, looks, touches—came together then. "It's true, but it's only half the truth. You're afraid if you're loved you'll be like your father, and you're afraid if you love you'll be like your mother." The fear of hurting and the fear of being hurt—and both of them were driving him away from her—not because he didn't care, but because he did. "You won't know that neither one of those needs to be true until you face those old temptations. And until you do that, you won't know if you belong here or anywhere else. I've done that, thanks to you. Now you have to do it, too. To stop running and to face those demons you thought you were leaving behind. Because you haven't left them, Cal, don't you see that? Just like your Aunt Eva remained in her prison even when she could have left it, you carry your demons around with you. They're inside that shell you retreat into. But there's also a man with life and love and joy inside there, if you'll let him out.

"I pray you do, because I love you, Cal."

He stood, fully dressed. Ready to leave. "I never wanted you thinking you're in love with me."

She laughed, and half meant it. "You don't think I've tried not to? From the start I tried not to. But mistletoe and puppies and blizzards conspired against me. Mistletoe, puppies, blizzards and you. I never had a chance."

Chapter Fourteen

Matty walked into Taylor's office and dropped into the chair.

"Cal's gone. Left this morning. Spent Tuesday lining up another hand so the Flying W wouldn't be short." She huffed as if in irritation, but Taylor saw the telltale sheen of tears. "As if some fill-in could replace him—the idiot. He packed up yesterday, loaded his truck and left at first light."

"Did he say anything?"

"Not much. Said he was sorry to be leaving me in the lurch. Said 'Thanks.'" Taylor could hear the single, laconic word in his low voice, and knew, as Matty did, how much it encompassed. "Said you wouldn't be his lawyer anymore, so he had to take care of things himself. You had to know he'd go, Taylor."

"I knew."

"Do you think that was wise?"

"It was the only thing I could do. I couldn't watch...I

couldn't.'' Taylor looked to her friend for understanding
and received it. Matty came around the desk, put her arm
around Taylor's shoulders and squeezed.

''I know, I know. I'm sorry. I just hope to God it shakes
him up hard enough to loosen some of those stubborn bolts
in his head.''

''Did he…did he take everything?''

''No. Left his furniture and most of his books. Took
clothes, a couple paintings, a candlestick—if you can believe that.'' She shook her head. ''And he took Sin.''

''Good,'' Taylor said firmly. ''If there's anyone who
needs unconditional love, it's Cal.''

One look at his father's last assistant, and Cal knew that
Christina had hired this one. She had medium brown hair
going gray, less chin than forehead, thick glasses and a
nervous air.

''If you want anything, Mr. Whitton, just buzz. It's the
red button, on the right.''

''Greg Salisbury should be here in five minutes, and the
meeting starts in twenty. If I think of anything I can't do
without before then, I'll get it myself, or I'll open the door
and ask you.''

''Oh. Yes, sir. Of course, Mr. Whitton.''

''No, wait. One thing I do want—don't call me Mr.
Whitton.''

''Not…but—I mean, yes, sir, uh, sir.'' She was backing
out of the room the entire time.

''Thank you, Ms. Markham,'' he added just before the
door closed, leaving him alone. Alone in his father's office.

It hadn't changed since the last time he'd been here, the
week before Great-Aunt Eva died.

His father's portrait still hung in the place of honor over
the antique sofa. Anyone who ever sat on the thing soon
learned the error of his ways—and a lesson in the ego of

Laurance Whitton—because the only comfortable seating faced the portrait.

Cal looked at it now. It showed a vital, driven, savvy man. A man who not a soul on this earth honestly mourned.

A man who'd had a woman who truly loved him, until he drove her away.

A sensation of cold moved up Cal's neck and across the base of his skull.

Before he could decipher its cause, a knock sounded and Ms. Markham ushered in a man a few years older than Cal, with a streak of gray in his dark hair and an easy smile.

"Mr. Salisbury," Ms. Markham murmured before disappearing.

"It's nice to meet you, finally, Cal. Sorry—I should call you Mr. Whitton. I've talked with Taylor so much about your situation, I guess I picked up her habit."

"No problem. Matter of fact, I'd prefer it to Mr. Whitton."

The lawyer frowned. "That might not be a good idea. I understand you're not sure you want the people here to know about your life in Wyoming, is that right?"

"That's right." Once this was over, he planned to disappear. He doubted he'd go back to Knighton. But having the vultures from his old life know they could find him there would close off the possibility completely. He wasn't ready to do that.

"Then we better stick with Mr. Whitton, and leave Cal for Wyoming. You're not going to win any friends when this gets out."

He nodded. The gesture felt awkward, wrong somehow. Giving up being Cal Ruskoff was harder than he'd have expected. He missed the name. He missed the life. He missed the man.

By dissolving this company, you'll dissolve their lives right out from under them without another thought, simply

*because it's what suits your purposes. Isn't that what you
father would do?*

Oh, yes, Laurance Whitton always did what suited hi
purpose without a second's thought. Now Bennington Cald
well Rusk Whitton was about to tell a roomful of stranger
that he was going to do what suited his purpose. Was Tay
lor right? Was it a futile gesture to try to get back at a ma
he could never get back at? Was it to even the score in
game with only one player left?

"Sorry it can't be simpler," Salisbury said, "but con
sidering you're about to dismantle the company these folk
work for, it's probably a necessary complication. If yo
want to look over these valuations—"

"It's as simple as you make it."

*I found myself telling this five-year-old that it reall
wasn't as simple as Mama Abedelia made it sound. Tha
there were circumstances and obligations that could com
plicate right and wrong tremendously, and that gray wa
the only universal color. But in the end, it's as simple a
you make it.*

"What?"

"Just thinking aloud. Sorry."

"No problem." The lawyer picked up where he'd lef
off, talking about valuations done for tax purposes.

Cal interrupted him. "These valuations—they're th
same kind that would be done for converting the compan
to worker-owned?"

Salisbury looked up. "No. But Taylor had that kin
done, too. I wondered…"

A discreet knock on the door presaged Ms. Markham
opening it halfway to announce, "Everyone's gathering i
the conference room, Mr.—uh, gentlemen."

"Thank you, Ms. Markham."

"Sooner we get this started, the sooner it'll be over,'
Salisbury said.

Something in the other man's neutral voice caught Cal's interest. "You're not looking forward to this, are you?"

"Can't say I am."

"I should have known that was why Taylor picked you."

He shrugged. "We've been friends a long time. Well, are you ready?"

Cal glanced at the portrait again, then started to shrug out of his suit jacket. The lawyer's brows rose like an elevator.

"No, I'm not ready. In fact—" He broke off to stride to the door, fling it open to reveal the startled face of Ms. Markham, and announced, "There isn't going to be a meeting—not today anyway. Ms. Markham, tell everyone to go back to their regular work and I'm sorry to have wasted their time, then order in sandwiches, because Mr. Salisbury and I have a lot of work to do."

The woman's mouth worked before she got out, "What kind of sandwiches, sir?"

Cal laughed. "Beef, of course! Roast beef. In fact, order in roast beef sandwiches for everyone in the company. Oh, and Ms. Markham, get the flower shop in Jefferson, Wyoming, on the line. If there's more than one flower shop, get Dave Currick of Knighton, Wyoming, on the phone and ask him what the hell he was talking about."

He shut the door, then turned back to the gaping lawyer. "Now, let's get started. And call me Cal."

Almost two months of silence. Of not even hearing anyone else mention Cal's name. And then two phone calls referring to him in one day.

Taylor had thought the wordless looks of sympathy from Matty, Dave and Lisa were bad enough. Even Ruth Moski had patted her arm in a consoling manner. As for her family, the Larsen radar was working all too well. She hadn't told them anything, yet she'd received calls from her parents and each sibling, plus her sister-in-law, asking if something was wrong.

At least when Lisa buzzed and told her line two was Greg Salisbury from Connecticut, Taylor was braced for what the topic was going to be.

"Thanks for the client from hell, Taylor."

"What do you mean?" Cal had been the client from hell for her, but the same reasons wouldn't apply.

"He doesn't listen to a damn thing I say. Sits across my desk from me, and tells me what he wants, stays silent while I tell him all the reasons that's not a good idea, then says to do it his way, and have it done a month faster than it's humanly possible to do."

"You're lucky he comes to your office," she murmured. A vision of Cal astride a horse, with the greening mountains and blue sky as his backdrop, swept in. And that was another thing to blame on his insistence that she go to the Flying W all those times—too many vivid memories of Cal in the life that had suited him so well.

A harumph came over the long-distance line. "I'll give him this, he's sharp. And quick. Never had anybody pick up the ins and outs of the P-and-S faster."

A purchase-and-sales agreement? Was he selling after all? She couldn't afford to jump to that conclusion, she couldn't afford to hope. "He's a good businessman. Wait until he finds a company to run—the right company for him, one he can build up his own way. And when he does, invest in it."

"First I have to survive what he's doing to dispose of this company. *He* sure doesn't seem to care about the hornet's nest he's stirred up. And the grieving widow is a definite hornet. But he never notices—he just keeps doing what he wants."

Just like his father.

"He's seen Christina?" The ache under her breastbone grew barbs.

"Seen her? He's practically had to peel her off him a few times. Maybe she's not a hornet, maybe she's a leech. Either way, she hasn't budged him any more than anyone else has."

Emotions hit Taylor like gusts of wind, not allowing her to recover from one before the next hit. Relief—Christina had not ensnared him again. Joy—he had faced one of his demons and come through it. Sorrow—surviving that demon hadn't yet allowed him to return to Knighton. Fear—more demons, perhaps not as enticing as his ex-fiancée, but broader and deeper, remained.

"Having your plan to follow has been a lifesaver," Greg went on. "Great work, by the way. That's really why I called. To say thanks. Your plan has made this go a lot faster than it would ordinarily. Although not fast enough to please my client. The man is definitely in a hurry about something. "

Her plan…her plan to convert the company to worker-owned. He wasn't dissolving Bennington Chemical.

She couldn't formulate an answer, but Greg didn't seem to notice.

"Yeah, this plan to sell his majority ownership to the employees is a thing of beauty. And he's sweetened the deal even more."

She fulfilled her end of wrapping up the phone call automatically. Her heartbeat had picked up an irregular rhythm, like an added grace note. She feared it might be hope.

The fact that Cal was turning the company over to its employees didn't necessarily translate into his coming back to Knighton. And it certainly didn't mean he'd come back to her.

With the second phone call, an hour later, she had no opportunity to brace herself. Matty had called at least every other day "to chat," so Taylor had no reason to suspect this one would be different.

"Have you heard?"

"Heard what, Matty?"

"The animal rescue group's been funded for as far into the future as anyone can conceive, and Dr. Markus got a whopping donation for the clinic he wants to build. Somebody paid the back taxes on the Widow Brontman's place. Ruth and Hugh Moski's granddaughter suddenly got money to go to medical school, too."

"How wonderful for them," Taylor said when she could manage words.

"All anonymous gifts from some unknown benefactor. Word is the paperwork comes from some law firm in Connecticut."

She hadn't needed that confirmation to know. It was Cal. Clearing the books before he closed them? A lesson he'd learned from his father. Just like he'd learned from his father to fear love, with a refresher course from Christina.

He swore he'd hated his father all his life, but if Cal hadn't loved his father, the man couldn't have hurt him so bitterly. And he'd loved Christina enough to plan a life with her.

To protect himself from more of the kind of pain they'd inflicted, he'd perfected the habit of leaving what he loved. His home. Sailing and the ocean. Oh, yes, Cal had learned well to see danger in what he loved...and in loving itself. He'd grown to love Wyoming and the Flying W and cattle ranching. How could she even think he might return?

And her? It was the proverbial no-win situation. If he felt he was caring deeply for her, he would cut himself off from her as he had cut himself off from sailing. The only way he would come back was if he was sure he didn't care.

Then another thought occurred to her.

Cal had taken Sin with him.

He *had* let himself love that dog—whether he'd admit it or not—so he hadn't cut himself off from love entirely.

But that left a big leap—from letting himself love a dog, to letting her love him.

Cal backtracked when the doorbell rang barely a minute after he'd entered the rental town house. Almost like someone had been waiting for him.

Christina stood under the outdoor light, the harsh shadows making a travesty of her practiced smile.

"Hello, Benning. May I come in?"

He shrugged and turned away, letting her decide whether to follow. She did, closing the door, then backing up a step as Sin charged in from the back. Cal had paid a bundle to have a Sin-sized doggy door installed so he could access the fenced backyard. And that was on top of practically having to buy the furnished unit to get permission to have a dog.

"What a sweet doggy."

Sin gave a slow swish of his tail, more like a cat's stay-away lashing than his usual happy greeting.

"What do you want, Christina?" Cal crossed to the built-in minibar.

She sat on the love seat, stroking one palm over the cushion next to her in invitation. "Is that any way to greet me? After all we've been to each other."

He sipped the Scotch he'd poured over ice. "What do you want, *Stepmother?*"

"That's not funny," she snapped.

He sat on the straight-backed upholstered chair across from her. Sin leaned against the chair, casting doleful looks at Christina. Cal wondered what she'd do if she knew she was sitting in Sin's favorite spot. He hadn't changed the no-furniture rule, but he'd not only spotted dog hair on the cushions, he'd seen Sin looking out the nearby window, and that could only be accomplished by sitting in that spot.

"That's our legal relationship. And that's the only one we have."

Today's meeting with the board, the corporation lawyers and Christina's lawyers had gone for twelve and a half long—sometimes acrimonious—hours. He was more tired than after the hardest all-day session at the Flying W. What he wanted to do was take off this suit and throw a stick for Sin for a while. Forget all the legal and financial wrangling he had to go through to get this company off his hands.

A transformational process…

That's what that woman from the Wyoming flower shop had said fireweed was good for helping someone get through.

It had been a strange conversation last month. No, the month before. God, it seemed as if he'd been mired in meetings forever.

Ms. Markham had efficiently put through the call to the flower shop. Only then had he realized he had no clue why he was calling. It wasn't as if he'd intended to send flowers to—to anyone. He'd sputtered out something about Dave Currick telling him to call.

"Currick?…Currick? Oh, yes. Indian paintbrush."

"What?"

"Indian paintbrush," she'd repeated firmly, as if that explained everything. "Wedding bouquet. What wildflower are you interested in?"

"Wildflower? I'm not interested in any wildflower."

"No? I thought perhaps that was why Dave Currick suggested you call. He was so interested in Indian paintbrush, and wanted to know all about its properties. The essences of flowers have great benefits, you know. Each flower, especially wildflowers, can aid you in different ways, help with different situations. Although Dave Currick came at it from the other end—having a wildflower he was interested in, and then finding out the properties of its essence met his needs exactly. He was quite struck by that. So if there was a wildflower you had a particular association with or—"

"Fireweed." He'd had no intention of saying that, but it came out.

"Ah, fireweed. Such an interesting choice."

"I didn't choose—" he'd started. He'd thought Dave was nuts when he'd gone on about this flower shop before Cal's departure, and now he wondered about his own sanity.

"No, of course not. It chose you. Ah, yes," she continued, not letting him speak, "fireweed is excellent for a transformational process. That's to be expected, given its ability to grow and bloom after a fire. It's quite remarkable the way it can help you break old patterns by facing your fears. It breaks down the resistance so many people have to change, especially deep change. And of course it brings more stability by deepening your connection to the earth."

Nonsense—had to be. What the hell did flowers know about his life? He'd rallied enough to demand suspiciously, "Do you know Taylor Larsen?"

"No. Should I? Is that who you would like to send fireweed essence to?"

"No. I, uh…no. Send it to this address." And then he'd heard himself giving the office address for Bennington Chemical. At the last second he'd made it in care of Ms. Markham instead of in his own name, but still, he'd been shaking his head at himself ever since.

"You're right to shake your head," Christina said. "It doesn't have to be that way, Benning."

Cal stared at her. What on earth had she been talking about while he'd been thinking about fireweed and Taylor?

"I've wondered where you were all these years. Wondered how things might have been if I'd made a different choice. We can find out now what we've been missing. There's no reason we can't."

"Yeah, there is," he countered, up to speed now. "Because I don't have any interest in knowing."

"I don't believe that. Not after…well, let's just say I'll

never forget, and I'm sure that you won't, either.'' It was a beautifully delivered speech, with her head tipped down as if she were shy, combined with a slow survey of his body that was decidedly not shy.

"And I'll never forget the lessons you taught me, Christina.''

She smiled, obviously not catching his undertone. "I knew that if I could see you, it would be all right. Because we understand each other. We have something between us.'' With fluid grace she shifted to sitting on the coffee table near him. "Is that why you wouldn't let me be at the meeting today, because when you see me…?''

She ran her nails over the fabric covering his thigh.

Sin yawned loudly, and Cal almost laughed.

"I excluded you from the meeting to avoid this scene. Give it up, Christina. No matter how hard you try to vamp me, the plan's going through.''

"You don't believe I've come here just for you, Benning? You didn't used to be so humble.'' She tilted her head back, offering her lips.

"Even if you came here just to have sex with me, never thinking it might influence me to halt the plan and leave you in charge of Bennington Chemical, it's no sale. I'm not interested.''

It took her a long moment of studying his face to see the truth of his words. Then her facade crumbled.

"I worked too hard to let you give away Bennington Chemical. It's not yours to give away—it's mine!''

"Wrong. Read the will.''

"You're cheating the stockholders. You can't do this.''

"I'm the main stockholder, and the others agree the long-term benefits outweigh the loss of immediate income. A very good lawyer drew up that plan, and you'll find I *can* do this.''

"You're punishing me! You're being spiteful and vindictive, just because I chose your father over you.''

"Christina, this has nothing to do with you."

Her expression shifted and he knew she didn't believe him. In fact, she'd become more convinced of the opposite.

"Benning, what we had was so good. If you two hadn't been so much alike, your father never could have won me away. Actually, it was like falling in love with you all over again."

She moved in close, running her hand from the middle of his chest up to the opened collar of his shirt.

He hardly noticed.

If you two hadn't been so much alike.... You're just like your father.... Your father thought nothing of crushing people in order to get what he wanted. He rolled over them or used them as it suited his purposes. And that's what you intend to do.

But he hadn't done that. He was turning the company over to the employees, just like Taylor had urged him to do. So why had Christina's phrase opened the wound over Taylor's words?

"I never stopped wanting you," Christina said. "We wouldn't have had to stop if you'd been more cooperative back then."

"What about that little vow you took with my father, something about forsaking all others."

"You *are* still angry at me," she said with a pout. "You know that's not how the real world works."

"You mean people keeping their vows, and marrying because they love somebody instead of for money and power? A couple years ago, I would have agreed with you. But now..."

"Now. Yes, right now, Benning. That's what we can have." Christina stood, wrapping both hands around his free hand and tugging.

He couldn't even see the woman in front of him for the memory that filled his mind.

Taylor holding a candle up into a darkness all around

that included him. Holding that candle up to cast its light.
While her other hand protected the flame from the gusts
and drafts and sighs and storms that threatened it. Holding
that delicate flame up so he could see it, so he could see
her, even when the candle sputtered and the wax burned
her. Even when he was part of the crosscurrents that buf-
feted the fragile fire and threatened to extinguish it.

Holding up her heart to lead him, if he let himself follow
its light.

*A man who'd had a woman who truly loved him, until
he drove her away.*

His own thoughts. His own assessment of his father, of
the man Christina and Taylor had said he was like. As
different as they were, he'd never doubted the ability of
either Christina or Taylor to read people. To read him.

Christina had used the ability to manipulate him.

Taylor had used the ability… Taylor had…

He stood, some half-formed notion of following the light
motivating him. He'd forgotten Christina, until she rose,
too, and started to guide his hand to her breast.

"Now," she murmured in a throaty voice. "Now can be
our time."

He jerked his hand free and stepped away.

"Not our time—your time. To leave."

Cal was back.

But that was all Taylor knew. Just the bare word of it
from the stool-sitters at the café when she'd gone for a take-
out salad for lunch.

"I see Cal's back in town. Saw him driving through like
he was heading to the Flying W 'bout nine," Hugh Moski
had said to her, clearly expecting that she already knew and
would fill in more.

"So I hear." She paid her bill in a hurry and returned
to her office.

She considered, as she dropped off Lisa's order in the

outer office then headed inside to hers, asking Lisa if she knew anything, or could find out anything. She considered calling Matty. She considered calling the foreman's cottage. She did none of those things.

Had he come back to pack and go for good? He could have asked Matty to do that, though asking for help had never been his forte. He could have hired someone or he could have sent some underling to do it, though letting anyone else into his private space had never been his way, either.

So she could see him coming back to pack up what was important to him, and heading out. Without a word to her? Maybe.

That would hurt.

Nearly as much as his going for good would hurt.

But she would survive, and she had Cal to thank for that knowledge. Cal had dragged her out of her own self-protective shell as surely as she'd kicked him out of his cave by making him go back East. It was an important lesson. If only for that, she would never regret loving Cal Ruskoff.

Eventually she'd get over the pain. She was sure of it. Because no one could go on hurting this much forever.

But she wouldn't get over it this afternoon, and not while he was back in town.

She packed the files she'd failed to open once in the past two hours into her briefcase, shut down the computer she hadn't looked at and tidied her desk. She'd reached the outer door before she stopped. Who was she kidding? She turned around and dropped the briefcase on her desk, then headed out again.

"I'm leaving, Lisa."

"Do you feel okay? Is there anything I can do?"

"I feel fine, and there's nothing you can do. Thank you. Why don't you close up the office and take the rest of the afternoon off, too."

Taylor shut the door behind her before Lisa could answer. With her head down, she was almost to her car when she became aware of another presence in the parking lot. Her heart slammed hard, then seemed to reverberate in her chest with the force of the blow.

Cal.

She knew it before she looked up and saw him leaning against the passenger door of an unfamiliar pickup beside her car. He wore his old jeans, old boots, the familiar hat and the plain leather belt. Only his shirt indicated a change. It was new, dark blue and good quality. But he'd rolled the sleeves up in his customary way, and he had his arms folded across his chest, at complete ease.

She heard a steady thumping and wondered if it was her heart, and if he could hear it, too.

"Hello, Cal. I heard you were in town."

"We've been waiting for you, Taylor."

His gesture to the open window explained the "we." Sin sat there looking out the window. He'd grown, his coat was fuller, lustrously healthy. She realized it was his tail wagging against the seat that was making the rhythmic sound she heard.

At least one of them had clear feelings about this reunion.

"Why didn't you come into the office?"

"I didn't want to interrupt your business."

So he wasn't here on business. But she'd known that. And at some level she'd also known he wouldn't come into town and slip away again without seeing her. He had too much honor.

He pushed off from the truck door and was opening it. "Let's go for a ride."

She shook her head. "Say what you have to say here and—"

"I have something to show you."

"Cal, I don't—"

"I don't like to remind people of their debts, but if it takes reminding you that I took this mutt off your hands, and I pulled you out of a blizzard—"

"All right!" If he was so determined to do it his way, she simply didn't have the energy to fight him. She just wanted this done.

They were turning into the Flying W before he spoke again. "I told Matty she needs to hire a new foreman."

"I see. Well." Taylor cleared her throat and blinked fast. "Thank you for telling me directly, Cal. For not letting me hear it through the grapevine, or just letting time pass until it was obvious you weren't coming back. I do appreciate that."

"You've got it wrong, Taylor. I'm staying."

She blinked again, but for a totally different cause.

"I'm buying the Bartuck place on the north end of Lewis County. I'm quitting as Flying W foreman because I'm going to run my own ranch. I'm following your advice about Bennington Chemical. The employees are tickled. A couple of the stockholders are ticked, but that's okay. Your colleague in Connecticut's working out. And every legal type I've encountered has been real impressed by your work. Said they couldn't believe someone with that ability was holed up in Knighton, Wyoming."

"I'm not holed up. I'm living my life. A good life."

"That's what I told them."

She glanced at him, but his profile remained impassive. His next words did nothing to sort out her confusion.

"Christina came to the place I was staying in Connecticut last week."

"Christina? Your…"

"Stepmother? Ex-fiancée?" he supplied. "Yeah, that one."

She looked straight ahead. They passed the cluster of Flying W ranch buildings that included his house—his former house—without slowing. "What did she want?"

"She wanted to get back together."

"Oh."

"Don't be an idiot, Taylor."

An immediate flame of justifiable anger consumed her. It felt good after trying for so hard and so long to be understanding and rational. She jerked around to face him. He was grinning. That only made her angrier.

"Idiot? You've got—"

"A lot of nerve? Yeah, I do. But you're not showing the sense I know you have if you think I'd consider Christina for a second." The smile was gone and his voice had changed when he spoke the next words. "And you don't know me as well as I thought you did."

Taylor swallowed, trying to hold down the hope that kept rising up like bubbles that refused to burst.

"If it comes to that, you didn't listen to what I told you about Christina, either," he said with the old bite in his voice.

With that pointer, she said, "She came to see you because she wanted you to stop the agreement with the employees. To keep the company and let her run it."

"Yep. That's exactly what she wanted. But that's not what she got. I signed the papers before I left. There'll be more before it's all over, but the deal's in place. Just the way you laid it out. I think the employees are considering you for employee of the year—or sainthood."

"It was a fair agreement—nobody was cheated."

"No. But the current employees of Bennington Chemical aren't accustomed to being treated fairly."

Another legacy of his father, she supposed. She wasn't a violent person, but if the man hadn't been dead, and she could have gotten her hands on him...well, she supposed entities better suited to doling out justice than she was were probably taking care of Laurance Whitton.

"Christina said some other things, too."

Taylor wasn't going to give him another opening to accuse her of idiocy, so, she bluntly asked, "What?"

"She told me people don't keep their vows, and they don't marry for love in the real world—they cheat and scheme all in the name of money and power, and love is just another weapon to be used in that war." He shot a look at her, then pretended he needed to watch the road ahead. "I said I would have agreed with every one of those statements a few years ago. And then I started to tell her that now I wasn't so sure. Then I stopped."

Her heart had lurched with unshakable hope until those last three words.

"What stopped you, Cal?"

"Because I *was* sure." He braked the truck, then sat staring straight ahead, the engine still running. "I'd seen all those bad things in the real world, but I've seen the good ones now, too. One's no more real than the other."

"I'm glad."

He turned off the engine and faced her. "You don't look glad."

She looked at him then, knowing tears were caught among her lashes, hoping they wouldn't fall.

"I am, Cal. I can't think of anything in this world that I wanted more than for you to open your heart, so you would see the good in life, so you could *live* the good in life."

"Nothing you wanted more? Not even being loved back, when you said you loved me?"

She understood his need to ask. Because she'd been his guide of sorts, and he was still feeling his way, exploring the possibilities, but it was becoming an increasingly painful lesson to teach.

"Not even that. Because you couldn't really love while you kept believing the things you believed."

He cupped her cheek, and so much in her wanted to turn

into the touch, to close her eyes and pretend everything
was okay.

"You showed me how to believe new things."

Gratitude. That was what she heard.

He'd learned to open his heart and she would rejoice in
knowing how much happier his life would be from now
on…later, after she'd cried out the pain burning her throat
and searing her heart. She turned her head, away from his
touch.

"Cal, please, I want to go back now."

He swore under his breath.

"Not until I've shown you what we came up here for."
His grim tone was matched by his expression when he
came around to her side of the truck and opened the door,
silently waiting for her to get out.

From that expression she knew the fastest way—the only
way—to get this finished was to do what he wanted.

He took her elbow and steered her to a spot that over-
looked a slope down to a creek bed, then a rise up the
opposite hill. The entire area was covered with an under-
coat of green that was topped with spikes of purplish-rosy
flowers.

"I wanted you to see this, Taylor. It's fireweed. All
grown-up and blooming."

Only then did she recognize this as the same spot they'd
come to when he'd lectured her about fire walls, and where
sprouts of green had made her feel so hopeful.

Cal kept talking. "You knew fireweed comes back first
after an area's been burned, but did you know it likes dis-
turbed ground to grow in? And it helps people with trans-
formations."

"It's beautiful, but…?"

He took her left hand. When she tried to tug free, he held
on tighter. "I told you love was a weapon people used to
manipulate the person who was weak enough to love. It
took me a while, but it finally hit me, when I saw Christina,

what an idiot I'd been for lumping everybody together. I'd
handed you that weapon almost from the start, and you've
never once used it against me, even when I gave you plenty
of reason to. But you were wrong about one thing—'' he
sounded almost belligerent ''—even when I didn't believe
in it, I did love you. I do love you.''

Taylor gaped at him, sorting through his absence, the
grim challenge in his voice, the field of wildflowers. They
all came into focus when she met his eyes.

They held the familiar heat, but the ice was gone. Gone
completely, and in its place was a light she'd seen only
rarely there.

''Oh, Cal, you idiot!''

She flung herself into his arms, knowing he'd catch her,
and he did. His hold was strong and sure, even as uncertainty lingered in his voice.

''I'm no bargain, Taylor. I've made a start, but I've still
got burned-out stretches inside. Will you be my fireweed,
take hold where it looked like nothing could grow, and help
me change?''

''Try and stop me. Just try and stop me.''

Epilogue

"I still don't understand how you got that rash," Matty said, staring at the red patch that remained on Taylor's arm more than a week later.

As hostess, Matty had taken Taylor's arm to draw her into the Slash-C main house, where Dave and Matty were having Cal and Taylor over for dinner.

Taylor felt heat rising up from her chest across her throat and into her face. It wasn't from embarrassment, but from memories. Making love in a field of fireweed probably wasn't the smartest thing to do for someone with sensitive skin, but she would do it again anytime Cal wanted.

Especially if he volunteered again to smooth lotion over all her prickled flesh afterward.

She glanced at him, saw the deepened grooves and the light in his eyes, and the heat spread lower.

"Taylor probably got the rash tramping around checking out the place Cal's buying," Dave offered blandly.

But Taylor caught an exchange of looks between him

and Matty, and heard the understanding in Matty's drawn-out "Oh." If Taylor hadn't already been bright pink, she would have blushed.

"We have been looking at the place," she said, trying to redirect the conversation. "It's going to need a good deal of work to get it in shape."

"I could get started now if my boss wasn't making me finish out the summer," Cal grumbled.

"Hey, I let you be gone two months," Matty shot back, "so quit griping."

The exchange didn't fool anyone, since the four people in the room knew Cal had been the one to insist that he pick up the reins as Matty's foreman until she found a replacement and he could close on the purchase of his ranch in the fall.

Matty gestured for them to sit on the couch, then perched on the arm of the easy chair Dave sat in. "Well, you've got plenty of experience with turning around a run-down place after bringing the Flying W back to life."

"Helping you bring it back," he corrected.

"You should have driven a harder bargain for that company back East and you would have had all the money you'd need."

"I'll have plenty of money." He gave Taylor a significant look, and she felt a fresh surge of heat. Money for things like a family. They'd talked about starting one last night, and then they'd done more than talk about it. A lot more.

"Looks like you got too much sun, Taylor," Matty said, with a devilish glint in her eye. "You should be more careful."

Cal made a noise between a snort and chuckle, put his arm around her shoulders and took her hand with his free one. "Honey, I don't think this announcement is going to hold until dessert."

Taylor tore her gaze from her soon-to-be husband and looked at her friends, both grinning widely.

"We wanted you to be the first to know," she started. And got no further with their plans for a fall wedding, and a move into the main house at Cal's new ranch—their ranch.

Matty burst out laughing, leaving it to Dave to explain. "I think my wife is trying to say we *were* the first to know—at least Matty was—and long before you two finally woke up."

"You mean the snowstorm," Taylor said.

"Before," Matty got out, still laughing.

"When you maneuvered me into bringing Sin out to him."

"And me into keeping him," Cal added.

"Before."

"New Year's Eve and your mistletoe ambush," Cal said.

"Before," Matty insisted. "Hey, you guys have to let me plan a party for you to celebrate, okay? This'll be fun. We can have it here and invite everyone."

Dave pretended to groan, shaking his head as he told Cal, "Run. Run while you have the chance—Matty's planning again!"

Cal's arm tightened around Taylor. "That's okay, her last plan turned out." Just before his lips touched Taylor's, he added, "Turned out fine."

*   *   *   *   *

Available in August from

JOAN ELLIOTT PICKART

A brand-new, longer-length book
in the bestselling series,

The Baby Bet

*Party
of Three*

He was a hard-boiled cop with a child in his care.
She was a woman in need of his protective embrace.
Together they were a family in the making....

Available at your favorite retail outlet.
Only from Silhouette Books

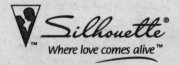

Silhouette®
Where love comes alive™

SILHOUETTE® MAKES YOU A STAR!

Feel like a star with Silhouette.

We will fly you and a guest to New York City for an exciting weekend stay at a glamorous 5-star hotel. Experience a refreshing day at one of New York's trendiest spas and have your photo taken by a professional. Plus, receive $1,000 U.S. spending money!

Flowers…long walks…dinner for two… how does Silhouette Books make romance come alive for you?

Send us a script, with 500 words or less, along with visuals (only drawings, magazine cutouts or photographs or combination thereof). Show us how Silhouette Makes Your Love Come Alive. Be creative and have fun. No purchase necessary. All entries must be clearly marked with your name, address and telephone number. All entries will become property of Silhouette and are not returnable. **Contest closes September 28, 2001.**

Please send your entry to: **Silhouette Makes You a Star!**

In U.S.A.	In Canada
P.O. Box 9069	P.O. Box 637
Buffalo, NY, 14269-9069	Fort Erie, ON, L2A 5X3

Look for contest details on the next page, by visiting www.eHarlequin.com or request a copy by sending a self-addressed envelope to the applicable address above. Contest open to Canadian and U.S. residents who are 18 or over. Void where prohibited.

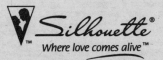

Silhouette®
Where love comes alive™

Our lucky winner's photo will appear in a Silhouette ad. Join the fun!

SRMYAS1

HARLEQUIN "SILHOUETTE MAKES YOU A STAR!" CONTEST 1308
OFFICIAL RULES
NO PURCHASE NECESSARY TO ENTER

1. To enter, follow directions published in the offer to which you are responding. Contest begins June 1, 2001, and ends on September 28, 2001. Entries must be postmarked by September 28, 2001, and received by October 5, 2001. Enter by hand-printing (or typing) on an 8 ½" x 11" piece of paper your name, address (including zip code), contest number/name and attaching a script containing 500 words or less, along with drawings, photographs or magazine cutouts, or combinations thereof (i.e., collage) on no larger than 9" x 12" piece of paper, describing how the Silhouette books make romance come alive for you. Mail via first-class mail to: Harlequin "Silhouette Makes You a Star!" Contest 1308, (in the U.S.) P.O. Box 9069, Buffalo, NY 14269-9069, (in Canada) P.O. Box 637, Fort Erie, Ontario, Canada L2A 5X3. Limit one entry per person, household or organization.

2. Contests may be judged by a panel of members of the Harlequin editorial, marketing and public relations staff. Fifty percent of criteria will be judged against script and fifty percent will be judged against drawing, photographs and/or magazine cutouts. Judging criteria will be based on the following:

   • Sincerity—25%
   • Originality and Creativity—50%
   • Emotionally Compelling—25%

   In the event of a tie, duplicate prizes will be awarded. Decisions of the judges are final.

3. All entries become the property of Torstar Corp. and may be used for future promotional purposes. Entries will not be returned. No responsibility is assumed for lost, late, illegible, incomplete, inaccurate, nondelivered or misdirected mail.

4. Contest open only to residents of the U.S. (except Puerto Rico) and Canada who are 18 years of age or older, and is void wherever prohibited by law; all applicable laws and regulations apply. Any litigation within the Province of Quebec respecting the conduct or organization of a publicity contest may be submitted to the Régie des alcools, des courses et des jeux for a ruling. Any litigation respecting the awarding of a prize may be submitted to the Régie des alcools, des courses et des jeux only for the purpose of helping the parties reach a settlement. Employees and immediate family members of Torstar Corp. and D. L. Blair, Inc., their affiliates, subsidiaries and all other agencies, entities and persons connected with the use, marketing or conduct of this contest are not eligible to enter. Taxes on prizes are the sole responsibility of the winner. Acceptance of any prize offered constitutes permission to use winner's name, photograph or other likeness for the purposes of advertising, trade and promotion on behalf of Torstar Corp., its affiliates and subsidiaries without further compensation to the winner, unless prohibited by law.

5. Winner will be determined no later than November 30, 2001, and will be notified by mail. Winner will be required to sign and return an Affidavit of Eligibility/Release of Liability/Publicity Release form within 15 days after winner notification. Noncompliance within that time period may result in disqualification and an alternative winner may be selected. All travelers must execute a Release of Liability prior to ticketing and must possess required travel documents (e.g., passport, photo ID) where applicable. Trip must be booked by December 31, 2001, and completed within one year of notification. No substitution of prize permitted by winner. Torstar Corp. and D. L. Blair, Inc., their parents, affiliates and subsidiaries are not responsible for errors in printing of contest, entries and/or game pieces. In the event of printing or other errors that may result in unintended prize values or duplication of prizes, all affected game pieces or entries shall be null and void. **Purchase or acceptance of a product offer does not improve your chances of winning.**

6. Prizes: (1) Grand Prize—A 2-night/3-day trip for two (2) to New York City, including round-trip coach air transportation nearest winner's home and hotel accommodations (double occupancy) at The Plaza Hotel, a glamorous afternoon makeover at a trendy New York spa, $1,000 in U.S. spending money and an opportunity to have a professional photo taken and appear in a Silhouette advertisement (approximate retail value: $7,000). (10) Ten Runner-Up Prizes of gift packages (retail value $50 ea.). Prizes consist of only those items listed as part of the prize. Limit one prize per person. Prize is valued in U.S. currency.

7. For the name of the winner (available after December 31, 2001) send a self-addressed, stamped envelope to: Harlequin "Silhouette Makes You a Star!" Contest 1197 Winners, P.O. Box 4200 Blair, NE 68009-4200 or you may access the www.eHarlequin.com Web site through February 28, 2002.

Contest sponsored by Torstar Corp., P.O Box 9042, Buffalo, NY 14269-9042.

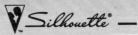

If you enjoyed what you just read,
then we've got an offer you can't resist!

Take 2 bestselling
love stories FREE!
Plus get a FREE surprise gift!

Conveniently Yours

SECRETS

A kidnapped baby
A hidden identity
A man with a past

Christine Rimmer's popular *Conveniently Yours*
miniseries returns with three brand-new books,
revolving around the Marsh baby kidnapped over
thirty years ago. Beginning late summer,
from Silhouette Books…

THE MARRIAGE AGREEMENT
(August 2001; Silhouette Special Edition #1412)
The halfbrother's story

THE BRAVO BILLIONAIRE
(September 2001; Silhouette Single Title)
The brother's story

THE MARRIAGE CONSPIRACY
(October 2001; Silhouette Special Edition #1423)
The missing baby's story—
all grown up and quite a man!

You won't want to miss a single one….
Available wherever Silhouette books are sold.

Silhouette®

Where love comes alive™

Visit Silhouette at www.eHarlequin.com   SSECY01

COMING NEXT MONTH

#1411 COURTING THE ENEMY—Sherryl Woods
The Calamity Janes
Widow Karen Hanson refused to hand over her late husband's ranch to Grady Blackhawk, a longtime nemesis, but had a different plan when it came to her heart. Now that forbidden passion had cooked hate into a fiery love affair, Grady needed to prove that it wasn't only the land he was after…but also her love.

#1412 THE MARRIAGE AGREEMENT—Christine Rimmer
Conveniently Yours
It had been ten years since Marsh Bravo had said goodbye to his love, Tori Winningham. Now he was back and ready to take responsibility for a child he hadn't known was his. But when unexpected passion led to a possible pregnancy—the only agreement to be made was marriage.

#1413 BACHELOR COP FINALLY CAUGHT?—Gina Wilkins
Hot Off the Press
Small-town reporter Lindsey Gray was guilty—guilty of loving police chief Dan Meadows from afar. Now up close and personal, these two had been thrown together by a job-related issue. But when Lindsey made a quick getaway, would the chief be too busy with the law to notice love?

#1414 TALL, DARK AND DIFFICULT—Patricia Coughlin
Former test pilot Hollis "Griff" Griffen endured his aunt's doily-filled Victorian only to cash in on her will—until he met antique expert Rose Davenport, and his intentions changed. But when Griff revealed his original motive, would Rose still think he was a rare find?

#1415 HER HAND-PICKED FAMILY—Jennifer Mikels
Family Revelations
Gillian Quinn was searching for her long-lost sister. Her good friend Professor Alex Hunter yearned to give his daughter, Shelby, a mother. But when she showed up on his doorstep, Gillian would need a few lessons in love before she learned that her search for family was over….

#1416 MILLIONAIRE IN DISGUISE—Jean Brashear
When multimillionaire Dominic Santorini met Lexie Grayson, he revealed everything, except his true identity. But soon the truth was out and Lexie discovered that her mysterious lover was also her new boss. Now, blinded by betrayal, could Lexie convince this handsome Greek tycoon that she wanted the man…and not his money?

When Cal Ruskoff was literally thrown into the arms of Taylor Larsen by a matchmaking friend, his world suddenly tilted. And when she became snowbound in his cabin, he looked temptation straight in the face again—and temptation won the battle. But Cal had secrets to keep...for the moment.

Taylor thought she'd managed to crack the shell that Cal retreated to. But when he hired her as his lawyer, she sensed she was being kept at a "safe" distance. Could she finally break down the barriers around his heart and show him she was meant to be his perfect match?

Life,
Love
&
Family

SPECIAL EDITION

Visit Silhouette at www.eHarlequin.com

SILHOUETTE
MAKES YOU
A STAR!
SEE DETAILS INSIDE

ISBN 0-373-24409-6

24409

UPC

0 65373 00450 5

SILHOUETTE®
BOOKS
®